Richelieu Plays
† Bridge †

Robert F. MacKinnon

MASTER POINT PRESS • TORONTO

Master Point Press
331 Douglas Ave.
Toronto, Ontario Canada
M5M 1H2
(416) 781-0351 Fax (416) 781-1831
Internet www.masterpointpress.com

Canadian Cataloguing in Publication Data
MacKinnon, Robert, F
Richelieu plays bridge

ISBN 1-894154-44-4

1. Title.
PS8575.K486R52. 2002   C813'.6 C2001-904148-9

Editor	Ray Lee
Cover and Interior design	Olena S. Sullivan
Cover Illustration	Leo Lingas
Text Illustrations	Alan MacKinnon
Interior format and copyediting	Deanna Bourassa

Printed and bound in Canada by Webcom Ltd.

1 2 3 4 5 6 7   06 05 04 03 02

Richelieu Plays Bridge
✝ Bridge ✝

Contents

Acknowledgements

The author wishes to acknowledge the invaluable assistance of Linda Lee who kindly went through the play of every hand and made many constructive suggestions for improvements in the commentary.

The following episodes, in slightly differing form, have previously appeared in:

Bridge Plus (editor, Elena Jeronimidis) 'The Rules of the Game';

International Popular Bridge Monthly (editor, Brian Senior) 'The Judgement of Richelieu', 'Richelieu and the Cardinals', 'The Great Masked Duplicate of 1625'.

Finally the author wishes to express his thanks to the above mentioned editors and to Ray Lee for their patient and active support.

Introduction

lexandre Dumas's great novel *The Three Musketeers* has for over 150 years continually renewed interest in the goings-on at the court of Louis XIII. Dumas had uncovered a vein of literary gold, for the court at the time was populated by an unequalled group of colorful characters: the beautiful, devout, and devious queen, Anne of Austria, secretly in love with the dashingly handsome Duke of Buckingham; the lascivious Duchesse de Chevreuse who could easily twist a man, even a Cardinal, around her little finger; Richelieu, the consummate schemer willing to sacrifice his soul in the pursuit of power. The key figure of the King is portrayed by Dumas as a shadowy character in need of protection from the wiles of his crafty Prime Minister, a view that has prevailed despite evidence that such was far from being the case. In fact, the King and the Cardinal operated together in a close, smoothly-functioning partnership.

In his editor's view, Dumas' novels were long enough without including bridge hands, so all references to bridge were expurgated, even though the protagonists were known to have engaged almost daily in the game. The omission was rectified in 1978 with the publication of Aksel J. Nielsen's *Bridge with the Three Musketeers* (Kaye and Ward, London) a highly biased account based on notes left by D'Artagnan's manservant. Planchet, like Dumas, wished to show his erratic master in the best light possible, but he stretches our credulity and does the King an injustice on his description of following hand in which the irrepressible Gascon plays in six spades missing two cashable aces:

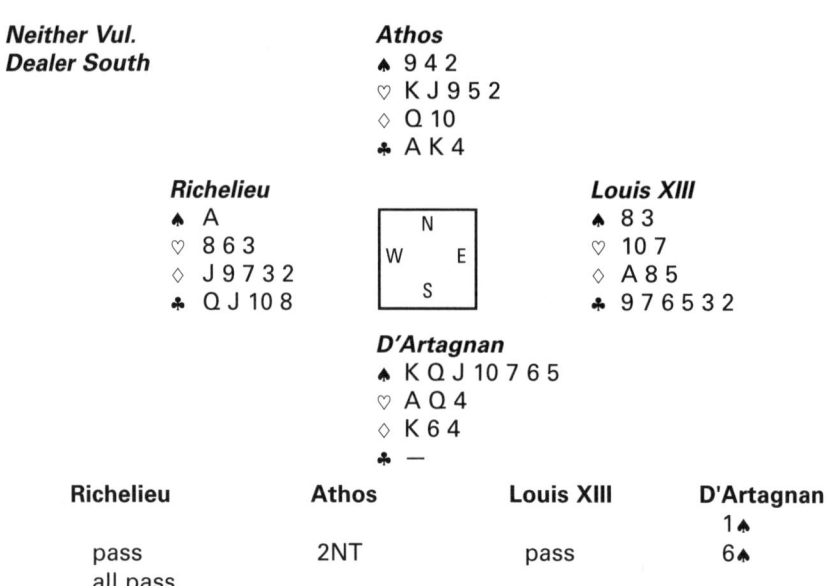

Neither Vul.
Dealer South

Athos
- ♠ 9 4 2
- ♡ K J 9 5 2
- ◇ Q 10
- ♣ A K 4

Richelieu
- ♠ A
- ♡ 8 6 3
- ◇ J 9 7 3 2
- ♣ Q J 10 8

Louis XIII
- ♠ 8 3
- ♡ 10 7
- ◇ A 8 5
- ♣ 9 7 6 5 3 2

D'Artagnan
- ♠ K Q J 10 7 6 5
- ♡ A Q 4
- ◇ K 6 4
- ♣ —

Richelieu	Athos	Louis XIII	D'Artagnan
			1♠
pass	2NT	pass	6♠
all pass			

The Cardinal leads the ♣Q and D'Artagnan takes the top clubs and discards two hearts from his hand before leading a trump to the ace. According to Planchet, the Cardinal woodenly returns a third club, allowing the slam to make as declarer can get rid of his losing diamonds on the heart winners in dummy. Louis angrily blames the Cardinal for this disaster. This is the kind of misinformation concerning the King and the Cardinal that has been circulating for three centuries.

One should not believe this implausible tale for one moment. One of the crosses that Richelieu had to bear was that Louis XIII was a stickler on partnership cooperation. Although the Cardinal preferred a free-and-easy approach to bidding and defense, frequently he had to suppress the creative side of his game for fear of raising the ire of the King who took a slip from orthodoxy as a personal betrayal. On the first club Louis would have played the ♣9 to show an even number in the suit. On the second club from dummy he would have played the ♣2 as a clear indication of a strong diamond holding. Richelieu would certainly have switched to a diamond in response to that suit-preference signal, the Bridge equivalent of a royal command, and Louis would not have failed to play the ♣2. If, inadvertently, he had played his clubs otherwise, Louis the Just would have been the first to apologize to his 'dear Cousin' for a careless play.

In Paris today there are many reminders of the servitor Richelieu, but few of his master. True, there exists a nondescript equestrian statue in the Place des Vosges and you may view Louis' portrait in the nearby Musée Carnavalet, but his tomb in the Basilica of Saint Denis has never been restored after its destruction during the French Revolution. If Louis XIII is remembered today it is most likely as the father of Louis XIV, the so-called Sun King, yet it was the father who left his country much the better for his having reigned over it.

We must also take exception to Dumas's characterization of Anne of Austria as a damsel in distress who cannot extricate herself from a mess of her own making without four bungling musketeers stumbling to her rescue. In fact, she exercised real political power, as did many women at that time. Female rulers of their countries who were contemporaries of Richelieu's included Catherine de Medici, Mary, Queen of Scots, Elizabeth I, Marie de Medici, and Christina of Sweden. In addition, many less exalted women played an active role in political life, especially in France. The Duchesse de Chevreuse was foremost of those. Richelieu's successor, Mazarin, must have had her in mind when he wrote to a Spanish minister in words that might as easily been penned by his predecessor:

'In Spain, as in all other countries, you have two types of women: coquettes, of whom there is an oversupply, and decent women, of whom there are but a few. The former think of not else but how to pleasure their lovers, and the latter of nothing but how to please their husbands. In either case, their sole aim is the gratification of their vanity and the fulfillment of their desire for luxury. But our French women! Whether they be virtuous or loose, old or young, clever or silly, all want to meddle in absolutely everything. A wife will not go to bed with her husband, nor a wanton with her lover, unless he first informs her of the affairs of the day. They must know everything, see everything, be informed about everything, and, now this is even worse, they must interfere in everything and mix it all up.'

As for our main character, Cardinal-Duc de Richelieu, his personality is so complex that it cannot be analyzed in its totality in one book. Each decade sees another interpretation of his life put in print, but in all the years since Richelieu's death in 1642, no biographer has topped the witty epitaph of Pope Urban VIII, who, on being informed of the Cardinal's passing, remarked extemporaneously, 'If there is a God in Heaven, he presumably has much to answer for, but, if there is no God..., well, he was successful.'

To finish this brief introduction we retell one incident that gives insight into the personality of the great statesman. When Montaigne died in 1592 his literary heir was his adopted daughter, a young lady by the name of Marie de Gournay. She compiled several editions of his works and produced some of her own fiction that was mannered in style and full of far-fetched romantic notions. By 1635 she had become out-of-date and something of a laughingstock amongst the fashionable literary crowd that surrounded the powerful Cardinal. When she dedicated her latest edition of Montaigne's works to Richelieu, he gave her an audience during which he amused his hangers-on by rather making fun at her expense by using some of the fulsome phrases that had appeared in her work, *L'Ombre*. The old lady was no fool; she gently rebuked the Cardinal in such a gracious way that he felt deeply ashamed of himself and humbly asked her pardon. Richelieu had always loved cats and was frequently found stroking a favorite feline sitting in his lap. He discovered Mlle de Gournay also was a cat lover. Later when he granted her a generous lifetime pension, it amused him to include also a pension for her cat, Piaillon, and not only for Piaillon, but also for Piaillon's soon-to-arrive kittens as well.

Our story encompasses the decade 1615-1625 when Richelieu, then in his thirties, was struggling to win the favor of the ruling royal family. How was he able to attain prominence and what role did Bridge play in his rise to power? That is what we shall describe. If before commencing on the Bridge segment the reader would like to learn more of the Cardinal's early days, his noble family, his education, and his surprising decision to become a priest, a historical summary is presented in the Appendices along with some comments on life in Paris at that time. Let us begin our journey back in time to those days when Fate shuffled and dealt the cards of Richelieu's destiny.

Richelieu Plays Bridge

Along The Corridors of Power

𝕴t is a bright, sunny day in mid-June, 1616. The Grand Gallery of the Louvre is packed with serious-faced men and their richly dressed womenfolk competing for an advantageous location from which to view the promenade of the young royal couple recently married and returned from the South. These jostlers normally have but minor connections with the Court, but on this occasion they have been allowed entry to pay their respects en masse to their royal patrons — patrons in name only, however, for it is the Queen Mother, Marie de Medici, who loosely holds the purse strings in her chubby fingers.

Standing apart from the hurly-burly is a tall, pale, red-lipped gentleman with long, blonde hair flowing to his shoulders. From his brown costume of heavy material one might guess correctly he is an Englishman. Beside him is a stocky, old gentleman with sun-tanned features whose clothes are finely made but of a fashion several years out-of-date. As we approach, the old codger, obviously a leftover from the glory days of Henri IV, is doing all the talking.

'It does one's heart good to see such a lively crowd, but the noise, the noise, Monsieur, is enough in time to impair the hearing. I'm sure your English court does not suffer from such a chaotic affliction. Ah well, we French like to talk, even if there is nothing to talk about — that's the way we are — and since the arrival of the new queen from Spain, there has been no lack of topics. Look at these young courtiers taking on new life, setting out new shoots, and now blossoming out in these colorful silks and satins we see displayed before us. What hats! If I were younger I'd purchase one of those with big, white, African plumes, like that one over there. Oh, what a great time to be young, Monsieur, and living in Paris! I envy the days and nights that lie before you, especially the nights. Take full advantage.'

'I intend to,' replies the Englishman, his eyes sifting through the crowd for a pretty face with pouting lips.

'I mean no disrespect, but His Majesty is as yet still a young sprout. Some plants take longer than others to grow to maturity and it is just a matter of time before he has the strength to claim his place in the sun, but, frankly, it can't be too soon for some good Frenchmen. His mother's a good sort, but a bit of a pumpkin, if you ask me, dominated by that countryman of hers, Concini — Zucchini, I call him. Oh, Monsieur, you smile. My similes grow agricultural, I fear. As you may have deduced, I prefer to spend my days in my little garden now, among my fruits and vegetables, returning to my roots as it were, and come to Court only to pay the necessary respects. Frankly, my bladder can't stand the waiting about for someone who may never appear.'

The Englishman silently continues his amatory survey — the complaints of old age do not merit a reply.

'I can point out some of the courtiers with whose names you may be familiar. That tall, elegant cavalier by the window is Bassompierre, France's greatest lover, although there are many who compete for that title. Ironically he's not French at all, but a German from Lorraine. The short, ugly man with the beautiful, blonde wife is Henry, Prince de Condé. She's the one who drove the old King mad with desire. Strange, is it not, how these ugly mugs get wedded to such beauty and grace. She doesn't look happy to me and no wonder — she just missed marrying Bassompierre. Ha, at last here comes someone who knows me.'

The old gentleman steps forward and makes a sweeping bow to a tall, heavy-set man with florid features and a stupid face who returns a smile and a bow that does not break his stride on the way by.

'That big lout was Hercule de Rohan, Duc de Montbazon. I knew him well in the old days. At least he recognized me and noted I'm still alive. His daughter has just come to Court and from all I've heard she emulates her old man's rakish ways. That would be justice well-served. Ah, now there's an interesting new fellow coming this way — see him, pale of face, pointed of beard, bright of eye, dressed in black and carrying a portfolio? That's Armand-Jean du Plessis, younger brother of Henri de Richelieu. He's a Bishop and Grand Almoner to the new Queen. Quite full of himself, isn't he? Don't be fooled, as so many are, by his overdone obsequiousness; he's a groveler, that's for sure, but grovelers get the gravy. You've heard what the Pope said of him? No? How's your Italian? — *Questo giovane sara un gran furbo* — ha-ha — *un gran furbo*, I like that. If he is to become a great trickster, and it takes one to recognize one, then I am content that this one will be on the side of France, for we could do with some more intelligence in the conduct of our foreign affairs. Frankly, Monsieur, and I trust this goes no further, I feel this marriage alliance with Spain benefits more the Spaniard, who wishes to surround France with corsets of steel and then squeeze us until our eyes pop. The old King wouldn't have stood for it. But look! Here come their Majesties!'

It hardly seems possible for more people to crowd into the corridor, but there appears along the passageway a contingent of Swiss guards followed by a procession of courtiers in the midst of whom walks a young couple to whom all bow or curtsy as they pass. The boy-king is a lad of medium height and build, with the full face of an immature adolescent. His black hair is long and curly, the look on his smooth face solemn and impassive. His bright eyes give evidence of a quick mind, but he seems ill at ease when the crowd of humanity presses close. At such times he avoids eye contact and turns to address the robust gentleman who walks beside him. The queen is alike to the King in years, but she seems more mature and gracious when acknowledging the tributes of her subjects. She is a pretty little thing, who moves with a dainty step and easy grace. She is dressed in the Spanish style; her father is Philip III, King of mighty Spain, but she is known as Anne of Austria because of her Hapsburg lineage.

'I venture to say the young King has much to look forward to,' observes the old gentleman after the procession has passed. As the tall Englishman turns to make his farewells, the old courtier says, 'You must depart? I must stay. I have enjoyed talking with you, Monsieur. It is always interesting to hear the opinions of an Englishman. Good luck to you, Monsieur. Adieu, adieu, and adieu,' he concludes with a well-executed deep bow and wide sweep of his hat.

ANNE OF AUSTRIA

A few days later Armand-Jean du Plessis de Richelieu again passed through the Grand Gallery, now divested of the clamorous crowd. Everyone present this time was important or could be important to his future. He gave effusive greetings to all and sundry. A smile was ever on his thin lips. Often his gaunt frame bent forward in repeated bows. He tarried not long with any particular group, but moved on purposefully, giving the impression of a man with pressing duties to which to attend, an impression heightened by the red leather portfolio he carried under his arm. His black costume was not clerical, yet it was appropriately austere and set him apart from the others moving along the corridors of power. His dress said, 'Yes, a man of obvious principle, yet one flexible in practice, not someone overly concerned with all the niceties,' exactly the impression he wished to convey — a priest to whom you could talk frankly, a priest with whom you could bargain as freely as with the devil. Bright sunshine poured through the open windows of the Grand Gallery as the Grand Almoner made his way to his appointment with the young queen.

Queen Anne was judged by courtiers to be the most beautiful woman in Christendom, but that was courtly exaggeration — at fourteen years of age she was still not fully matured. The Princesse de Condé at twenty years of age had better claim to that title. Anne was a slim blonde with green-flecked eyes and a snow-white complexion, and when she attired herself, as she did on this day, in her green dress with the long slashed sleeves caught at the elbow and wrist with diamond buttons, a black feather in her hair, and when the sun played upon her unblemished cheek and full red lips, as it did now, then a young man, even a Bishop, could not but help to be impressed. If asked at that moment when her white teeth sparkled in laughter, if she were not the most beautiful, dainty creature he had ever seen, then such a man would have said with all his heart, 'She is'.

'Your Majesty,' began Richelieu, 'I do not wish in any way to change the beliefs with which your father and saintly mother by her good example have inculcated within your heart. You look puzzled — *inculcated*? A new French word for your Majesty — it means to be impressed upon your heart by repeated example.'

He paused to collect his thoughts once more before proceeding. 'I do not wish in any way to change the beliefs with which you have come to us, but the outward shows of piety may take different forms in different countries. Like the fashion of one's clothes, those that may be seen as commonplace in our country, France, may appear quaint in the country of your father, Spain. And vice versa. So please bear with me, and in time you will see there is no spiritual conflict whatsoever engendered by the differences in our customs.'

'Thank you, Bishop,' replied the young queen, meekly lowering her eyes. 'You give my heart ease. I do not wish to give the King offense, but I do need some time to adjust to the French ways with which I am unacquainted. I must assure you, however, that observances of my religious duties are not in the way of being merely an outward show.'

Richelieu smiled pleasantly enough, but in his heart he felt a foreboding. The older members of the Spanish entourage played too strong a role in the new queen's household, acting to preserve the austere practices of Madrid which were highly inappropriate to the French Court and which certainly would serve to give offense if retained.

'Your Majesty, I am most honored to be allowed to serve a lady whose every thought proves worthy of her royal heritage. Turning now to more pressing matters, the Queen Mother has suggested I might instruct you in the French way of Bridge. It is, of course, imperative that Your Majesty quickly become familiar with the favorite card game of the Court, and, in addition, there is much to be learned from the game, for it is much more than a game, it is a lesson in life.'

'Yes, I am quite taken with Bridge, but, alas, have not had much experience at card play. I would welcome your kind instruction,' replied the queen sweetly as she had been coached to do.

'It is important for the sake of appearances not to play against any but your own attendants until your skills are sufficiently advanced to impress a French courtier. In the meantime I can provide some guidance. The game exercises the three powers of the mind: Memory, Intellect, and Will. By playing Bridge you will develop an ability to retain information, and also the skill of recognizing ahead of time what is important to commit to memory and what is not.' Queen Anne nodded solemnly in agreement, so Richelieu felt he could press on.

'We all have remembrances, Your Majesty. We cherish the pleasant and suppress the unpleasant. Has it not been said, 'Forgive then forget'? But Bridge does not distinguish between a pleasant card and an unpleasant card, a pleasant fact and an unpleasant one. Cards are cards and facts are facts; each must be taken at its face value. There is no forgiving and forgetting, only the utilization of what is known to be.'

'You mean facts as they appear in the Holy Scriptures, Bishop?' asked Anne.

'We speak here not of holy words, but evidence of men's actions as encountered in our daily life,' replied the Bishop, somewhat put off by the Queen's highly orthodox reaction. It was going to be harder than he had bargained for to bring this young woman to his practical way of thinking. He decided to skip to his final point.

'Of Memory, Intellect, and Will, the greatest is Will. One cannot expect to excel at Bridge, or indeed at any endeavor, without the will to do so. Bridge pits your interests against those of the opponent and it is often the strongest will that prevails. By playing bridge you will exercise your will power and learn not to give up hope even when the future appears darkest. Also you will learn not to lose your attentiveness when the future seems rosy...'

His discourse was interrupted by the Queen. 'Ah, don't say rosy, for the scent of the rose makes me faint.' She placed a hand to her forehead and closed her eyes, and Richelieu recognized this as a signal to end his lesson. Nonetheless he felt he had made progress, not realizing that his efforts to instill cold rationality in this warm heart would earn him only frigid hatred in the end. But why speak of 'cold' rationality and 'warm' heart? Is it 'colder' to plan one's actions for the maximum benefit and the least risk than to act impulsively and, through lack of foresight, to endanger the careers and even the lives of those around you, as Anne was to do repeatedly? Is not the selfish perpetrator of foolish acts showing a 'cold' disregard for the well-being of others, no matter how many warm tears of regret may later be publicly shed?

The Rules
of
the Game

he month of June 1616 was a busy one at the French Court, but not for Louis XIII himself. It had been expected that once he had returned to Paris after his marriage half a year previous, the King would begin to take on more of a role in the governing of the country. It was not happening. His mother, the Regent, kept him from the meetings of the Council, and Concini, her chief adviser, ignored him, sometimes adding rudeness to neglect. For his part, Louis pursued his quiet hobbies and neglected his child bride. Although they met formally twice a day surrounded by their attendants, warmth of feeling was not expressed during the rituals of these meetings. At this time the King, bound up in all the trappings of a kingship over which he had no control, had not the self-confidence needed to undertake a loving relationship. For Louis XIII, 'to love' always was to mean 'to dominate.'

Every morning Grand Almoner Richelieu waited upon the Queen and attempted to make her into a good Bridge player. He soon discovered that his pupil, although possessing intelligence sufficient for the fulfillment of her royal duties, was not a natural card player, but a task once taken up by Richelieu was a task never set down. A teacher of the young, like a doctor to the old, trades in excessive optimism. He decided to pursue a method of instruction in keeping with her rigid Spanish upbringing, that is, he drew up a list of rules to be followed faithfully.

Daily the list grew longer as in private sessions he partnered his pupil against two members of her Spanish household: her Lady-of-Honor, the Condesa de Las Torres, on whom old age had encrusted a patina of righteousness, and the sly Duque de Monteleone, Ambassador from Spain, to whom respectability was granted according to custom. Gradual progress was noted: honors started to be covered by honors, low cards began to appear at second-hand play, and so on.

Two of Richelieu's rules pertaining to opening leads were: *don't lead from a worthless doubleton in an unbid suit*, and *never lead trumps*. The following deal proved instructive, although not in the way Richelieu would have hoped.

De Las Torres
- ♠ 10 9 8 6
- ♡ 10 2
- ◇ Q J 8 7
- ♣ A 7 4

Queen Anne
- ♠ K Q 7
- ♡ 9 8 7 6 3
- ◇ 10 5 2
- ♣ 9 3

```
      N
  W       E
      S
```

Richelieu
- ♠ 5 4 3 2
- ♡ Q
- ◇ A K 6 3
- ♣ K J 6 5

Monteleone
- ♠ A J
- ♡ A K J 5 4
- ◇ 9 4
- ♣ Q 10 8 2

Queen Anne	De Las Torres	Richelieu	Monteleone
pass	pass	1◇	1♡
pass	pass	dbl	2♡
pass	pass	dbl	all pass

With neither side vulnerable Richelieu opened the bidding in the suit below his singleton and Monteleone overcalled in that suit. In the balancing position the Grand Almoner demonstrated for his pupil's benefit the function of the protective double. The ambassador rebid his values, not generally a wise practice, but he was familiar with the Queen's defensive abilities and rather fancied his chances.

In the final-pass position, Richelieu let his hot blood override his judgment. He was aware of the dangers of competing further with a 4441 shape but he felt that if his pupil were to advance, her mental clay would have to be fired in the furnace of competition where each card played was crucial to the outcome. To him will-power was the prerequisite to preeminence in any endeavor, and one did not cultivate will-power by coddling. Therefore, double!

The young Queen gave no thought to removing the double; she assumed that her partner must be well stocked in high cards and would be pleased when she showed up with much more defense than she had promised. Richelieu would hold four spades for his initial double, so she led the king in his promised suit with high expectation of praise from her hard taskmaster. The Duque was delighted by this gift; he took his ace and returned the ♠J to set up winners in dummy.

Anne was one of those timid souls who become flustered in times of crisis. Nothing appeared certain so she reverted to a 'safe' trump. This only aided the Spaniard as he could win Richelieu's ♡Q and enter dummy with a second trump to discard his two losing diamonds on the winning spades. The Queen took her ruff on the fourth spade, and returned yet another trump, allowing the Duque to draw the outstanding trumps in complete safety. Uncertain of the position of the cards after this faltering defense, Richelieu had come down to ◇AK6 ♣KJ, so Monteleone was able to manage ten tricks, having begun with a mere six.

Richelieu apologized profusely to the Queen, taking care also to compliment the Duque on his fine play and the Condesa on her fine pass on the first round that might otherwise have gone unnoticed, but inwardly he seethed. 'What a different story if the Queen had led from her worthless doubleton in clubs!' he thought. 'The ♣K takes the first trick and a club is returned, Monteleone winning cheaply, but he is trapped.'

This is the position that Richelieu envisioned:

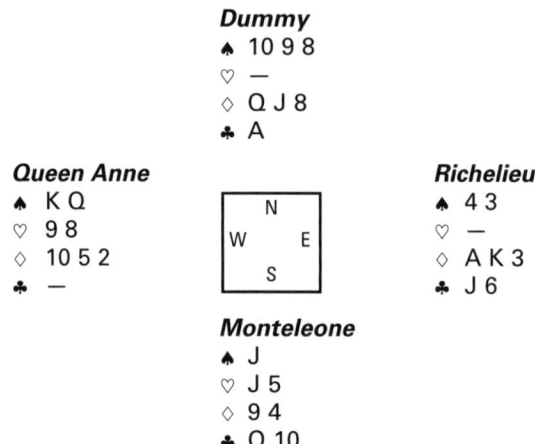

Dummy
♠ 10 9 8
♡ —
♢ Q J 8
♣ A

Queen Anne
♠ K Q
♡ 9 8
♢ 10 5 2
♣ —

Richelieu
♠ 4 3
♡ —
♢ A K 3
♣ J 6

Monteleone
♠ J
♡ J 5
♢ 9 4
♣ Q 10

Monteleone, having taken the second club and played on trumps, has returned to his hand with a spade to his ace. If he plays a club now, the Queen can ruff this and obtain a second club ruff, enough to set the contract, therefore declarer is forced to draw another round of trumps. If he plays to the ♣A thereafter, the Queen must refuse the ruff by discarding a diamond. Now in dummy, Monteleone must relinquish the lead, so the Queen's hand may be entered with the ♠Q. She can draw the last trump, assuring two spades, two diamonds, a club and a heart trick for the defense. Now there was a worthy lesson in defense.

'I do not wish to interpose my own views on what must be the superlative instruction of the Bishop,' began the Duque preparatory to doing just that, 'but if I may be so bold, this hand provides good instruction to Her Majesty on the rules that govern our actions at the bridge table.'

'Quite so, Your Excellency,' put in the Condesa, 'I once overheard King Philip say to the Grand Inquisitor, *When holding five trumps I look no farther*', and the Grand Inquisitor confirmed that view, adding he would do the same even with six.'

'A good rule to be sure, but I had another in mind. Can you not guess it?'

'I find it interesting that if the Queen, God forbid, were to break a rule and lead from her worthless doubleton in clubs...' began Richelieu, about to expound on his superlative seven-card ending.

'No, no,' interrupted the grandee with an impatient wave of his hand, 'I can always make my contract on any lead whatsoever provided I do not make the error of drawing more than one round of trumps before starting on spades. Of course, a lead of a low trump might tempt me into such an error, but, no, the rule I had in mind was *always take out your partner's takeout double*, not so? Here a contract of 2♠ by West is down one after the inevitable trump lead from the Condesa, but that is better than putting too much faith in partner's doubles.'

As Queen Anne dutifully added Monteleone's rule to her notebook, Richelieu could do nothing but grit his teeth, smile, and await a chance for revenge. All these references to trump leads, an action that he had expressly forbidden, had brought on one of his fierce headaches.

MORE RULES

Young Queen Anne was confused by the contrary advice she was receiving concerning opening leads. Her Grand Almoner had told her never to lead trumps, her Lady-of-Honor had recalled that her famous grandfather had always led a trump holding five (or more), and her Major Domo had spoken of benefits to be obtained indirectly from a trump lead. To resolve her difficulty she asked the advice of her ancient governess, a dignified old crow who went by the title of the Duquesa de Villequieras.

'Let's see, your Spanish advisor said to lead a trump and your French advisor said not to, but both sides agreed that it didn't matter one iota. So the answer is easy! Follow the French rule, for you are the Queen of France. In that way the French can never criticize your action no matter how ludicrous the result, for in so doing they would be heaping criticism upon themselves.'

Not entirely satisfied with this sensible solution, the Queen approached the Princesse de Condé, a young woman of the French Court who had treated Anne kindly from their first meeting. This was her comment.

'On leading trumps the best advice I ever got came from my brother, the Duc de Montmorency, who told me, *lead trumps when nothing else is better*. I find that works for me.'

Although one may not disagree with this admonishment in principle, it is of doubtful practical value and may even lead to some confusion in the mind of a novice, as did another rule of the same kind laid down by the normally lucid Richelieu: *on defense, take all the tricks that are coming to you*. In many a battle ambiguity has led to disaster, as it did on this deal played on the very next day.

De Las Torres
♠ 9 8
♡ 10 9 4
♢ 7 4 3 2
♣ K 9 8 6

Queen Anne
♠ A K J 7
♡ 6 5 2
♢ K 10 9 6
♣ 7 3

```
      N
  W       E
      S
```

Richelieu
♠ Q 5
♡ K Q 7 3
♢ J 8 5
♣ Q J 4 2

Monteleone
♠ 10 6 4 3 2
♡ A J 8
♢ A Q
♣ A 10 5

In third position, with both sides vulnerable, Monteleone saw his hand as a strong 1NT opening bid, so he made that bid, and was allowed to play there as Richelieu had resolved to give up on balancing doubles for a while. It was well the Spaniard made this bid, for if he had opened with a bid of 1♠, the result would have been a contract of 1NT for East-West, making eight tricks. On this basis one might think that Monteleone should have been held to five tricks in his own 1NT contract, but it doesn't always turn out that way.

Like many novices Anne liked to lay down an ace to have a look at the dummy before deciding how to conduct the defense. Fully aware of this propensity, Richelieu did not unblock his ♠Q under her lead of the ♠A. Seeing the ♠5 appear on his right, Monteleone wanted to make it appear safe to continue spades, so he played the ♠6. In fact, the best defense would be to follow Monteleone's suggestion and continue with a spade to Richelieu's queen, for then the Bishop could return a diamond through the ♢AQ. However, Anne was suspicious of Monteleone's card and she had a contrary nature in keeping with her Spanish upbringing. From what holding would Richelieu encourage with the ♠5? He would have to hold ♠Q5432, leaving Monteleone with ♠106, but Anne was not about to give the problem the benefit of the thorough analysis it deserved. Lazily she concluded that Monteleone must have had some motivation for his apparently deceptive ♠6, so she was not going to fall into the obvious trap of continuing spades and giving up a trick to declarer's ♠Q. She switched to a diamond.

Monteleone was happy to take his ♢Q and continue spades. Richelieu overtook Anne's ♠J and cleared the diamond suit. Monteleone exited with a spade to Anne's ♠7 and the Queen, following Richelieu's rule to the letter, stolidly began taking her diamond tricks to produce the following ending:

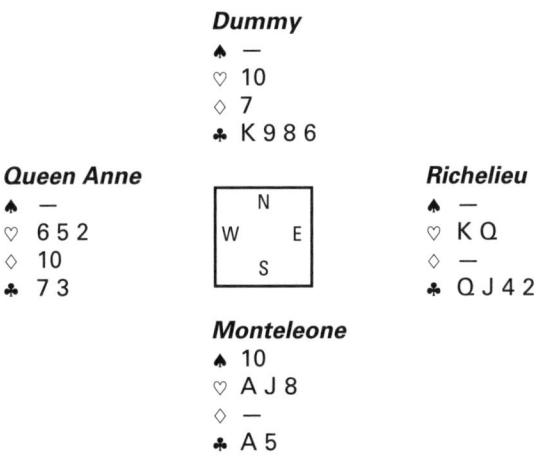

Dummy
♠ —
♡ 10
◇ 7
♣ K 9 8 6

Queen Anne
♠ —
♡ 6 5 2
◇ 10
♣ 7 3

```
    N
W       E
    S
```

Richelieu
♠ —
♡ K Q
◇ —
♣ Q J 4 2

Monteleone
♠ 10
♡ A J 8
◇ —
♣ A 5

Oh no! thought Richelieu when he realized what was happening. On the last diamond, he parted with the ♣4 and Monteleone with the ♡8. Lead through strength, proudly recalled the Queen as she laid the ♣7 on the table, but it mattered not what she led. Monteleone could win with the ♣A or the ♡A in his hand and make his contract easily by squeezing Richelieu in clubs and hearts on the play of the ♠10.

'May I ask how many points you held, Bishop?' asked the Queen breezily. When Richelieu admitted to 11, Anne commented, 'So did I. Isn't it strange that we both held 11 points, but I took five tricks and you took only one? If you could have taken just half as many as I, we would have set the contract.'

'You noticed that, did you, Your Majesty?' replied Richelieu as pleasantly as possible. 'Your Excellencies, I do believe my dear pupil is at last beginning to think like a true bridge player.'

THE ULTIMATE RULE

Richelieu had to admit to himself that his attempt to teach bridge by laying down rules was not working as well as he had hoped. Too late he was discovering that no sooner had his pupil absorbed a rule than a deal came along in which it failed miserably. A more religious man might think the Devil had had a hand in it. To a man of reason like Richelieu there were just two honorable alternatives:

1. follow the advice of Francis de Sales: retire from politics, return to his diocese, and serve the people; or

2. present prematurely to the Queen the ultimate rule that all rules are made to be broken.

He decided that with the next lesson he would embark on alternative #2 with alternative #1 remaining as a distinct possibility in the near future.

Anne was puzzled. It seemed that the more one learned the less one believed. Faithfully she reported the latest addition to her list to her old Spanish governess.

'Nonsense,' exclaimed the Duquesa de Villequieras, 'rules are made to be followed not to be broken. Scratch that last one.'

'But sometimes the rules fail,' observed the Queen.

'What do you expect?' retorted the governess, a pure Castilian Aristotelian, 'The rules are not at fault, it's the world that's imperfect.'

A year previous back in Spain this answer would have satisfied the Infanta, but by now she had been exposed to the influence of the emancipated ladies of the French Court. She approached for advice the Princesse de Conti, perhaps the most emancipated of that crowd, a novelist and the inventor of the beauty patch.

'In order to gain peace of mind we ladies must forget most of what has been taught us at an early age,' the Princesse affirmed. 'Don't take too seriously any rules that men lay down for us to follow, for in public men are always telling us to act in one way whereas in private they are hoping we do quite the opposite. You'll see. This Bishop has kindly given you a *carte blanche*. Use it. Remain as charming as you are, but do as you please. Above all, never, never try to explain your actions, especially to a man.'

Richelieu came to the next practice session with renewed optimism. He was sure he would encounter a hand in which he could demonstrate the advantage of breaking one of his own rules. It was exciting to speculate which rule that might be. Perhaps, *never open the bidding on less than twelve points*? That was certainly was a live possibility. Or *never bid notrump with a singleton*? There were so many candidates, but the first rule to be broken was, surprisingly, *never underlead an ace*. With the opponents now 60 up, game seemed inevitable after the bidding given below.

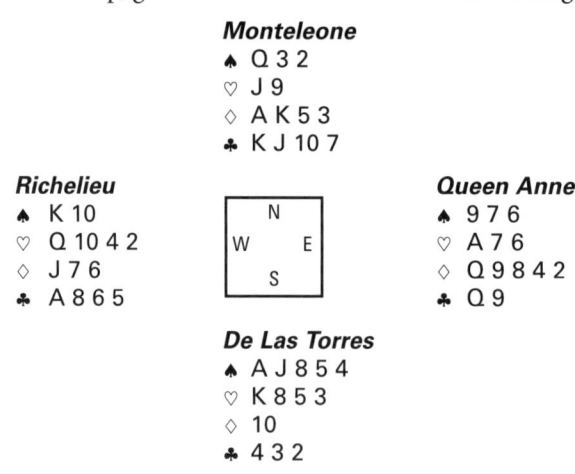

	Monteleone	
	♠ Q 3 2	
	♡ J 9	
	◇ A K 5 3	
	♣ K J 10 7	

Richelieu		Queen Anne
♠ K 10		♠ 9 7 6
♡ Q 10 4 2		♡ A 7 6
◇ J 7 6		◇ Q 9 8 4 2
♣ A 8 6 5		♣ Q 9

	De Las Torres	
	♠ A J 8 5 4	
	♡ K 8 5 3	
	◇ 10	
	♣ 4 3 2	

Richelieu	Monteleone	Queen Anne	De Las Torres
pass	1◇	pass	1♠
pass	1NT	pass	2♡
pass	2♠	all pass	

The unbid suit was clubs and the expectations were that dummy would hold the opponents' power in that suit. Rather than play the ace to guard against a singleton honor in declarer's hand, Richelieu decided to underlead his ace. There was the danger that the Queen might misread the situation, but that danger would exist no matter what the lead.

Instead it was the Condesa who misread the situation. She never expected the Bishop to break one of his own rules, so she saw no reason to put up the ♣K losing to the ♣A now marked on her right. Hopefully, she put in the ♣10 and lost to Anne's ♣Q. As it happened, the Queen was also on the lookout for an opportunity to break one of Richelieu's rules. It would not be too much to say her mind was ablaze with anticipation. She saw that here was an opportunity of breaking not just one rule, *always return your partner's suit*, but simultaneously a second rule, *never underlead an ace*. Boldly she placed the ♡6 on the table, doing Richelieu one better.

Once again the Condesa saw no profit in what was in her estimation a losing play, so she ducked the heart to Richelieu's queen. A second heart put Anne on lead once more and this time she switched to her remaining club. Richelieu won and led a third round, ruffed by Anne, so that in the end the defense took two clubs, two hearts and two spade tricks, setting the contract and saving the rubber.

The Spaniards made no comment on the play, although the Duque's brow was furrowed and the Condesa's cheeks were seen to take on an unaccustomed blush. Monteleone grew somewhat uneasy after this display by a man he had always considered a firm ally of Spain. Was this simply a demonstration of skill at card play, or did it have greater significance? Was the Bishop entirely reliable?

Anne saw new possibilities arising on several fronts and could hardly wait to talk again with the Princesse de Conti. Richelieu was satisfied that at last his pupil was grasping the essence of Bridge. He appended the following comment to his own write-up of the hand: *The truth is always complicated, whereas lies can be made simple as one desires. It follows that the confused mind, seeking simplicity, can most easily be led on by untruths.*

Anne of Austria

Anne was engaged to Louis when both were twelve years old. On being told to send a personal message to her fiancé, Anne wrote saying that she could hardly wait to be his bride. Her governess objected to this passage, saying it was unbecoming a lady. 'Haven't you always taught me to tell the truth?' replied the defiant Infanta.

Marie-Aimée de Rohan-Montbazon

𝔐ost historians through the ages have agreed that the greatest bridge player of his age was Armand-Jean du Plessis, but those whose contrary arguments have the greatest merit are those who espouse the cause of the flamboyant Marie-Aimée de Rohan-Montbazon, Duchesse de Chevreuse, Richelieu's most formidable opponent in the court of Louis XIII.

The Duc de Saint-Simon at a much later date wrote of her:

'Her charm and beauty are great, but her daring is greater still, and all three are ruled by the power of her brain, which in turn is ruled by her insatiable will to prevail. She always displays clear judgement, sure and precise, she is always exciting, ever imaginative and never lacking for clever stratagems.'

Here is what Cardinal de Retz recalled:

'I never saw another person whose swift intuition could so easily surpass the prolonged deliberations of lesser minds. She often produced brilliant expedients which to others appeared to come like great flashes of lightning.'

Thus, whenever Richelieu opposed the Duchesse at the bridge table, it became a classic confrontation between relentless rationality and uninhibited inspiration, with fierce willpower and high intelligence being exercised on both sides. Here is the story of their first encounter.

One afternoon in late July 1616 when Louis XIII was away pursuing his favorite pastime, trapping magpies, the Grand Almoner decided to drop by the Louvre and see how Queen Anne was coming along with her Bridge. He came upon Her Majesty at the card table with Charlotte de Montmorency, the Princesse de Condé, and her stepmother, the dowager Duchesse de Montmorency. It was good, he thought, that Her Highness had chosen the company of accomplished French women of varied experience over the usual crowd of matrons who had accompanied her from Spain. Only the darkly clad Duquesa de Villequieras was on hand as a kibitzer and Richelieu took a seat beside her from which to observe the play.

In fact, the Bishop was more interested in observing the Queen's winsome partner, a young maid-of-honor he had not previously noted in her entourage. He found in the newcomer's countenance much more to admire than in the doll-like face of the Queen. Marie-Aimée de Rohan-Montbazon at sixteen years of age was the epitome of French feminine beauty, an epithet that implies more than a dash of lively intelligence to augment pleasing features. Her hair was silky light auburn, her face a perfect oval, her eyes dark blue, sparkling and full of mischief. Her light eye-lashes were the longest Richelieu had ever seen and gave a deceptive impression of fawn-like vulnerability. She was not tall, but supple and athletic, her face tanned, in appearance more like a young boy-shepherd than a lady of the Court. Her full red lips, an indication of the womanly passions which would soon enough rule her heart, now curled in a smile which could make a man forget everything, forgive any-thing. As she studied her cards she waggled her tongue, the tip of which she allowed to protrude slightly at the side of her mouth, apparently unaware of the effect this was having on our Man of Reason. His heart skipped a beat. There was so much he could teach this nymph.

The Queen was on lead against the Princesse de Condé, who six years previ-ously had inspired the last, mad passion of Henri IV. She did not get along well with her husband, an infamous sodomite, the rebellious first Prince of the Blood and sec-ond in line to the throne. The Bishop gave no indication that he had just come from advising the Regent to toss this same Prince into the Bastille. If he had, the Princesse would not have expressed her gratitude for being rid of his unwelcome presence — quite the contrary, for she was greatly inconvenienced whenever her husband was sent to prison. When he was at large, she was free to go discreetly her own way while he amused himself with his pageboys, but when he was in prison she was under the social obligation of paying him highly visible conjugal visits. Furthermore, prison life restored his manly vigor.

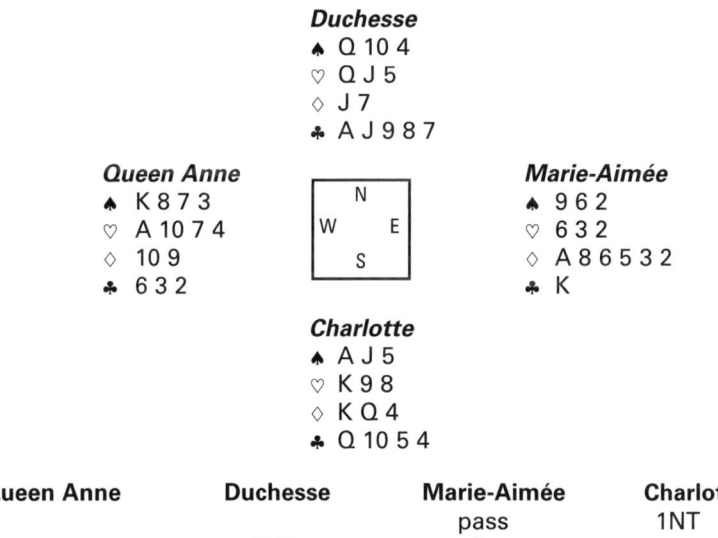

	Queen Anne	Duchesse	Marie-Aimée	Charlotte
			pass	1NT
	pass	3NT	all pass	

The young queen's pretty brow furrowed as she studied her cards. She held 7 HCP and her partner held a like number. Was it simply a matter of leading her fourth best, hoping to establish four tricks in the major suits and another in the minors in partner's hand? The bidding indicated that dummy would come down well provisioned in the minors, in which case the preponderance of declarer's strength would lie in the majors, she reasoned. Her passive nature led her to favor a diamond lead hoping to play through strength in the dummy giving nothing away, but she consciously rejected this as being unorthodox and returned to consideration of which major to lead. The ♡A was a sure entry to her hand, so that indicated a spade lead to establish tricks there. On the other hand, she needed less in hearts from partner to establish three tricks in the suit, but then the ♠K might not be the entry needed to cash them. Also, the run of a long minor might pinch her in spades, whereas the ♡A could be laid bare easily. Then again, on a spade lead declarer could hold up the ♠A whereas she might not be able to hold up the ♡K on a heart lead. Sigh.

After some time had been given up to a futile cycling through these thoughts, the Duquesa de Villequieras, whose continuously pursed lips gave the impression of someone sucking on a particularly bitter olive, leaned over and pointed with a bony finger at the spade suit. Anne shook her head, annoyed at this impertinence, and with a teenager's defiance decided on her natural choice after all. Marie-Aimée's heart skipped a beat when at long last the ◊10 appeared on the table; however, she suppressed her first impulse of encouraging with the ◊8. A few years hence she would be portrayed in the glory of full womanhood as Diana the Huntress, and even at this earlier age she knew that a good huntress mustn't frighten her prey. Her signal must be not so loud as to wake a sleeping doe, yet not so soft as to go unheeded. The ◊8, and even the ◊6, might provoke the desperate, and successful, play of the ♣A from the dummy. But could she afford the risk of the mildly encouraging ◊5? She recalled Anne repeating one of Richelieu's relevant rules: once one has chosen to lead a suit, one should continue that suit upon regaining the lead unless there is a clear alternative. Certainly such would be the case with this dummy on view, so Anne would need very little encouragement in the diamond suit.

With a solid stopper remaining in diamonds Madame la Princesse did not take much heed of the play of the ◊5 under the ◊J. However, she did not act without due caution. The long hesitation on the opening lead was an indication that the spade finesse was not working. Guarding against the ♡A being in the hand with long diamonds she led a heart towards her king thinking it best to lose immediately the trick in hearts that needed to lost. The club finesse could see her through in any event and even if the club finesse lost the diamonds appeared to be splitting evenly.

Queen Anne won the ♡A and continued diamonds, discouraged with the ◊6 from the innocent-looking young maid-of-honor. Still not anticipating any severe problems from the diamond suit, the Princesse took the club finesse, losing to the singleton ♣K. Now at last Marie-Aimée de Rohan-Montbazon showed the strength of her long suit, claiming four more tricks to set 3NT by two tricks.

'Oh, you did have diamonds! I found your suit!' exclaimed the Queen happily, clapping her tiny, white hands together as the diamonds cascaded from her partner's hand. The Duquesa clucked her tongue disapprovingly. For once Richelieu was in sympathy with the old crow. As he later wrote in his political testament, 'When success comes accidentally, that is unfortunate for one can draw no satisfactory conclusion from it.'

'Oh — *mon loup de loup*,' exclaimed the Princesse de Condé good-naturedly, 'that was an excellent lead, Your Majesty. Don't you agree, Bishop?'

'Most excellent, indeed!' responded Richelieu. 'Your Highness had no chance against such a remarkably clever defense.'

'Look, Your Majesty,' cried the young maid-of-honor, 'I held 6-3-2 in three suits.'

'And I held 6-3-2 in the other suit. That is most strange, isn't it, Duquesa?'

'Hrmmph,' replied the white-haired duenna. Apparently Bridge was not her game, but then, given her age and disposition, what could be?

'Bishop, I can see you have taught her well,' said the dowager Duchesse, stiffly rising from her chair. 'See if you fare any better than I can against these two young sharps.' Richelieu readily took both the seat and the compliments being offered. Quickly he gathered up the cards and began to shuffle; the dealer has the advantage of the first bid.

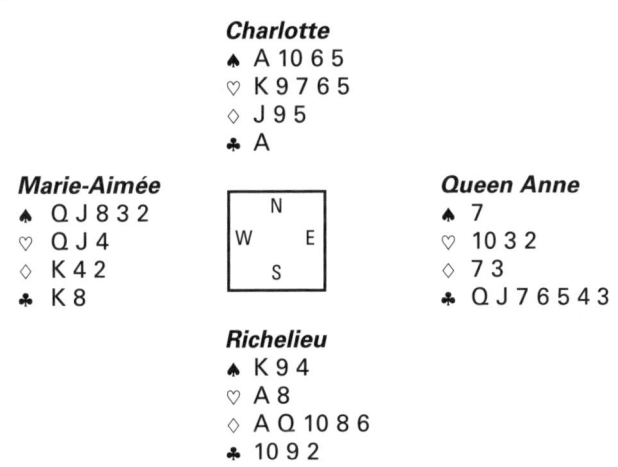

Charlotte
♠ A 10 6 5
♡ K 9 7 6 5
♢ J 9 5
♣ A

Marie-Aimée
♠ Q J 8 3 2
♡ Q J 4
♢ K 4 2
♣ K 8

Queen Anne
♠ 7
♡ 10 3 2
♢ 7 3
♣ Q J 7 6 5 4 3

Richelieu
♠ K 9 4
♡ A 8
♢ A Q 10 8 6
♣ 10 9 2

Marie-Aimée	Charlotte	Queen Anne	Richelieu
			1♢
1♠	2♡	pass	2NT
pass	3NT	all pass	

On lead against 3NT Marie-Aimée looked at her collection and considered each suit in turn. On the bidding none appealed except clubs. As her partner could hold two or three high card points at most, it appeared the only hope was that Anne held the ♣Q and some length. As a surprise attack combined with an unblocking maneuver, she decided that the ♣K had much to recommend it. Richelieu was somewhat dismayed to see this unexpected lead, and dismay led to frustrated anger when the diamond finesse lost and he found himself down three tricks. The novices had done it again!

'You did not fare as well as I did, Bishop,' chided the Princesse de Condé. 'At least I held it to down two,' she laughed. 'Next time maybe you will support my suit and avoid bidding notrump without a stopper in the fourth suit,' she added sharply, not yet convinced that his air of superiority was not misplaced.

Richelieu's cheeks took on an unaccustomed blush as he battled to control his emotions. He would have liked to reply sarcastically, 'If I were playing with a good partner naturally I would have bid 3♣, without the fear of being misunderstood,' but he didn't; he didn't because of course, it wasn't true. After a brief but fierce internal struggle, he bowed graciously to the Princesse and turned to the young lady on his left, smiling his most ingratiating smile.

'Well done, indeed, Mademoiselle. You serve Her Majesty well by putting your own interests aside so as to enable her to take the glory of the setting tricks. There is a lesson for Life in this hand, Duquesa,' he added, but the old lady had nodded off.

'Bishop Luçon,' whispered Marie-Aimée, taking advantage of this lapse in surveillance and looking into his eyes, her long, curly eyelashes flickering, 'do you think you might get the King to agree to having some targets set up in the Grand Corridor so Her Majesty might practice at the bow? We would so much like to join His Majesty's hunt, but are afraid to disgrace ourselves with a misplaced arrow.'

Richelieu was shocked by the boldness of this request, but the Queen added her voice to the request.

'Yes, please. It is rather boring stuck here in our apartments when we could be out in the forests with His Majesty. I once shot a deer while hunting with my father,' she exclaimed excitedly.

'Yes, why not?' added the Princesse easily. 'It would seem most natural that a young wife would wish to be by her husband and share in his every joy. I used to shoot, myself.'

'What sort of targets did you have in mind, Mademoiselle? Rabbits? Squirrels? Something perhaps a bit larger?' asked Richelieu, eager to please.

'Larger, much larger,' replied Marie-Aimée readily, 'Men!'

'Men! I hardly think...'

'Not real men, Your Grace, men of straw, of course,' giggled the young temptress.

The Princesse de Condé smiled. 'For now, men of straw on which to practice, but I think you will not always be content with such an easy target, Mademoiselle.'

'Pardon me, Your Highness,' replied the young imp, 'but I fear that it is men of straw who are to be my destiny; a gypsy fortune-teller said as much.'

'Men of straw have this advantage,' interposed the dowager Duchesse, who had just rejoined the group, 'they are easily set aflame.'

'Arrows may pierce their hearts, but being of little substance, they are easily put right again as good as new,' added the Princesse de Condé, throwing a sidelong glance at the Bishop.

'A nation of straw men is easily destroyed if they fall one by one, but bound together by cords of kinship, they can prevail even against the strong winds of evil fortune,' observed the Bishop severely, making a political statement in a voice loud enough to rouse the Duquesa from her nap, putting an end to the jolly conversation, as he intended it would.

Later Richelieu added to his diagram of the first hand this observation beside the Queen's hand: *Folly is more to be feared than Wisdom, since Acts of Folly are never based on Reason.* Underneath the second hand he wrote: *A young woman of wit and beauty thinks anything is possible and acts accordingly.*

Despite these disparaging words the Bishop gave the matter much thought and at last convinced himself that some advantage could be gained by following the young lady's suggestion. He persuaded the Queen Mother to set up a target range in her garden and invite her daughter-in-law over for crossbow practice and a friendly chat. It turned out that Anne was an excellent shot, but a shy conversationalist somewhat in awe of her domineering mother-in-law. Not content with the granting of this favor, Marie-Aimée, who was not shy at all, suggested the young ladies would like to try muskets next. Richelieu drew the line there. The repercussions would be unpredictable.

Marie-Aimée de Rohan-Montbazon

One day at Tours as she walked by a group of workmen one said loudly, 'There goes a beauty! I would love to be making love to her right now.' She laughed gaily, turned to them and called out, 'There's another one who prefers the work that others do.'

Richelieu
and the
Cardinals

$\mathcal{J}$f flour is to rise in an oven and become bread, it requires water, sugar and yeast. If a man is to rise in Court and become a power, he requires adaptability, servility, and sponsorship. Now that the reader has been introduced to the young ladies who would later constitute the Cardinal's most persistent opposition, let us return to the previous year, 1615, to the time before Richelieu had won the favor of Marie de Medici. The Queen Mother was Italian and, as such, supported the efforts of Spain to reunify Europe under one religion. To many Frenchmen this was a fit objective, whereas to others it appeared that she was putting the interests of foreign powers above those of the country she ruled. The French clergy was split on this issue. The Ultramontanists, led by Cardinal de La Rochefoucauld, advocated full support for the Pope, whereas the Gallicans, led by Cardinal Du Perron, were willing to give him only conditional support. Under these circumstances it was wise for a young cleric to keep his personal opinions to himself.

In early 1615 Richelieu was in Paris as a delegate to the Estates-General meetings. As an up-and-comer he had expected to be chosen as one of the keynote speakers, but he was passed over for this and given the less glorified role of a behind-the-scenes negotiator. While this gave him the opportunity to meet face-to-face with the deal-makers, the position entailed little more than dashing here and there as a glorified messenger boy. It was with the expectation of better things to come that the twenty-nine-year-old Bishop of Luçon arrived on the evening of January 20, 1615 at the sumptuous residence of Cardinal Du Perron in answer to a summons to take part in a few relaxing rubbers of Bridge after another hectic day of toing and froing.

It was well after nine o'clock before Richelieu was ushered into the card room where sat the three most influential prelates of France: the Cardinals Du Perron, La Rochefoucauld, and Sourdis, the latter being a president of the Estates. After kneeling before each and kissing their rings, Richelieu took his seat as the elderly Du Perron dealt out the cards. The game progressed quickly. Richelieu was nervous in the company of such exalted personages, but not too nervous to notice that the Cardinals had a distinct preference for playing in 3NT contracts, regardless of distributional or high card deficiencies. It seemed their attitude was that 'all roads lead to 3NT' and if a hand could not be played in 3NT, it should be tossed in. The other condition of the game that was remarkable was that these were the only men he had ever encountered who could play effectively and talk seriously at the same time.

After two rubbers the conversation turned to the real purpose behind their summons: what the Cardinals were planning for Richelieu's future. This was the deal on which all was revealed.

La Rochefoucauld
- ♠ Q 10
- ♡ Q 9
- ◇ A Q J 2
- ♣ A K 7 5 2

Du Perron
- ♠ K 9 7 2
- ♡ A J 8 7 2
- ◇ 8 4 3
- ♣ 10

Richelieu
- ♠ J 8 6 5
- ♡ K 10
- ◇ 7 6
- ♣ Q 9 8 6 4

Sourdis
- ♠ A 4 3
- ♡ 6 5 4 3
- ◇ K 10 9 5
- ♣ J 3

Du Perron	La Rochefoucauld	Richelieu	Sourdis
pass	1♣	pass	1♡
pass	2◇	pass	3NT
all pass			

Du Perron initiated the revelations.

'By the way, Armand, please give our best wishes to your brother, Henri, on his recent marriage. Pass.'

'It's very useful to have an older brother who can give you some leverage at the Court — a club,' put in La Rochefoucauld.

'Thank you for your good wishes, Your Eminences. I certainly shall pass them along. Pass,' said Richelieu appropriately.

'Yes, Henri has a very good heart. One heart,' commented Sourdis. 'That makes you all the more valuable to our organization, Armand.'

'Tonight we have been discussing your future,' revealed Du Perron. 'I suppose you have wondered why we passed over you in the selection of the public speakers at the Estates-General. Pass.'

'The reason was,' explained La Rochefoucauld in his turn, 'that we didn't want you to get embroiled in public debates on such politically sensitive topics as the limitations on papal authority and the acceptable justifications for tyrannicide. No, you and your brother are very much diamonds-in-the-rough who can do with a bit of judicious private polishing before being put on public display. Two diamonds.'

'I shall serve in whatever humble capacity you see fit,' assured Richelieu, 'without complaint. Pass.' In truth he was somewhat piqued at not being given a more prominent role.

'Of course you will, Armand, we never doubted that,' said Sourdis reassuringly. 'The time has now come for you to be informed of our great plans for the future — three notrump,' declared the president of the clergy. As expected this was passed out.

'Knowing you as I do, I imagine it will not come as a great surprise,' said Du Perron, placing the ♠2 on the table.

'You will not be disappointed in what we have to offer,' said La Rochefoucauld, laying his cards on the table. It was indeed a fine dummy.

'Our plan is for you first to ingratiate yourself with one of our major allies within the Court — the Queen,' said Cardinal Sourdis, calling for dummy's top spade. 'We want you to become a member of her clique — now a small club,' he added pointing at the ♣2.

This *was* a surprise.

'The Queen!' Richelieu exclaimed, rising with ♣Q. He paused to consider this unexpected development. Marie de Medici, as Regent, suffered from no dearth of toadies.

'Not the Queen Regent,' said La Rochefoucauld, correcting a possible misunderstanding.

'We are thinking of something new for you: the post of Grand Almoner to the *future* Queen, provided you feel comfortable in that capacity,' indicated Du Perron.

As it appeared that the defense could make at most four tricks on a spade return, Richelieu tried the effect of opening up declarer's suit.

'What of the King?' he asked, placing the ♡K on the table.

'The King is the key,' stated Sourdis, 'but any precipitate move in that direction could prove highly dangerous. It's all a matter of timing,' he added craftily. Eventually he played the ♡3.

'I am most honored and shall serve where best I can,' the Bishop commented, much pleased that the ♡K was standing up. 'Meanwhile, shall I continue on as usual?'

'I shall inform you if a change is required,' replied Du Perron, coolly signaling encouragement with the ♡8.

Richelieu continued with the ♡10, Du Perron overtook with the ♡A and claimed down two.

The Cardinals knew they had chosen the right man.

As for Richelieu, he realized his mother had been right to insist on his learning Bridge at an early age, telling him, 'Armand, when courting favor it is sometimes useful to have a useless accomplishment.'

Richelieu
and the
Young King

he Bishop of Luçon, intellectual, scholastic, and an excellent orator, had made a hit with the closing address of the Estates-General in February 1615. He was deemed to be just the man for the task of elevating Louis' mind. At the time Louis was a chubby youth of thirteen years of age, extremely shy with girls, but good at handcrafts, a lover of the outdoors — in short, the ideal Boy Scout. From experience, Richelieu knew what middle-aged matrons wanted most (flattery fraught with classical allusion) but he was somewhat at a loss as how best to entertain the royal cub. The sylvan haunts of hoof and wing that served others as common ground over which to approach the King and win his favor did not appeal to the urbane prelate. In the end he adopted the style of an overly friendly schoolmaster and that resulted in his first major flop.

One rainy afternoon in March 1615, Madeleine de Souvré, daughter of the Governor to Louis XIII, hurried down the Grand Gallery with a large book under her arm. It was not to return an already long overdue item to the Royal Library that she was in such great haste, no, she was late for her tryst with the Duc de Montmorency. Due to her nearsightedness she nearly collided with the man she least wanted to meet.

'Oh, here you are, dearest,' said her father, who was also nearsighted, 'I have been looking for you everywhere. Come with me to the lecture I have arranged for the King.'

'I'm sorry, Daddy, but I simply must return this book to my friend instantly.'

'Richelieu on Bridge will be a rare treat,' said the Maréchal, myopically scanning the far wall, 'I am hoping Bridge will provide His Majesty with a casual environment in which to learn the logical thought processes that lead to good judgement and intelligent planning. You would benefit greatly, Young Lady.'

'I'm sorry, Daddy, but ...'

'Planning is paramount. You wouldn't be in such a rush now to return your friend's book if you had planned better. Time and timing, they go hand in hand. Bridge teaches one to plan ahead for the golden opportunities that come along all too infrequently. As for Bridge and timing ...'

'But, Daddy, I have this terrible headache right now.'

'No more 'buts'. As your father I must insist, Madeleine. Amongst other things the Bishop will be describing all the positive responses to the Canonical Club; you won't want to miss that, surely.'

At this point Madeleine swooned. She was saved from a potentially nasty bump by a handsome young man who happened by at the right time and caught her as she fell.

'Most excellent timing, Henri,' exclaimed Souvré. 'Don't worry about her, it's just one of her dizzy spells. Look, I'm in a bit of a rush, the King's lecture and so on, so could you see to it that Madeleine gets put to bed immediately and is given something warm and stimulating?'

'Maréchal,' replied the Duc de Montmorency, 'I shall attend to it p-personally.'

Richelieu began his lecture with a survey of national characteristics, which he felt would be useful to the King in the context of foreign affairs. He started with the English.

'Beware the Englishman, Your Majesty — his is a perverse and contrary nature. He is not content playing methods adopted by the rest of the civilized world, but persists in utilizing his own peculiar bidding system. He tries to convert others to his way through the distribution of books by clever authors that purport to be on card play, but into which are woven multitudinous examples of this strange scheme to which every Frenchman may feel a justifiable revulsion.

'When during the reign of your good father I was in England on a secret mission, disguised as a salty tar, I had occasion to play at the Mermaid Club against two of the best of the English players, Sir Francis Bacon and Ben Jonson. I must in truth report this encounter as a cautionary tale. Although I support the rights of any citizen to employ the weak notrump, never would I recommend the use of it to Your Majesty — it lacks sufficient dignity and is subversive in the extreme. Here is such an opening bid,' said the Bishop, indicating a large display board be brought forth by two handsome pageboys with long, curly locks.

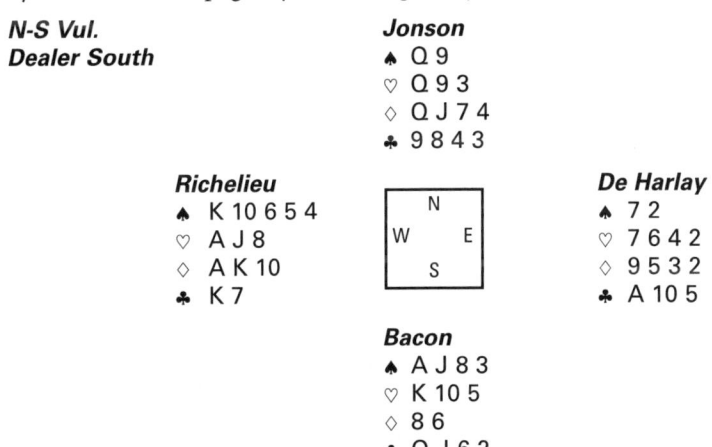

N-S Vul.
Dealer South

Jonson
♠ Q 9
♡ Q 9 3
◇ Q J 7 4
♣ 9 8 4 3

Richelieu
♠ K 10 6 5 4
♡ A J 8
◇ A K 10
♣ K 7

De Harlay
♠ 7 2
♡ 7 6 4 2
◇ 9 5 3 2
♣ A 10 5

Bacon
♠ A J 8 3
♡ K 10 5
◇ 8 6
♣ Q J 6 2

'When Sir Francis opened 1NT, I asked the meaning of the bid and was informed with much alcoholic prolixity that it was natural and promised 10 to 12 HCPs. They call this bid *Sweet Kate*. Note that, Your Majesty. Note well the bare 11 HCPs in the South hand with the wide-open diamond suit. Note the vulnerability.

Note the position — first hand opening! And it is a minister of the crown who acts thusly!' Richelieu laughed a bitter laugh, then added fervently, 'Thank *le Bon Dieu* for the English Channel, Your Majesty! Yes, thank you, dear Lord! Long may its waters froth and churn like their sour beer in the stomach and continue to keep those English far away from the hallowed ground of France.'

'Amen,' added Souvré and the assembled courtiers.

'Well, naturally, I doubled this miserable contract, as who would not? I led my fourth highest from my longest and strongest, which I am sure Your Majesty recognizes as the proper lead against a NT contract. The ♠9 wins in dummy — ah, the luck of the Devil to find such a dummy, *n'est-ce pas*? The ♣3 is played to the ♣Q and my king. Naturally I think this is a finesse with Sir Francis holding the ♣A, so I now play the ♡J as an unblocking play, hoping to set up tricks in my colleague's hand. Pah! The accursed dummy wins again, and the ♣9 is led to the ♣J. The club exit puts my partner on lead. When I discard the ◊10, Bacon unblocks the ♣8 in the dummy. De Harlay returns a spade, but he is too late. If only he had won the ♣A at the first opportunity! But I do not blame him; how was he to know? I win my king and I exit a spade. Sir Francis plays a heart: I win, I cash my top diamonds, but by now declarer has seven tricks by way of two hearts, two clubs and three spades.'

The audience began to buzz as most had not followed the play exactly, the Bishop having run through the play too quickly. Richelieu paused, took out a handkerchief and wiped his brow. His face had turned quite pale at the recollection of this humiliation. Regaining his composure, he gave a wan smile and raised his narrow shoulders in a Gallic shrug.

'Ah, well, Your Majesty, what can one do? *C'est magnifique, mais ce n'est pas le Bridge.* Give the Devil his due and perhaps learn something. The Lesson, I respectfully submit, is: don't desire to have all the power in your own hand. A balance of strength is always more effective. So, Your Majesty, I advise you to keep this principle in mind when dealing with your ministers of state.'

Richelieu bowed low as the courtiers responded with a flutter of applause. They were all for sharing power with the King.

'The English are so boring,' said the King with a yawn, 'Don't you have some stories of Spaniards?' Louis was scheduled to be married to the Infanta Ana by the end of the year.

'Spaniards?' replied Richelieu, taken aback by Louis' adverse reaction. Keenly feeling a need to regain some lost ground, he shuffled nervously through his papers. If a doubled 1NT contract did not raise sufficient interest, how about a grand slam, always so appealing to the superficial mind?

'For true excitement, no one matches the Italians — but Your Majesty knows that full well, for is not your mother sprung from that boisterous and lovable stock? And in all of Italy, for sheer excitement, nothing matches the consistorial *Sanctum Sanctorum Bridgium*, where the Cardinals play exclusively what is known as the Canonical Club. All strong hands are opened with a bid of one club. And do you know their definition of a strong hand, Your Majesty? It is anything with sixteen points or more! Imagine that, a strong hand — sixteen points. How presumptuous!' The Bishop's thin laughter was accompanied by some polite chuckles from some of the older courtiers who once followed Henri IV, but many of the younger politicians refrained from any show of compliance to these dangerous, mocking remarks directed at papal authority. Richelieu indicated a second display be brought forth.

'Excitement, Your Majesty? What of this grand slam played by Cardinal Barberini in 1607?'

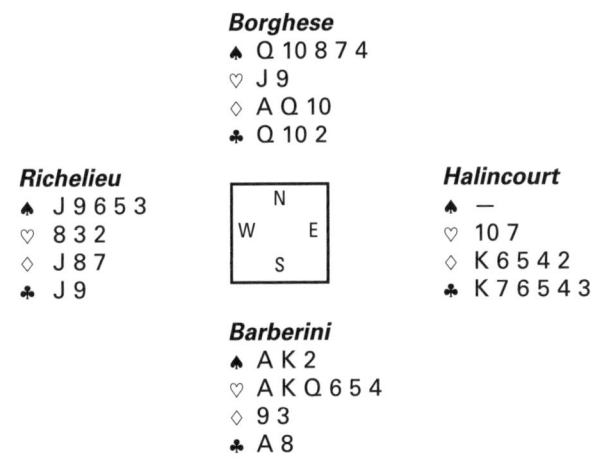

Borghese
- ♠ Q 10 8 7 4
- ♡ J 9
- ◇ A Q 10
- ♣ Q 10 2

Richelieu
- ♠ J 9 6 5 3
- ♡ 8 3 2
- ◇ J 8 7
- ♣ J 9

Halincourt
- ♠ —
- ♡ 10 7
- ◇ K 6 5 4 2
- ♣ K 7 6 5 4 3

Barberini
- ♠ A K 2
- ♡ A K Q 6 5 4
- ◇ 9 3
- ♣ A 8

'Since with sixteen or more points they open one club, and because their faith is strong, the Holy Fathers can open the bidding on values which to call adequate would strain the credulity of men of lesser faith. Here Cardinal Borghese saw fit to open the bidding with 1♠. In this view he would be close to those of the heretical British. The world of politics is like our own true world, spherical, so although the Italians and the British are thought to be at opposite ends to each other, so far apart are they that they actually meet at a point of agreement,' said the Bishop moving his thin arms in a circular motion to demonstrate his point. The British and Papal delegates exchanged glares, agreeing to agree that Richelieu was totally wrong in this concept.

'Indeed, global geometry is such,' continued Richelieu, 'that the greatest distance between two extremes can be the point halfway between the two. Thus, a man of moderate opinions may find himself attacked from both extremes by those who share the commonality of opposition to the voice of reason.'

Richelieu sniffed with satisfaction as the young king nodded his comprehension. Having made a point in favor of Reason, the Bishop returned to Bridge.

'Hearing a bid of 1♠ from his partner, Barberini immediately applied the screws of the Inquisitional 4NT. After a response of 5◇ indicating one ace (that at least was a blessing), an artificial bid of 5♡ inquired of the ♠Q, since spades were the agreed trump suit. When Borghese bid 6♠ to confirm possession of that card, you may well imagine my excitement at the defensive prospects. Alas, it was not to be an auspicious hand as the crafty Barberini now bid 7NT!

'In such company it would be wondrous to receive, although inappropriate to seek, divine assistance, so I had to content myself with the safe lead of a heart. You see the advantages in Barberini's approach of keeping one's intentions hidden to the last possible moment. Whether in the management of the play of cards or in the management of affairs of state, secrecy and diligence are so necessary to success as to dwarf all other attributes.'

Once more Richelieu paused until the King stopped wiggling in his throne and nodded an acknowledgement that he had got the message.

'The Cardinal took the ♡J in dummy and played a spade to hand, then paused to plan his play. I could well feel admiration for this keen mind as he plotted his steps in the face of the unexpected bad break in the suit on which he had placed such great hopes. So must statesmen plan coolly in the face of unexpected calamities, and not give up hope. In fact, what appears at first to be bad news often ends up as being a blessing in disguise. Never give up hope, Your Majesty. The trick is to turn events to your own advantage, as I shall now demonstrate.'

A large chart held up by two more apple-cheeked pages showed this six-card ending:

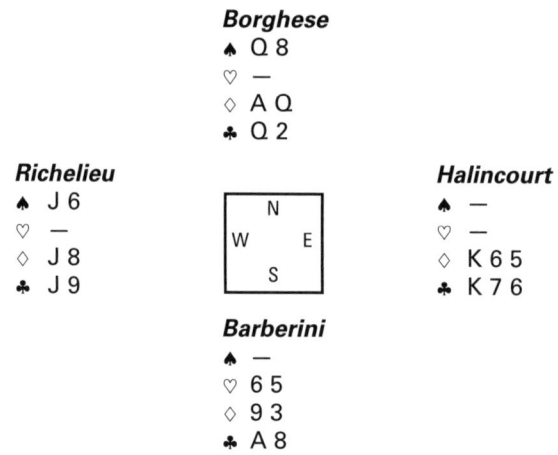

'Barberini had taken the marked finesse in spades, then played off his winners in the heart suit. On the ♡6, I threw my ◇8 and declarer discarded the ♣Q from dummy. Because I had begun with a long suit, spades, and had not discarded clubs earlier, he placed the ◇K with Halincourt. The Cardinal played his last heart and, after I had parted with my last diamond, threw the ◇Q from dummy. A diamond to the now bare ace caught me in an embarrassment. I had to keep two spades, so could keep just one club. On the play of the ♠Q from dummy, Halincourt suffered a similar martyrdom — he had to keep his ◇K and so also had to come down to a single club. Now the Cardinal's ♣8 proved to be his thirteenth trick. What a remarkable man, Your Majesty! I had witnessed a far-sighted play that could serve as a model for optimism in the expectation of good fortune and diligence in the face of adversity. Note also the selection of a notrump contract when holding two strong suits as a guard against a bad division of trumps. This is like carrying two strings to one's bow. It would not be surprising if someday he were to be elected Pope to the advantage of all Christendom.' (Indeed, this Cardinal Barberini was to become Pope Urban VIII in 1623.)

After the lecture the King's boyish, thirty-eight-year-old companion, Charles d'Albert de Luynes, asked Louis if he had enjoyed the Bishop's talk. Louis shrugged — obviously the Bishop had failed to impress. The lad felt he had been talked down to and thus belittled. Instinctively he recognized that the flow of words was not driven by the force of sincerity.

'I was bored,' Louis replied simply. 'I don't think Monsieur de Luçon can be much of a player — all he could talk about were his failures. By the way, Luynes, I was wondering, do you find my mother exciting in any way?'

'Er... no, Your Majesty,' responded the 'Scout Master' carefully, 'She's not the type one could ever refer to as 'a good sport'. But listen, why not let's go out and fly a kite.'

Henri II, Duc de Montmorency

Montmorency was the epitome of the gallant nobleman. Once he was approached in his courtyard by a suppliant who begged a rather large sum of money ($150,000) to invest in an enterprise that couldn't fail, or so he claimed. The Duc, scarcely breaking stride, unhesitatingly granted his request. Two years later when the man returned with the loan in hand plus the profits earned on the investment, Montmorency refused the money saying, 'It is repayment enough that you have returned as promised.'

Richelieu's
Bad
Dream

is brilliant successes at the Estates-General had cost Richelieu much in the way of nervous energy. He lingered on in Paris for a while but when promotion did not follow quickly, his mind sank into a deep depression that only peace and quiet could cure. Six months in retreat at the Priory of Coussay, spent on a critical study of Jesuit writings, acted as a cold compress on a fevered forehead.

✝ ✝ ✝

One hot afternoon in August 1615, a lethargic Richelieu sat at his window over-looking the priory gardens. From his accustomed armchair he had a full view of the road to Paris. If there were to come an urgent message recalling him to Court, it would be along this road the messenger would gallop. At the moment there was not to be seen in motion even a farmer in an oxcart. In Richelieu's lap rested an open book, the latest word from the Jesuits on insubstantial squeezes. As he gazed at the pastoral scene before him, he became drowsy, his eyelids grew heavy, his hand slipped from the book, and he commenced to dream of a magnificent triple squeeze. La Rouchepousay, Bishop of Poitiers, was in the dream acting as his part-ner against two of the resident monks.

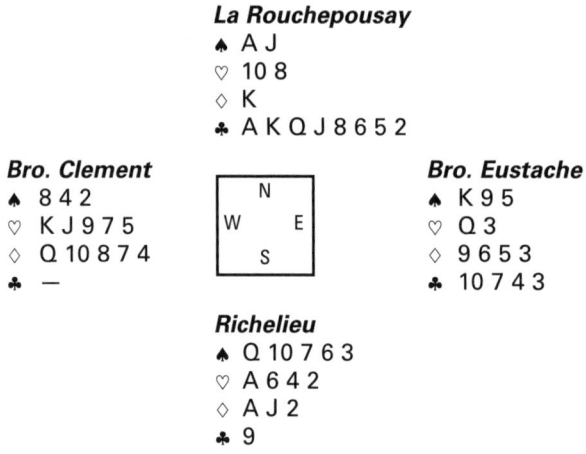

La Rouchepousay
- ♠ A J
- ♡ 10 8
- ◊ K
- ♣ A K Q J 8 6 5 2

Bro. Clement
- ♠ 8 4 2
- ♡ K J 9 7 5
- ◊ Q 10 8 7 4
- ♣ —

Bro. Eustache
- ♠ K 9 5
- ♡ Q 3
- ◊ 9 6 5 3
- ♣ 10 7 4 3

Richelieu
- ♠ Q 10 7 6 3
- ♡ A 6 4 2
- ◊ A J 2
- ♣ 9

Clement	La Rouchepousay	Eustache	Richelieu
			1♠
2♠	dbl	2NT	pass
3◊	3♡	pass	3NT
pass	6♣	pass	6NT
pass	pass	dbl	all pass

The hot-headed Henri-Louis Chasteignier de La Rouchepousay was an implacable scourge of witches and heretics. Also, he was at all times a trying Bridge partner. When Brother Clement showed a weak hand with hearts and an undis-closed minor, La Rouchepousay doubled, ostensibly suggesting penalty. This allowed Brother Eustache to ask for an identification of the minor. The Bishop then made a nebulous forcing cuebid in hearts. When Richelieu admitted to a stopper in that suit, La Rouchepousay made a wild leap to slam in his long suit, which Richelieu concluded at length was a 'choice-of-slam' bid. Somewhat uneasily he corrected to 6NT, hoping for a diamond lead.

Brother Clement took his time searching for the killing lead. His thick lips moved silently as he scratched the orange fringe at the back of his bald head.

'Come along now, Brother Clement, we don't want to cut deeply into Vespers,' remarked La Rouchepousay impatiently.

'Do you need a review, Brother?' urged Eustache. 'I doubled.'

'It's not easy, but here goes,' said Clement finally, placing the ♡J on the table.

Richelieu counted twelve tricks, but the opening lead had fouled his communications. No matter, the Brothers had trouble keeping track of the cards, so there was a good possibility of a squeeze and endplay on the run of the clubs, especially if they were played quickly. This was the position after the play of the last club from dummy:

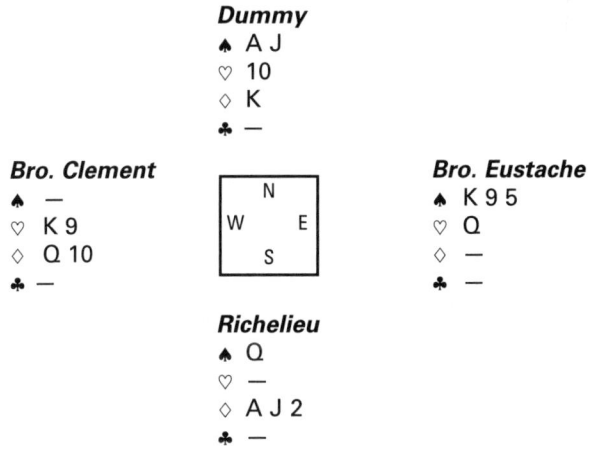

Richelieu dreamed he cashed the ♠A with great hope of a squeeze and endplay, but Brother Clement surprisingly was up to the challenge — he unblocked the ♡K. Richelieu cashed the ◇K then exited from dummy with the ♡10, but Brother Eustache won the ♡Q and took the ♠K for the setting trick.

'What a devilish lead!' exclaimed La Rouchepousay, 'I believe that was the only one to beat it. A low heart lead eats up the queen and the endplay becomes inevitable.'

A sneer crept across the face of the normally respectful Clement.

'Yes, no matter what you pretend, you aristocrats are not the only ones capable of benefiting from reading *Bellarmine on Squeezes*,' he stated brazenly. 'You, Monsieur,' he said rudely, pointing at Richelieu, 'who taught you how to read? Your mother, no doubt, and she was common like us.'

'And who called you her 'little sickling' and nursed you through your childhood illnesses? It was your mother and she was one of us, no doubt about it,' commented hefty Brother Eustache, baring his yellow teeth in a manner most threatening.

'Say this isn't true, Armand,' pleaded La Rouchepousay, whose ancestry was officially beyond question.

'Ravillac won't be the last man of religion to use his knife for something other than cutting cheeses,' said Clement, drawing a vicious-looking blade from the sleeve of his cassock.

'If anyone is in league with the Devil, it's you,' accused Eustache, rising from his chair as someone grasped Richelieu roughly from behind by the shoulder.

'Scoundrels!' exclaimed Richelieu, preparing to defend himself. As he emerged from his troubled dream he saw a solicitous Brother Clement bending over him, a look of concern on his face.

'A thousand pardons for disturbing your rest, Monseigneur, but look there, coming down the road in a cloud of dust, surely that must be a royal messenger by the looks of him.'

The royal messenger brought a summons to a meeting with Marie de Medici in Poitiers. The Queen had a strong heart, but a weak mind. The phrase 'out of sight out of mind' might have been invented for her, but there was a noble thread running through her weak fabric. Devout and Italian, she believed the pope should be obeyed unquestioningly. Valuing money highly, she believed that those who were bribed should stay bribed. Loyal herself, she believed that those whom she brought to power owed her a lifetime of service. If the world were a better place she would have been a successful ruler, but the world is what it is and she was doomed to repetitious disappointment and failure.

Six weeks later La Rouchepousay escorted a fully recovered Richelieu into the presence of the Regent who was seated on an elevated throne surrounded by several ladies and courtiers in magnificent attire. On her right sat her oldest friend and staunchest supporter among the French ladies, Louise-Marguerite de Lorraine, Princesse de Conti, not the gentlest or most submissive or most beautiful of women, but clever, honest, practical, and high-spirited.

What the Queen lacked in beauty she nearly made up for in a dazzling display of jewelry. Her naturally rosy red cheeks and stocky frame were evidence of robust good health and overflowing confidence. And why not? Her cherished dream of a double royal marriage with Spain was soon to be realized and thereby she imagined she would be establishing peace in her own time in a Europe unified by the One True Faith. Richelieu bowed as humbly as his high churchly status would allow. He was disappointed in not seeing some spark of recognition in the Regent's eye.

'Ah, at long last we meet,' greeted the Queen of France heartily, extending a pudgy hand topped by a large ruby ring, 'We have read your inspiring book and taken much good instruction therefrom.'

'I am honored, Your Majesty,' replied Richelieu, who had written many books. Not wishing to appear backward, he added audaciously, 'Would Your Majesty be referring to my most recent humble work, *Fifty Rules of Catholic Conduct?*'

'I was not! But you must send us a hundred copies to be distributed to the ladies and gentlemen you see around you. They could use some moral instruction. But no, Bishop, I was referring to your *Bridge for Novices.*'

'Your Majesty is most kind, but I feel I should not accept great credit for merely setting down on paper that which must be obvious to most players of experience, namely, that in Bridge, as in Life, Reason should govern our actions. Reason dictates tolerance of and allowance for the weaknesses of our fellow participants; my methods follow simply and logically from this primary assumption.'

The Queen nearly swooned upon hearing these words. How often had she stood in dire need of the allowances that the Bishop so eloquently advocated. As she and the Bishop went on to discuss at length the reduction in the requirements for an opening bid when holding a long suit, the Princesse de Conti turned to whisper to the handsome soldier who stood nearby, 'I seem to recall that crooked nose.'

François de Bassompierre, Marquis d'Harouel, was a soldier more noted for his invasions of friendly bedrooms than of hostile territories. However, he had risked his life in battle many times in the past and would do so again in the future, except that now he took risks not in a quest for glory, but for a reaffirmation of the value of a life that even in its thirty-sixth year threatened at times to become stale.

'You may recall he gave the closing speech for the clergy at the Estates-General last year,' he replied, taking the opportunity to press close as he whispered in her ear.

'I remember now, I liked that speech for it was the shortest by far,' said the Princesse, turning her head to give the gallant an encouraging smile. 'A long sermon is the triumph of zeal over wit.'

'And, like Bridge, a victory of invention over necessity.'

'What are you two whispering about?' demanded the Queen sharply.

Bassompierre bowed apologetically. 'We were expressing the fervent wish that we might be allowed the pleasure of playing Bridge with the Bishop during our visit to fair Poitiers. We are anxious to discover if the Bishop plays as well as he preaches.'

The Queen hooted joyously. 'What a splendid suggestion! You others, why didn't you think of it? Bassompierre. you shall partner me and, Bishop, you shall have the Princesse de Conti. Come back tonight at ten.'

'Now see what you've got us into,' whispered the Princesse as she curtsied.

'Me?' retorted the Marquis as he bowed. 'Don't you think I had better plans for this evening?'

Bassompierre was one of the most successful gamblers of his day and often acquired at the card table the wherewithal to support his extravagant tastes. Richelieu was as sound as any contemporary, but six months of Bridge with the innocent brothers in holy orders at Coussay had dulled his practical skills, as the following hand demonstrated.

Princesse de Conti
♠ 9 8 7 5 4 2
♡ K J 9 4 3
♢ —
♣ 4 2

Marie de Medici
♠ —
♡ Q 10 2
♢ 9 7 5 4 3 2
♣ Q 7 5 3

N
W E
S

Bassompierre
♠ Q J 6 3
♡ 7 6 5
♢ K 10
♣ K J 8 6

Richelieu
♠ A K 10
♡ A 8
♢ A Q J 8 6
♣ A 10 9

Marie	Conti	Bassompierre	Richelieu
pass	pass	pass	2NT
pass	3♡	pass	3♠
pass	4♡	pass	4NT
pass	5♣	dbl	5NT
pass	5♢	pass	6♠
all pass			

Richelieu had written extensively on the use of transfers after notrump opening bids, but he was not certain to what extent they were used by court ladies. When the Princesse rebid hearts he decided the safest course was to launch into the ace-asking 4NT that serves so well to cover over a multitude of bidding sins and lacks of faith. The 5♣ response gave Bassompierre the opportunity to double for a club lead. He reasoned that it was better to indicate a lead, no matter how ill-advised that might turn out to be, than to leave the Queen to her own devices.

Richelieu showed that all aces were present with 5NT then bid 6♠, leaving it to the Princesse to correct to 6NT if necessary. In that tentative way the right slam was reached. Marie de Medici led her fourth highest club to Bassompierre's jack and Richelieu's ace. When the spade ace was played, the Queen smugly held up the ♢7 for display, looked into Richelieu's eyes and solemnly raised an inquisitive eyebrow. Richelieu hid his disappointment behind a gracious smile.

'Thank you, Your Majesty,' he said with a polite nod of the head, 'I am about to lead a diamond next.'

The Bishop cashed the ♢A, discarding a club, to which Bassompierre followed with the ♢K! In the Priory of Coussay falsecarding against a bishop was punishable by extra garden duties, so Richelieu convinced himself that the Marquis had been dealt a 4441 distribution with a singleton diamond. In that case the contract had been doomed from the start. With a heavy heart he ruffed a club to dummy and led a spade. When Bassompierre didn't cover, Richelieu won with the ♠10 in hand feeling that he had been given a reprieve. Here is how he pictured the four hands after five rounds of play:

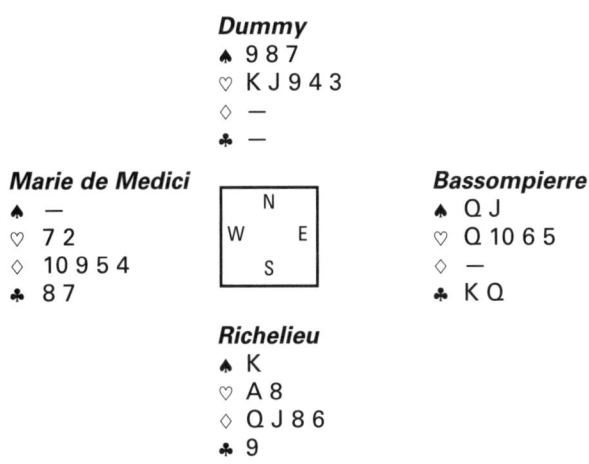

Dummy
- ♠ 9 8 7
- ♡ K J 9 4 3
- ◇ —
- ♣ —

Marie de Medici
- ♠ —
- ♡ 7 2
- ◇ 10 9 5 4
- ♣ 8 7

Bassompierre
- ♠ Q J
- ♡ Q 10 6 5
- ◇ —
- ♣ K Q

Richelieu
- ♠ K
- ♡ A 8
- ◇ Q J 8 6
- ♣ 9

Although Bassompierre's play of not splitting his honors couldn't materially affect the result, Richelieu now saw the opportunity of a swindle. He would lead the innocent-looking ◇6 and if the dull-witted Regent, not grasping the trump situation, careless failed to cover, he could pitch a heart from dummy, the Marquis would be compelled to ruff with a natural trump trick, and another unmakable contract would be made. Imagine the elation when the Regent ponderously played low on the ◇6; imagine the consternation when Bassompierre calmly produced the ◇10. What a revolting development! The would-be swindler had been swindled. This outcome served to reinforce Richelieu's conviction that 'what surprises never pleases.'

Marie de Medici clapped her chubby hands gleefully. Obviously the dictum applied only to the victim. 'Oh, Bassompierre, you are marvelous. You are so lucky, Madame, to have such a handsome gallant at your feet,' she gushed.

'At my feet, yes,' remarked the Princesse, 'but he has the audacity to aim higher,' to which the Queen hooted in good humor.

'True enough,' admitted Bassompierre. 'Of all your various parts it is your tongue I most admire, dear Lady. Like a good cider it is sharp without being bitter, sweet without being cloying, cooling and warming at the same time.'

'Marquis, your words are homely; the words conjure up images of frothing at the mouth. Could you not at least say my lips are like rosebuds?'

'I like a good Normandy cider provided it is virgin pressed,' commented the Queen inappropriately, 'It makes a good tonic.'

Richelieu felt somewhat left out during these exchanges, uncertain as to how best to reintroduce in a gracious manner a reference to his *Fifty Rules of Catholic Conduct*. His military training had taught him that a frontal attack on an established position can be costly, so wisely he decided to advance obliquely over neutral territory.

'Please excuse me, Your Majesty, but I cannot let another moment pass before congratulating the Marquis on his superb jettison of the king of diamonds.

Without that card being played I would surely have made my contract. I bow before your superior skill in all humility.'

'You mean you could still have made it even after my brilliant club lead?' exclaimed Marie de Medici.

'Yes, Your Majesty, I failed; the hearts couldn't have lain more favorably,' admitted Richelieu contritely with bowed head, overacting outrageously.

'Well! You are an honest fellow to admit it so openly — a welcome change, I must say. Humility is not only the humblest of virtues but also the rarest. We could use more of it around here.'

A timid courtier approached the Queen and asked, 'Is it Your Majesty's desire that I fetch some cider?'

'What?' exclaimed Marie de Medici. 'Not now, you numbskull, I need a clear head. Fetch me my Arabic elixir.'

Richelieu's nightmare of public humiliation had come true, but in government service mediocrity cloaked in false humility is often preferred to immodest ability. Thus, he gained much from his bad play. His humble confession of faults did what many commendations of virtues had failed to do, win an important Court appointment: Grand Almoner to the young bride, Anne of Austria. On the other hand Bassompierre was to pay dearly for his display of cleverness. Although he had been told by his mother often enough that the best medicines taste bitter, Richelieu as Prime Minister could never trust the man who so easily had made a fool of him in earlier days at Poitiers.

Richelieu
Tells
a Joke

The influence that the Cardinals could exert on the mind of the devout Queen Mother together with the favorable impression she had formed of the handsome young Bishop of Luçon bore fruit. By September 1616, Richelieu was ready to move on to higher appointments after having stood for five months on the threshold of power. The arrest in July of the Prince de Condé proved that the Italian faction surrounding Marie de Medici had gained the ascendancy, but at what cost and for how long? These and other questions Richelieu hoped to discuss with Cardinal Du Perron, the influential Grand Almoner to the King of France.

He was ushered into the study where Du Perron greeted him cordially from behind a large desk covered with papers. The Bishop was shocked to see how Du Perron had aged since the Estates-General — his famous great beard had turned entirely white. What had once bristled with rectitude now drooped with resignation.

'Forgive me for not rising, Armand, but my lumbago is giving me a problem today. Sit there and I shall ring for chocolate.'

After a polite exchange on failing health, bad weather, and the marked decrease in the morals of youth, the Cardinal took a sip of bitter chocolate and got down to particulars.

'We are pleased with your progress to date as Grand Almoner to the young Queen; even the Duquesa de Villequieras is mightily impressed with your piety. However, winning favor with Spanish matrons is one thing, winning favor with young Louis is quite another. Let me say in all frankness that your first attempt was a disappointment to me. It appears His Majesty perceives an insufficiency in your persona. What is the term he used? A wet mitten? A limp garter? Whatever. I'm not sure of the term young people use nowadays, but the message is clear and unfavorable.'

Richelieu was taken aback. A wet sock, was he? He had it on reliable authority that Louis had called the Cardinal 'an old poop', but he didn't respond in kind, replying simply, 'I understand, Monseigneur, but I thought piety would be most becoming in a Grand Almoner and...'

'Quite, quite, Armand,' interrupted Du Perron impatiently, 'piety has its place, but now it is time to move on and cultivate more pleasing characteristics if you are to progress in politics where amiability outweighs saintliness and faults find favor. The timing is right to display your humane side. Do you have a sense of humor, Armand?'

'I believe so, Monseigneur.'

'Yes, I'm sure you do, but here I am not talking of sharp wit, which is dangerous when it cuts too near the bone of truth, but broad humor which at the very worst is seen as the wisdom of a fool. Merry jests make one popular. Marie de Medici likes a good joke if it's not too long and is a bit risqué. To get to the point, do you know any jokes, Armand?'

'Yes, Monseigneur, I heard many good jokes when as a young man I underwent military training, but I hardly think they are repeatable at Court.'

'Don't be too sure on that point. Tell me your best joke, Armand, and let me decide if it's suitable or not. Mind you, it must possess novelty, or you'll be laughed at.'

Sacre bleu! mused Richelieu to himself, I thought that the whole purpose of a joke — in fact its entire *raison d' être* — was to be laughed at. If one tells a joke and is not laughed at, what's the good of it? Richelieu searched his memory for a jest suitable for Du Perron's ears.

'Ah!' he exclaimed at last, 'I remember one told me last year by an Abbesse in Luçon. I'm sure it can't have traveled this far.'

'Perhaps not, but a good joke, like bad news, travels fast. Proceed,' said Du Perron with an impatient wave of the hand. He leaned back in his chair, closed his eyes and pressed his fingertips together, listening to Richelieu's version of...

The Story of the Three Wishes

The angel Gabriel was sent down to France to seek out and reward those who were doing the Lord's work. In Bordeaux he found a young rabbi who was leading a holy life and preaching against greed. When Gabriel asked what he would like as a reward, the young Jew replied, 'Twenty gold pieces. Oh, it's not what you think: on New Year's Eve I shall distribute the money amongst those of my flock in greatest need.'

Done. Next in Lyon the angel found a pot-bellied priest who was leading a holy life and preaching against gluttony. When asked what he would like for a reward, the priest replied, 'Twenty ripe cheeses. Oh, it's not what you think: on Christmas Eve I shall give them to those who are going to bed hungry.'

Done. Finally in Montauban the angel found a white-haired Huguenot who was leading a holy life and preaching against adultery. When asked what he wanted for a reward, the elder answered, 'A vial of love potion from the Fountain of Youth. Oh, it's not what you think: I'm going to slip it into my wife's gruel.'

Gabriel frowned and said, 'I find your request inadequate — you should think again.'

'You're right,' admitted the old fellow sheepishly, 'add a spoonful for myself.'

When Richelieu finished the story, he anxiously awaited the Cardinal's verdict, but Du Perron's eyes remained closed and he continued to breathe quietly. I've put the old poop to sleep, feared Richelieu, but a moment later a thin smile played across the Cardinal's lips.

'Yes, I call that a fine joke. It has everything: structure, repetition, variety, a taint of prejudice, ambiguity, and a twist at the end, besides which there's a very profound meaning to it that I haven't yet fully fathomed. Let's see if I have got the main point. The Huguenot by forever preaching against the temptations of the flesh had aroused his own desires, but not wanting to commit a mortal sin, he plans to drug his aged wife secretly in order that he might satisfy his own lust within the bonds of holy matrimony. However, and this is the tricky part, the wife having been thus stimulated, might not be fully satisfied by the short-lived vigor of her aging husband, therefore, to keep her from sinful adulterous acts, the preacher would have to be prepared to satisfy fully those desires he himself had aroused. The angel Gabriel understood that immediately.'

'That is how the Abbesse explained it to me, Monseigneur.'

'I think I could use this jest in my introductory remarks at the next Assembly of the Holy Orders, but a story suitable to a gathering of monks is not necessarily one suitable for the young King. You'll need something less of the cloister and more of the street. Here, I have written what I think would amuse his childish mind. Practice it in private. Embellish it if you like, but be ready by Friday, when I will arrange for you to meet His Majesty informally. That will be your opportunity to spring my merry jest on him.'

On that Friday Du Perron suggested to the King that he cut short his morning sermon so as to provide an opportunity for the Cardinal to pay his respects to Queen Anne in her apartments. As expected, the fifteen-year-old was happy to be let off early, so the King and the Cardinal appeared prematurely in the Queen's sitting room, finding her still in conference with her Grand Almoner, Richelieu.

'Perhaps the Bishop can stay for a moment while I pay my respects, for I wish to have a word later,' suggested Du Perron, and again the King did not object.

After a brief, formal exchange with the Queen there was an awkward moment as Louis stood with hands on hips awaiting the churchmen's departure.

'I have noticed quite a few newcomers arrived in the town recently,' noted Du Perron with a casual air, 'it appears to be more than the normal migration.'

'Yes, and that reminds me of a funny story, perhaps you haven't heard it, Your Majesty,' added Richelieu on cue.

'How can I tell until I hear it?' replied Louis sourly. 'Is it long?'

'Well, it goes like this...'

The Adventures of the Country Bumpkin

A country bumpkin came to Paris to seek his fortune. Although his back was strong, his head was weak. On his first morning the wonderful smell of Parisian cooking reached his nostrils and he felt the pangs of hunger something fierce for he was still a growing lad. He went up to a man selling pies from a cart.

'I see your pies are five *sous* each, ' he said, 'so how much for three?'

'You mean you have never learned to multiply?' replied the pieman, whose face had all the slyness of a fox, 'Let me show you how it's done. Don't worry, I won't charge you anything for the lesson.'

Using the point of his pastry knife he drew in the dirt. 'See, there's a three and there's a five, so put them together and you have thirty-five. That's multiplication.'

'Huh, thirty-five *sous* is too expensive,' replied the ignoramus putting away his purse.

'Wait, young master,' called the pieman, 'I don't want you to go away hungry. Let me teach you division. I'll sell three to you at half price. Let's see, half of thirty-five is seventeen and a bit, call it seventeen. Only seventeen *sous* for three, *sacre bleu*, I'm selling at a loss.'

'Agreed before you change your mind!' said the bumpkin swiftly. 'And to think my mother warned me that you Parisians were shrewd.'

Richelieu paused to accept the polite laughter of the Cardinal and the assembled courtiers and ladies.

'Ho-ho,' said the King mirthlessly, 'I don't believe a word of it.'

'Your Majesty, I am mortified,' remarked the Cardinal with mock surprise, 'You don't believe what a Bishop tells you?'

'No. I don't believe what even the Pope tells me unless it is written in the Scriptures.'

'Well, it is merely an amusing story,' admitted Cardinal Du Perron, making a partial confession.

'His Majesty is quite correct not to believe what he is told even by a churchman, as he shall see from what happened next to the country bumpkin,' said Richelieu.

'Is there more?' asked Du Perron, greatly surprised.

'Yes,' said Richelieu and he related...

The Second Encounter

Later as he walked along the Seine he came across a drunken priest propped against the embankment. The old drunkard could spot them a mile away.

'Give me ten *sous*, young master,' he begged, putting out a dirty hand.

'Why should I, Reverend Father?' asked the young man.

'It's for the good of your soul. Have you never heard we must all pay for our sins?'

'But I have never sinned, Father; I have lived all my life with my parents and have never been in Paris until this very morning.'

'In that case,' said the priest, 'how about giving me a little in advance?'

Richelieu was pleased when this second installment was rewarded with more laughter than the first. Queen Anne was especially amused, wrinkling her nose and showing her fine, white teeth. This was a side of her Almoner she had not seen before.

'Is that true, Cardinal? That a sin can be paid for in advance?' asked the King.

'Of course not — it's only a funny story the Bishop dreamed up to make us laugh.'

'A pity, for that could be useful for all concerned,' Louis observed.

'If Your Majesty so pleases there is a third adventure concerning *l'amour*,' offered Richelieu.

'Oh, very well,' agreed the King, seeing that the ladies were clapping their hands in eagerness to hear it.

The Third Encounter

An amorous young wife whose husband was away for the day buying wine for his shop saw the young man coming down the street with his pack over his shoulder. She recalled that Queen Margot had claimed that one brawny bumpkin was worth two Parisian pipsqueaks. Here was the perfect opportunity for satisfying her curiosity in that regard, so she did not hesitate to invite him into her house to stay the night.

Thinking it was a lodging house and seeing how well laid out it was, over his supper the lad wondered at the lack of guests.

'Young man,' laughed the hussy, 'don't you realize my husband is away and I invited you here so we could make love all night long without interruption? Silly fool, I'm not going to charge you anything.'

'Well, a priest told me this morning that we must always pay for our sins, so seeing as I don't have to pay, then it can't be a sin,' replied the gullible young man.

(*Good grief, thought the Cardinal, what kind of monster have I here unleashed? It's a blessing the Duchesa de Villequieras' bladder has absented her from this debacle.*)

Just before midnight (*continued Richelieu*) as they were about to accomplish their third ecstasy in the master bed, the wife heard her husband's voice calling from the street below. She threw on her nightdress, hurried down, and unbolted the door.

'Husband,' she panted breathlessly, 'I have to tell you there is someone sleeping in our bed — my young cousin just arrived from Gascony looking for employment.'

'*Mon Dieu!* What a large family you come from!' exclaimed the husband. 'It's a fine thing when a man finds he can't sleep in his own bed.'

'We can make do on the smaller bed. It will be like old times. Hurry,' said the hussy whose appetite for love-making had returned with renewed fierceness. 'Oh, by the way, my cousin is not too bright, so don't believe a word he says.'

'Oh, very well,' said the husband, shedding his pantaloons, 'but tomorrow get him out of here bright and early — I don't want any fools living in my house.'

The story was received with much merriment from the courtiers, red-faced indignation from the Cardinal, and wide-eyed interest from the King.

'Obviously the man was himself a fool,' Louis concluded. 'His wife was deceiving him.'

'Quite correct, Your Majesty,' said Cardinal Du Perron.

'All those relatives — they were her numerous lovers.'

'Quite so.'

'Well, if I were he, I'd chop her head off.'

To this pronouncement the ladies in the court expressed their consternation. The faint-hearted grew pale behind their fans.

'But if you were he, a mere wine merchant, you yourself might lose your own head for exacting such a revenge,' suggested the Cardinal.

'Not at all. I'd ask the King for a pardon and he would grant it,' said Louis the Just.

'And so he should,' said Richelieu ahead of everyone else, bowing low.

Louis scowled. In his enthusiasm Richelieu had gone too far in presuming to judge he who aspired to be the supreme judge on all matters within his kingdom. It was proving difficult for the Bishop of Luçon to please the King, but the impression he had made on the courtiers was most favorable.

Marie de Medici

The royal children were raised away from the Court at St. Germain-en-Laye, a few miles west of Paris. One day the Queen expressed a motherly desire as follows, 'If I had my wish I would have one foot in Paris and the other in St. Germain.'

'In that case, Madame,' remarked Bassompierre, 'I'd like to be at Nanterre,' (which lies mid-way in between).

The Concinis

The year 1616 saw the amiable adventurer, Concino Concini, at the height of his considerable power. He had amassed a great fortune and influenced the affairs of state solely through his control over his fellow Florentine, Marie de Medici. Here was a woman who needed a man always nearby to guide her thoughts, make her laugh, and provide preposterous flattery. The handsome Concini used ever-reliable methods; at times he was called upon to add physical substantiation to his airy adoration, a matter of increasing difficulty as he advanced into middle-age suffering from a double hernia. Concini admitted even to himself that he had been lucky. In 1600, penniless, he had left Florence for France as a minor attendant to the Medici bride. As a nobleman, he lowered himself by marrying the Queen's foster sister, friend and confidante, Leonora Galigai, a strange creature, dark, ferret-faced, hunchbacked, a dealer in spells, horoscopes, and portents. He never regretted it for his wife turned out to be passionate, forgiving and clever. It was she who made their fortune. After the assassination of Henri IV the couple jointly controlled the widow whom in private they referred to as *La Balorda* — The Stupid Lump. The emergence of Richelieu was like the appearance of a small dark cloud on the horizon of an otherwise bluest of blue skies. The Bishop of Luçon was a highly intelligent, political animal whose interests spread well beyond matters of religion. As the Italian saw it, an old bull is wise to protect his pasture from any young bull that happens along, especially a black one clothed as a priest. How then to deflect the oncoming charge? The new man was incorruptible and had the strong backing of the Church, but he had an obvious weak point: a lack of ready cash. If he could be made indebted well beyond the limit he could repay, he would of necessity become Concini's creature. It was worth a try.

When Richelieu received the Regent's invitation for an evening of Bridge, he saw behind it the hand of the crafty gambler and sensed the danger. He could ill afford to lose at their customary high stakes, but neither could he afford to turn down an invitation that was tantamount to a royal command. Concini was to partner Marie de Medici, there was hope in that, whereas Richelieu was to take as partner a lady-in-waiting of his choice. Who? Having given the matter much thought, Richelieu decided upon Concini's wife. She was cunning, true, but purposeful cunning is easier to read than aimless stupidity, and he knew ahead of time that she was not to be trusted. As there would be many witnesses to the match, overt cheating would be out of the question, so a bit of luck in the cards might see him through what was going to be a formidable test of card-reading skills and partnership manipulation.

The unlucky never rise and when he needed it Richelieu always found luck to be on his side. So it was this evening; however, his luck was dissipated to a great extent by deliberate misplays on the part of Galigai. Each misplay was followed by profuse apology in broken Italianate French, which Richelieu accepted with a cheerful mien. The baser the mistake the lower he groveled. Nonetheless, when the final rubber began, the score was slightly in his favor and he made slam on the first hand after this double-dealing auction:

Galigai
♠ 9 7 5 4
♡ K 10 9 3
◇ 6 4
♣ A K 4

```
      N
  W       E
      S
```

Richelieu
♠ K Q
♡ A J 8 7 5
◇ A K Q
♣ 7 6 3

Richelieu	Galigai
1♡	2♣
2♠	3♡
6♡	pass

'Scusi, Signore,' apologized La Concina from behind the black veil she always wore in public as protection against the evil eye, 'but I am not certain I am bidding the hand in the *bestissimo* way — is *possible* we miss a *grando* slam.'

Concini led the ◇2 and Richelieu was rather put out by the evidence of the depths to which the ugly creature opposite would degrade herself in open company — he didn't concede that some people actually bid this way all the time. Be that as it may, as he had bid non-descriptively himself, he found himself fortuitously in a slam which would make provided he could find the trump queen. The Bishop decided that, rather than guess early in the trump suit, it would be better to take the slight risk of an adverse ruff and explore the distribution by playing first on the side suits, perhaps taking advantage in the play of his unusual bid in spades. It would interesting to observe his opponents' reactions.

His first move was to go to dummy with the ♣K. Concini followed with the ♣8 and Marie de Medici with the ♣10, so superficially it would appear that clubs were held in even numbers on both sides. Richelieu did not believe this for one instant. During the evening's play it had become evident that Concini had acquired the lazy habit of always falsecarding. Perhaps this was due to his many easy successes against compliant competition; at any rate it was a safe practice to adopt with his current partner who was not up to drawing inferences from the spot cards. However, at least at Bridge, always lying is nearly as bad as always telling the truth. Richelieu assumed the Regent's card was truthful and that she held four clubs whereas Concini was lying and he held three, as with five clubs he would have led one.

Next, the spade suit. Richelieu led the ♠4 from dummy towards his doubleton ♠KQ. The Regent pounced on this card with her ace like a cat on a mouse and returned the ♠3. When Concini, who had followed to the first spade with the ♠8, could not ruff on this round, the Regent's surprised expression told Richelieu that here was a woman who had started with four spades. So consistent with his false-carding practice Concini had begun with three spades; therefore, his hand initially consisted of three spades, four diamonds, three clubs, and thus, three hearts.

It was possible the opening lead of the ◇2 was from a three-card suit, but that was all the more reason to place Concini with the longer hearts. As a further test of this hypothesis, Richelieu returned to dummy with the ♣A and led the decoy ♡10 from dummy. When the Regent did not cover the honor, as was her wont, he over-took with the ace and ran the ♡J. He was right, Concini had been dealt the ♡Q tripleton and the slam was made. Richelieu could not deny himself a small reward.

'Well bid, Madame,' he said with a bow towards his furious partner, 'I think I would have stopped in game myself, but you saw the added value of four hearts to the king-ten-nine and made the forcing raise of 3♡ rather than jump to 4♡. Well bid indeed. I don't think seven is there — no, I had to lose the ace of spades.'

'Monsieur de Luçon,' asked Concini with a smile, 'may I inquire as to the meaning of your 2♠ bid? You held only doubleton, is it not?' He had never perfected his French, and his strong accent was a constant reminder of his foreign origins.

'Yes, just the two,' replied Richelieu smoothly. 'but the 2♠ bid was what we call in France a reverse. As my partner had bypassed spades, I felt that a reverse to two spades would safely convey the playing strength of my hand with much more conviction than 2◇. Happily my clever partner was able to interpret my intent,' he concluded with a second gracious bow directed across the table. The black veil conveyed agitation with a brief flap.

'Oh, Bishop, you explain even the most difficult concepts with such clarity,' lauded the Regent, with admiration shining in her calf eyes.

Now safe from financial ruin, Richelieu overbid the next hand to a close game, hoping to put a successful end to a dangerous encounter.

N-S Vul.
Dealer North

Galigai
♠ A J 9 6 4
♡ J 8 7 5
◇ A 10 7
♣ K

Concini
♠ 10 7 2
♡ 10 4
◇ 9 4
♣ A J 10 8 7 4

```
      N
   W     E
      S
```

Marie de Medici
♠ Q 8 3
♡ K Q 9 6 3
◇ K J 6 5
♣ 5

Richelieu
♠ K 5
♡ A 2
◇ Q 8 3 2
♣ Q 9 6 3 2

Concini	Galigai	Marie	Richelieu
	1♠	pass	2♣
pass	2♡	pass	3NT
all pass			

After her little companion had opened the bidding, Marie de Medici spent some time staring at her cards, while fingering thoughtfully her favorite ten-diamond cross that hung around her thick neck. Finally she managed a deep sigh and a pass. This action was not lost on Concini, who proceeded to make an unusual lead, with the smiling comment, 'I don't know if this is right, but I am often liking to lead dummy's *secondo* suit.'

The ♡10 was covered with the ♡J, ♡Q, and ♡A. Richelieu saw the ♡875 would provide a second stopper in the suit. Eight tricks were assured, so one more was needed, either a fifth spade trick or a third diamond trick. Since the spades might provide five tricks in an emergency, it seemed safe to assure a club trick first, then to decide on how to tackle the diamonds, if the ♣K were allowed to take a trick.

When Richelieu led the ♣2 towards the dummy, Concini took his ace and returned his remaining heart. The Regent took the ♡9, then the ♡K, followed by a low heart to the dummy's ♡7, setting up her fifth heart. The passivity of Concini combined with the activity of the Regent gave them the look of defenders who saw clearly that the hand with the long heart trick had an entry. That entry was most likely the ♠Q: whether or not he held the ◇K, Concini would have assumed that Richelieu needed to take the spade finesse in order to make his game.

If Marie de Medici had been an expert, Richelieu would have been less certain of the position, but he felt sufficiently confident of his grasp of that lady's capabilities to back it with an otherwise risky play: he led the ♠J from dummy. Marie de Medici automatically covered this with her ♠Q, taken by the Bishop's ♠K. Richelieu now cashed the ♣Q and noted the Regent's hesitant discard of the ◇6. Reading the position correctly, he successfully finessed Concini for the ♠10. Now he could claim his nine tricks and with them what was for him a considerable sum of money.

There was brief moment of silence as each player became lost in his or her reflections on the play. Richelieu and Concini shared a common thought: what would have happened if the Queen Mother upon winning the ♡9, instead of trying to set up an extra heart trick for the defense, had returned the ◊J in an attempt to destroy declarer's communication?

'What happened?' demanded Marie de Medici hotly, 'I never made my good heart, Concini.'

Neither gentleman saw fit to voice his misgivings on her defensive priorities. Richelieu turned deferentially to Concini as if to say, 'Yes, tell us, do.'

The amiable Concini spread his hands in a graceful gesture of submission to fate. 'It was well played,' he said, complimenting his opponent. As an experienced gambling man he could recognize a good play when he saw one and the loss of a few thousand *écus* was something he could easily afford. 'As for you, Your Majesty, your good heart will always be your greatest asset, next to your beauty, of course, even though it may not always bring you the profit it deserves. Now let's see how much these two rascals have stolen from us.'

Galigai lifted her veil and glared at the Bishop, her eyes blazing with resentment. She hated to lose, even though technically she had won.

'I donate my winnings to the relief of the poor,' the hunchback declared, hoping to gain some satisfaction from depriving Richelieu of his winnings through example.

'How gracious,' replied the Bishop. 'It just so happens that I have an appointment with Grand Almoner Du Perron tomorrow afternoon, so I shall be able to handle this matter expeditiously. I shall come by, when convenient, to collect your donation for distribution through his holy office. Naturally your name will be made known to those who receive its benefits and be assured they will forever hold in their hearts the deepest gratitude for the gracious lady from whom such largesse so readily flows.'

For effect he returned a fierce gaze directly into the eyes of the superstitious woman sitting opposite. Much alarmed, she quickly restored the protective veil.

Richelieu sent half his winnings to his ailing mother, bought some fine new clothes, purchased some expensive books that he later donated to the Sorbonne, and invested the rest in a speculative and successful chocolate venture. Leonora Galigai never fulfilled her promise of charity, but she was impressed by the Bishop's ability and helped him advance in his career, thus gaining his gratitude. This led to his obtaining the post of secretary of state for foreign affairs in November, 1616. However, she was short-sighted in another direction; events would show that it was not the clever Richelieu but 'that simpleton', Louis XIII, for whom she and her husband should have reserved their worst fears.

The
Marquise
de
Rambouillet

he condition of France had greatly deteriorated once the restraining hand of the prudent Duc de Sully had given over to the Regent the keys of the royal treasury. Now the country faced bankruptcy while some at the top prospered beyond all reasonable expectation. The most visible of these fortunate few was the foreigner Concini. Thus Richelieu's victory over the hated Concini was celebrated by 'true Frenchmen' in taverns throughout Paris.

Many were the invitations to high-stakes games in the homes of the wealthy, but Richelieu turned them down on the grounds of ill health, which was not entirely untrue. As his reputation was established, what had he to gain by gambling for stakes at which he could ill afford to lose? Therefore, it was with some surprise and delight that in late October 1616, the Marquise de Rambouillet received an apologetic letter from Richelieu belatedly accepting the long-standing invitation to dinner and cards on the condition that the table be limited to four players. This limitation well suited the purposes of the Marquise who primarily wanted to obtain the Bishop's opinion on some ideas she had concerning the promotion of French culture and woman's place in a new 'enlightened' society.

Richelieu was ever eager to seek out those who presented themselves as persons of taste and refinement, and such was the reputation of the beautiful Marquise, wife of the Master of the King's Bedchamber. Catherine de Vivonne had been born in 1588 of an Italian mother while her father was serving as French ambassador to the papacy. Like many of mixed parentage, she championed a culture to which she could lay only a partial claim, as if extraordinary efforts were required to establish her legitimacy.

The four players were to be the Marquis and Marquise, Richelieu, and, a surprising choice — this coming as it did from a promoter of women's causes — Bassompierre. He had fathered many bastards by women from the highest to the lowest stations. While in public he treated each lover with the courtesy owed a princess, in private he worked hard at implementing their ruin. Recently he had become Colonel-General of the Swiss Guard posted at the Louvre, the duties of which position would not in any way interfere with his active love life. After dinner, as the card table was being prepared, the Colonel-General drew Richelieu aside for a private conversation.

'Now, my dear Bishop, I have a very important favor to ask, or at least to me it is important,' began the handsome courtier. 'May I beg this favor?'

'I am honored,' replied Richelieu with artificial warmth. 'If a lowly prelate can be of service to a distinguished soldier of France whom the King holds in highest regard, then he has but to be asked, and if the favor is in his power to grant, it shall be granted. I trust your endeavor is not directed towards an illegitimate end,' added the Bishop jokingly.

The gallant flicked his mustaches for effect. 'You see, dear chap, it is this: could we make the bridge game as brief as possible? There is a certain lady in the Louvre who would be most inconvenienced if my departure were to be delayed much beyond half an hour after ten.'

'There is no problem, I assure you, as I, too, am feeling feverish and would welcome an early return to bed.'

The gallant patted the Bishop's shoulder in a comradely fashion. 'Good man,' he said with a wink. 'You know, Bishop, I just today learned of a curious fact of which you may be unaware. It is common knowledge that tides and women are governed by the moon, but did you know that all the ladies of the court begin menstruation within hours of each other? I am assured this is true by the King's physician. Curious, is it not?'

Richelieu, who forever admired the workings of the mind, felt that the functioning of the human body did not bear up as well under close inspection. 'Really?' he said, managing politely to express mild interest on a distasteful topic. At times he found Bassompierre altogether too Germanic.

'Héroard swears it is true and why should he lie? It seems when a lady newly comes to court, she is not fully accepted until her menses comes to coincide with the others. I wish it were otherwise, for there are always days of the month on which I must seek my diversion far afield.'

Bassompierre's bright eyes twinkled with amusement as he gazed at the Bishop's face, waiting to see if he had managed to provoke a fitting comment.

'Indeed, I have heard it said that, although a man's passion is sometimes constrained by his conscience, the only curb to a woman's passion is lack of opportunity,' replied the Bishop.

The great lover laughed. 'True enough, but would we men have it any other way?'

The bridge proceeded in a perfunctory manner, punctuated by many comments by Richelieu along the lines of: 'Madame must not underlead an ace', 'Madame must count the tricks needed at the beginning of the play', 'Madame should not bid notrump without a stopper in an opponent's bid suit, even if it did succeed on this occasion.' At last Richelieu faced a problem in which he was able to demonstrate a principle through exemplary play.

N-S Vul.
Dealer North

Marquise
♠ Q J 2
♡ 9 8 6 3
◇ A Q 7
♣ J 9 4

Marquis
♠ A K 9 5 3
♡ A 10 4 2
◇ 6 4
♣ A 8

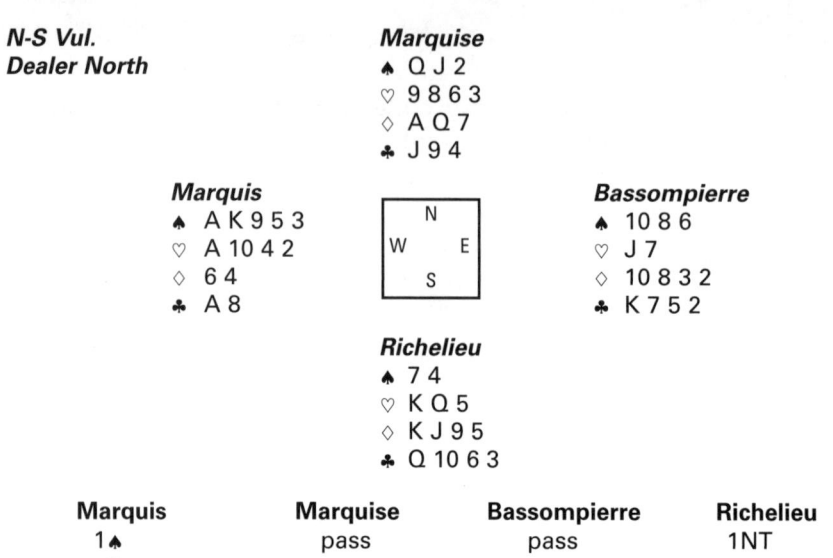

Bassompierre
♠ 10 8 6
♡ J 7
◇ 10 8 3 2
♣ K 7 5 2

Richelieu
♠ 7 4
♡ K Q 5
◇ K J 9 5
♣ Q 10 6 3

Marquis	Marquise	Bassompierre	Richelieu
1♠	pass	pass	1NT
all pass			

The Marquis led his fourth-highest spade which was taken by the ♠Q in the dummy. Richelieu saw he had seven losers, so seemed destined to go down one, but that had not yet happened and Rambouillet was not the brightest of players. It appeared likely that the top clubs were divided, therefore the Marquis must hold the ♡A for his opening bid. There would be no harm in playing off the diamonds.

On the third diamond the Marquis discarded the ♡4 and on the fourth, the ♣8, after taking a long look at the four hearts remaining in dummy. Richelieu led the ♡Q from his hand on which the Marquis played low, hoping to see his partner win the trick with the ♡K and play a second heart through declarer. Of course this was a dream without substance, but the Marquis was one of those players who see only the cards in their own hands. When Richelieu exited with a spade towards the ♠J in dummy, the Marquis was forced to take his six tricks then give Richelieu his contract by leading to the ♡K at the end. Seventy points was sufficient to score up a vulnerable game.

'How marvelous!' commented the Marquise, clapping her hands, 'I was right not to raise to two, wasn't I?'

'Perfectly correct,' replied the Bishop, 'Well bid, Marquise. But now I must ask a favor of the Colonel-General, one to which he has graciously consented earlier. I would like to take this opportunity to speak with the Marquise concerning some matters of Christian charity that would not long engage the military mind and he has kindly offered to allow us some time together for this purpose.'

'The Bishop is being diplomatic,' stated Bassompierre. 'In fact, it is I who must return to the Louvre to attend to an important matter which requires my immediate attention.'

'Well, in that case, you won't be needing me any further this evening, my dear,' said the Marquis brightly, 'so, if you will permit, Colonel-General, I would consider it an honor to be allowed to accompany you to the palace, for I, too, have left too long undone matters that must now be attended to expeditiously.' This excuse was plausible, since the Marquis was sometime Master of the King's Bedchamber.

Bassompierre was able to speak briefly to Richelieu before he left. 'Bishop, here is a piece of advice from an older man who has had much experience with the opposite sex: on those rare occasions when their conversation wanders from the purely autobiographical, it is best not to put up a counter-argument. Agree with what they say and they will become agreeable. There will be time enough later, if you so desire, to modify their views, since once they give their bodies, they are more than willing to surrender their minds as well.'

Richelieu was surprised that a man who was the object of desire of so many ladies should be a man who felt towards them such contempt. To invite Bassompierre's love was to seek an injury. Were refined ladies aware of his attitude, or was it, in some perverse manner, one of the reasons for his attraction?

'What you say is true enough,' agreed Richelieu, 'for it is Woman's undying wish to be admired for everything.'

In order that the Marquise not be left unaccompanied, a young lady was summoned to the drawing room. She was somewhat unattractive: pale of face, flat of chest, severely clad in a high-necked wool dress. Her blonde hair was pulled straight back and tied with a black bow. Her only attractive features were her bright, blue eyes.

'This is Hortensia, my English cousin, who is visiting us in Paris to learn our ways,' introduced the Marquise, whose fulsome beauty showed to even better advantage in the presence of this scarecrow. Thus the addition of this chaperone to the company acted on the mind of Richelieu in a way quite contrary to the intent of promotion of virtue. The English cousin, who appeared to a Frenchman's eye to be barely fifteen years of age, gave all the indications of being a most suitable candidate for the cloister, except that in her hand she carried a volume bearing the title *The Marvelous Adventures of Ali Pasha,* reading material of which a holy mother would hardly approve.

'I must first take you to task, Bishop,' began the Marquise with firmness, 'for did you not chastise me for bidding notrump without a stopper in the opponent's bid suit, yet on this last hand did you not do just that?'

Hortensia smiled at the prelate and irreverently raised an inquiring eyebrow.

'You do me an injustice, Madame, to think that I would preach one course for others and follow another myself,' replied the Bishop inaccurately. 'I would fear to lose your esteem on this apparent contradiction which arises from the different circumstances under which the two seemingly similar actions were taken. My bid is classified as a rear-guard action in the passout position. As such, it is allowable to bid notrump on the assumption that partner probably holds useful undisclosed values in the opponent's suit, since no raise had been forthcoming from opener's partner. Your bid, on the other hand, was made directly after the opening bid, with no such assurance.'

'I trust you are correct,' answered the Marquise, not totally convinced, 'so please excuse the inability of a poor novice to comprehend this concept immediately. I do not yet see the reason why one might not *always* bid with a reasonable expectation of partner's holding. I have so often found that partner holds just the right cards to make a contract viable, but that too often partner lacked the courage to act upon this happy circumstance.'

Cousin Hortensia now felt free to enter the conversation even though she had little knowledge of the matter under discussion.

'From what you say, Cousin, I gather that bridge partners are alike to two shy lovers, each pining for the other to offer the first evidence of love. A word once spoken, a sign once given, happiness and bliss prevail, but if each waits over long upon the other, the result is but sadness and regret.'

Based on this declaration Richelieu felt he must revise his original estimate of the precocious young female: perhaps Hortensia was not the potential novice he had assumed her to be.

'Yes, Mademoiselle, it pays to be bold in this world, but what is once done cannot be undone,' cautioned the Bishop. 'Action without forethought is often regretted and delay possesses the virtue of reasonable safety. This, at least, is the accepted view. It is best to conform to the views that are generally held, even if one thinks that these so-called truths are agreed upon only for the sake of expediency. Later on in life you will come to see that rules possess validity for subtle reasons a young mind cannot fully grasp.'

The Marquise nodded in solemn agreement, then commented, 'Resolve is a manly trait women fain would emulate; our indecision arises from fear, our prevalent emotion.'

Hortensia added, 'With a lover as with a bridge partner, to the woman's mind, boldness is the *sine qua non*. We admire most what we don't possess ourselves.'

Richelieu felt some anger with this comment, as in it he read criticism of his well-reasoned advocacy of the prudent course of action. 'I have noted that male boldness attracts the weaker sex to such an extent that boldness is often the only characteristic a suitor need possess in order to win favor. However, too often a woman of gentle mien will be deceived and read into eagerness an emotion of greater substance. So it is with bridge: a bold bid may succeed in capturing the contract, but when the bare truth is displayed in dummy and the shallowness which lay behind the bold words is revealed, disappointment and regret are all too often the consequences.'

'The hour grows late, so if I may, I would beg your indulgence now to listen to a proposal which lies close to my heart,' said the Marquise with a forgiving smile. 'I feel myself fortunate to be able to count on obtaining your frank opinion. False praise may please but it does not illuminate.'

The Marquise was given leave to say her piece by a slight bow in gracious acknowledgement. She continued, 'While not wishing to be critical of the royal authority, I must in truth say that, for whatever purpose or reason, the Court does not appear to be a place in which men and women of sensibility can gather to discuss matters of the intellect. There is no forum in Paris for an exchange of views from which both sexes may benefit. There should be. It is unfair that to be admired we women must possess ability and at the same time deny it.'

'From what I've heard,' interposed Hortensia, 'it is no wonder the Court is so well supplied with confessors — the supply needs must answer the demand.'

Richelieu closed his eyes tight and drew in his breath. He began to suspect this outspoken Hortensia to be an English heretic. Presently he reopened his eyes and, without reference to the English cousin's remarks, calmly bade the Marquise continue.

'Well, to be brief, my idea is this: why not convert part of this house into a bridge club for ladies of refinement and gentlemen of ability? Here they could meet in intellectual pursuits free from the encumbrances of vulgar intercourse. Politeness and decorum would prevail; arguments would be banned, discussion promoted. Decorative but not outlandish dress would become the fashion, something akin to what Hortensia is wearing now would be suitable; the low bodices of the Court ladies direct thoughts in the wrong direction. Famous players, like yourself, would provide public instruction. Musicians would entertain during the intervals. Bridge could be the whetstone on which to sharpen the wits.'

Richelieu voiced his reservations. 'It is natural for ladies to wish to adorn their minds with learning and bridge skills, but unfortunately men and women talking freely together will arouse suspicion. Also, many players, although they be quick-witted enough, are sly deceivers who would advantage themselves of your hospitality and the access you provide those with more gold than gray matter.'

'Polite society is based on the dual assumptions that a gentleman will publicly flatter a lady with his advances and that, in public at least, a lady will reject them. We would weed from our garden of culture those of insufficient discretion.'

'Like Adam and Eve being expelled from the Garden of Eden,' supplemented Hortensia. Was she mocking her hostess? Richelieu had too little experience of *les femmes anglaises* to judge the intent of her remark. He could never understand French women, so what hope had he with regard to the exotic English variety?

'My house would be the meeting place of poets and philosophers...' continued the Marquise, but Richelieu was quick to interrupt with a wave of his delicate hand.

'Poets are a mistake. Rhymers are shallow; the ideas they express in verse seldom stand up under an unbiased analysis. As for philosophers, I fear they would be a waste of time, Madame. Why disturb the minds of your fair guests with puzzles that have baffled the greatest thinkers for centuries? Better to hear from authorities of the Church how the wisest have resolved such questions as, for example, who is more to be blamed, Adam or Eve?'

Hortensia was not to be denied her opinions. 'I fear we poor women already know the answer to that one, but surely there are many problems of interest that fall outside the realm of religion and which can be discussed profitably. For example,' she continued eagerly, 'I have read in this book of the wonders of the flying carpet.

You smile, Bishop, and I agree the concept is fanciful in the extreme, but does it not suggest a great need in the matter of transportation? Why is there not a carriage that can pass smoothly over a muddy road or a plowed field? Why is there not a ship that can navigate accurately in a rough sea? Such conveyances would be of immense practical value in warfare, would they not?'

The Bishop was impressed and said so. 'Mademoiselle, I am impressed. Yes, there are many problems worth the consideration of great minds, problems of the type on which Leonardo da Vinci spent so much effort. I must confess to a problem of great practical value which has always puzzled me, and please excuse me if I give offense without intent to do so, but, that problem is how to determine paternity with absolute certainty. This is an important matter of state, especially,' he conceded to the Marquise, 'in a court where licentiousness is rampant.'

'No offense was taken,' assured the Marquise eagerly. 'This is exactly the type of problem which should be investigated thoroughly, and one on which women could voice a valid opinion based on their peculiar experiences.'

'If there were such a method,' added Hortensia, 'then there would no longer be any excuse for keeping ladies imprisoned at Court or in castles. A lady would gain the freedom to go out into the world and seek the companionship of men without the fear of false accusations and unmerited disgrace. At last women would be liberated from the confines of the harem, just like the heroine in this book I am reading.'

What folly here have I provoked? thought Richelieu, coming to the realization that conversations with intelligent ladies often lead to dangerous ground. He resolved in future to remain within the safe confines of Fortress Platitude and not sally forth to where he risked being ambushed by the light cavalry of Woman's Wit within the Forest of Conundrums.

(As the reader will not meet the pale Hortensia again within these pages let us here recount what became of her. She traveled to southern climes to improve her health. There she blossomed. While sailing about the Greek islands she was captured by Saracen pirates, 'married' to the captain, and, having survived several Mediterranean sea battles in which she played an active role, took up residence in Beirut in a most beautiful white mansion overlooking a twinkling sea as blue as her sparkling eyes. She was adored by her four, lively children, but at times strongly felt the need for solitude. At those times she took long rides into the desert and camped out with hospitable Bedouins under a dazzling canopy of bright stars.)

THE TWO PRINCESSES

Where was Bassompierre as the midnight hour approached? He was comfortably ensconced in the apartments of his lover, the Princesse de Conti, enjoying a snack while playing Bridge with the Princesse de Condé and her brother, Henri, the Duc de Montmorency. Seven years previous the General had been the favorite of the old Duc, an illiterate warrior who couldn't even write his own name, and had been happily engaged to Charlotte de Montmorency, now the unhappy wife of one of the nastiest of the Bourbons. Having been disappointed once in that direction he did not feel the least inclination to rekindle an interest in that fair lady.

Much more to his current tastes was the Princesse de Conti. Louise-Marguerite de Lorraine was one of those women who improve with widowhood, as do so many. At forty-two years of age, she had that mature beauty that attracts the true lover of womankind. Her slim body could still excite sudden passion, while her skills could sustain that passion in ways that were unknown to the feckless ingenue. She had written a naughty, thinly disguised account of the libidinous enterprises of the late Henri IV that, apart from locale, was widely admired for the accuracy of its details. Bassompierre had foolishly proposed marriage, but the Princesse had wisely refused him, recognizing that they both cherished their freedom.

Young Montmorency was handsome, a superb horseman, brave and resourceful when called upon to command troops in battle. He had been raised in the atmosphere of the Court, rigid in form but licentious in habit. It is significant that one of his earliest loves was Angelique Paulet, *La Lionne*, the most famous singer of her day — significant in that the Duc was unable to express himself at all well in speech. Many a sentence was begun then halted, as the Duc sought in vain for the words to match the thought, finally putting an end to the struggle with some expressive hand gesture. His lips moved, but no intelligence was imparted thereby. It was said of him that he possessed the most eloquent arms in France.

'So how was the Bishop this evening — his usual prissy self, I assume,' asked Louise-Marguerite, viciously biting off the head of a marzipan figurine with her sharp, little teeth.

Bassompierre shrugged. Easygoing himself, he did not much like it when his consort was in one of her nasty moods. 'Better than usual, actually,' he replied blandly. 'He's not such a bad chap, if you know how to handle him.'

'He, being a flatterer, must be f-f-flattered,' commented Montmorency, helping himself to *puits d'amour* with an apricot jam filling.

'Frankly,' affirmed his sister with a toss of her pretty blonde head, 'I can't stand the man: he smells of the sickroom.'

'He has never enjoyed good health,' explained Bassompierre, picking from a silver salver his favorite, an apple tart with a whipped cream filling, 'but he's a clever fellow and the Regent would do well to follow his advice.'

'Don't be so sure of your ability to handle him. People who have had poor health in their youth tend to develop strong willpower,' observed Louise-Marguerite displaying her novelist's analytical nature. 'Not like you, Francois, who can't resist the least temptation. You must have been a disgustingly healthy baby.'

'I am being criticized for having a pastry you yourself provided?' retorted the General indignantly before biting defiantly into the flaky crust and splashing cream on his mustaches.

'She wasn't thinking of tarts,' suggested Montmorency, 'at least, not the kind of tarts that have c-c-c-cream c-coming out the t-top.'

Bassompierre swallowed quickly and opened his mouth to protest, but the Princesse de Condé intercepted him.

'Fear not, Marquis,' said Charlotte with an acidic smile, 'it is the perverse nature of us women to give our love to those whom we least esteem.'

'We women first venture to give our love without reason, then we hazard our respect, also without reason,' explained Louise-Marguerite, patting the Marquis's arm lightly.

'You women never know what you want,' commented Montmorency. 'If desired hotly, you want cool respect; if respected coolly, you want......' He shrugged and waved his hand, scattering flakes of pastry on the rich, red, Turkish carpet.

'Germans say 'A Mistress inspires Love; a Wife commands Respect; a Mother engenders Fear',' stated Bassompierre, now deliberating over the candied fruits.

'Nonsense!' replied Charlotte indignantly. 'A lady commands respect no matter the position in which she finds herself.'

This statement was followed by a moment of silence as each member of the company recalled her husband's notorious sexual preferences. Blushing, she nibbled vigorously on a cinnamon biscuit stick. Finally her brother could no longer hold back his amusement and gave forth a loud snort. Her three companions began to snicker.

'By the way, how *is* Prince Pillion getting on in prison?' asked the Duc with an innocent air.

'You are wicked!' proclaimed the Princesse angrily, but in a voice too closely resembling that of her old governess, now her step-mother. Then she too gave up the pretense and joined in the jolly laughter.

'We are *all* wicked,' affirmed Louise-Marguerite, 'that's why we get along so well together.'

'Speaking of a lady's position, it has always been my contention that a Lady's position is beneath, but in closest proximity to, her Lord,' continued Bassompierre grandly.

'It is said that Queen Cleopatra was wont to place herself above Caesar,' replied the Princesse de Conti, who read history as well as wrote it.

'Ah, well, turnabout is fair play, *n'est-ce pas?*' asked Montmorency with a naughty look at his sister.

'Only middling fair, dear brother. Now let's stop stuffing ourselves with sweets and start playing Bridge,' chided the Princesse de Condé, firmly steering the conversation from ever shallower waters. Also, she was in grave danger of putting on weight and wanted to remove the temptations of the sweets from her mind.

Bassompierre was a gambler, with cards as with life. When his luck was running, he gained vast sums at the Bridge table, which were quickly spent on pleasures and whims, and when it was not, there were always those, like Montmorency, who were good for a loan until Dame Fortune again smiled. The worst that would happen was that his unpayable debts would become larger while remaining equally unpayable.

Louise
♠ A Q 4
♡ J 10 9 7 6 2
♢ Q 5 4
♣ A

Charlotte
♠ 8 6
♡ K 5
♢ K 10 9 2
♣ Q J 10 7 4

Montmorency
♠ 9 7 5 3
♡ 8 3
♢ J 8 6
♣ K 9 6 2

Bassompierre
♠ K J 10 2
♡ A Q 4
♢ A 7 3
♣ 8 5 3

Charlotte	Louise	Montmorency	Bassompierre
pass	1♡	pass	1♠
pass	2♠	pass	3♣
pass	4♣	pass	4NT
pass	5♠	pass	5NT
pass	6♠	all pass	

The Princesse de Conti opened the bidding in her six-card suit. When her partner bid spades, she thought he might have a five-card suit, so she wanted to make an encouraging move and not merely rebid her hearts. If it turned out he had heart support, he could always show it on the next round, she reasoned.

The General was a firm believer in the efficacy of the 4-4 fit. Once Louise had raised his spade suit, he gave no thought to maneuvering the contract back into the heart suit for which he held such good support. Instead he bid 3♣ as a nebulous 'help-suit game try', to see if his partner had control of the suit. When she showed excellent control in that suit, Bassompierre pushed to slam via the usual key-card asking 4NT.

Charlotte had an easy lead of the ♣Q, taken by the ♣A. Bassompierre immediately played a heart to his queen, losing to the ♡K. The princess forced dummy with another club, but it was to no avail — declarer could ruff, unblock the ♠AQ and come to hand with the ◇A, then claim his contract by drawing trumps and throwing losing diamonds from the now established dummy.

'François!' chided Louise-Marguerite. 'Once more you hogged the hand and failed to support my hearts. You are a beast, sir, and I shall never forgive you!' She put her tiny hands over her face to hide the tears that were welling in her eyes.

'Please don't be angry, and please, please, don't cry, and make those pretty eyes all red,' begged the Marquis. 'Look, I'll show you, 6♡ must fail the way the cards lie. Don't you think I would have put you into a heart slam if I thought it was the right contract? Of course, I would!'

'Yes, he's right, Lou-Lou,' comforted her fellow-princess. 'Look here, 6♡ must always go down, since I held both red kings. But that is not to say he is not a cad.'

'Is that right?' sniffed the injured party, peeking through her fingers, prepared to be convinced.

'Of course it is, dearest,' said the gallant, kneeling beside his companion's chair and putting a comforting arm around her shoulders. 'Look, next time you can play the 3NT.'

'Oh, b-b-brother!' commented the Duc disgustedly. He saw the wisdom of not admitting at this time that he wouldn't have found the diamond lead necessary to defeat 6♡. While he didn't mind losing the money, he hated suffering the agony of domesticated bridge.

Montbazon

y March, 1617 clever men like Bassompierre could see the Regency was nearly at its end. Even Concini began planning for retirement in warmer climes with his vast plunder. How the end would come was not clear, as young Louis XIII seemed barely capable of blowing his own nose much less asserting himself and taking up the royal duties that were rightfully his. At present he was under the influence of Charles d'Albert de Luynes, whose position as royal favorite was due almost entirely to his skill at falconry. Those who would conspire to overthrow Concini could not move without the King and the King would not move without his falconer.

It is especially dangerous to conspire against a regime that is beginning to feel its vulnerability. Late one evening at the Louvre three men were seated around a card table in a small room awaiting Luynes, ostensibly for a game of Bridge. Their desultory conversation had navigated around politics and had beached on the safe topic of women.

'Then I take it, *Messieurs*, from what you say, that you do not subscribe to the poetic view that love of a woman is an experience that elevates a man?' observed Richelieu dryly.

'I can see women as a means of elevation, yes,' replied Bassompierre, making an upward sweep with his right hand. 'In particular, I see them as a flight of stairs; wide or narrow, straight or curved, in palace or in cloister, all are made for mounting.'

'But isn't there something special about v-virgins?' asked Montmorency. 'They are like pretty f-f-flowers. As you stretch out your hand to pick one, you p-pause for an instant to admire the b-beauty that is about to... to... go poof.'

'Nonsense, *mon ami*, virgins don't go poof!' exclaimed Bassompierre. 'They hang about like shiny green apples on the bough; the best of them are made into tasty tarts and each year brings along a fresh crop.'

'I fear you belittle virgins, who are like the gold in our Treasury,' stated Richelieu emphatically. 'Although 'tis true that gold coins are minted to pass freely among men, a certain percentage must be maintained in their pristine state to stand as a guarantee of purity. So it is with virgins: we are the richer for their existence, even though they are withheld from circulation.'

At that moment the Duc de Montbazon poked his head in through the door, smiled broadly in his friendly manner, and joined their conversation uninvited. 'Have you heard this one? How is an old virgin like an old mare? They have both done a lot of naying in their day,' offered Montbazon, laughing heartily at his own stale joke. How long had he been listening at the door? wondered the three conspirators simultaneously.

Hercule de Rohan, Duc de Montbazon, Master of Hounds, was a soldier of strong physical presence, one of the Old Guard who rose under Henri IV. He was exceedingly gruff in manner and crude in speech, lacking in wit, and unable to formulate a useful suggestion on any matter of importance. Agreeably incompetent, his loyalty was never questioned by whomever currently held power. Thus his mental limitations became a valuable virtue in a court full of clever but untrustworthy intriguers and he continued to rise majestically like a hot-air balloon to ever-greater heights.

'Waiting for Luynes, are you, *mes braves*?' he asked with his familiar, brusque camaraderie. 'Well, he'll be awhile; he's tied up with the King right now, discussing snares and what not.' He sat himself down heavily in a chair at the table and puffed out his cheeks. 'Whew, that was a hell of a day of hunting, I'll tell you. The King has not much in him to remind us of the Old Boy, but the lad sits well in the saddle. Lots of deer, but we didn't spot even one of your virgins in the forest, ha-ha!' Bassompierre for once was at a loss for words, Richelieu had temporarily exhausted himself on the subject of virgins, while Montemorency's arms hung limp at his sides.

'But come along now, let's deal up a hand to pass the time while we wait for Luynes.' suggested the unwelcome guest. 'I can't stand Bridge, but I'll be the dummy. The Bishop and I against you dumb suckers at double the usual stakes. Don't worry, Bishop, I shall assume all the risk for half the profits.'

Montbazon took up the cards before him in his huge, hairy hands and began shuffling vigorously, too vigorously, for he fumbled and the cards went flying through the air in all directions.

'Holy dogshit!' exclaimed the Master of Hounds as he bent over to retrieve cards from the floor. The other three couldn't help laughing at this crude fumbler in spite of themselves. Montmorency took the opportunity to shrug at Richelieu, indicating he for one had no idea why the old buffer was imposing himself on their meeting.

Montbazon's bidding was as crude as his humor, but his method of shuffling proved effective as he dealt himself a grand slam.

Montbazon
♠ K J 6
♡ A K Q 5
◇ A J 8 6
♣ 8 5

Bassompierre
♠ Q 10 9 7 5 3 2
♡ J
◇ Q 10 7 4
♣ 2

```
      N
  W       E
      S
```

Montmorency
♠ 8 4
♡ 10 9 6 3
◇ 9 3
♣ 10 9 7 6 4

Richelieu
♠ A
♡ 8 7 4 2
◇ K 5 2
♣ A K Q J 3

Montbazon	Richelieu
1♡	3♣
3◇	3♡
3♠	4♡
5◇	5♡
5♠	6♡
6♠	6NT
7NT	pass

Bassompierre saw in his hand his favorite card. It was as if he was looking in a mirror at his own likeness, for was not he known as *The Knave of Hearts*? He led it reluctantly, since holding it usually brought him good luck.

'I had a hell of a time getting you to bid notrump, young fellow. If I'm paying for the hand, I want you to play the damn thing,' said Montbazon as he placed the dummy on the table one suit at a time. 'Look at those spades, pretty good… and the solid hearts… didn't expect diamonds like that I'll wager, and, of course, you have those buggers.' The force of his fingers bent the cards so fiercely that they remanded bowed after he released them.

What an ignoramus! He doesn't know the value of playing in the 4-4 fit, thought Richelieu as he counted up thirteen tricks in a heart grand slam. Impatiently he played a second top heart from dummy and was surprised by the 4-1 split, which meant there was a heart loser and that Montbazon, the man he had just rated an idiot, was correct and he, who aspired to become known as the greatest player in France, had been wrong! No matter, five club tricks and a diamond finesse would see the 7NT contract home, so Richelieu cashed the last heart honor and played two rounds of clubs, preparing to make a claim on a finesse, but another nasty shock occurred when Bassompierre showed out on the second club. There was nothing to do now but play out his clubs to this position and hope for a miracle:

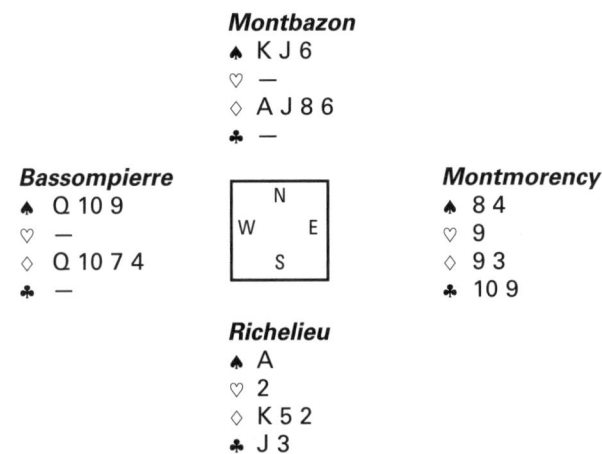

Montbazon
♠ K J 6
♡ —
◇ A J 8 6
♣ —

Bassompierre
♠ Q 10 9
♡ —
◇ Q 10 7 4
♣ —

Montmorency
♠ 8 4
♡ 9
◇ 9 3
♣ 10 9

Richelieu
♠ A
♡ 2
◇ K 5 2
♣ J 3

The diamond finesse had to be right, so it was a matter of squeezing Bassompierrre out of a fourth diamond on the lead of the ♣J. Once the diamond appeared from Bassompierre, the only hope lay in the diamond suit. The ♠6 was discarded, the ♠A cashed, the finesse for the ◇Q taken, and the contract claimed shortly thereafter.

'*Pardieu*, that was well done, Bishop,' exclaimed Bassompierre. 'You had me in the vise for sure. Nothing we could do, Montmorency.'

Montmorency shrugged and put his arms in motion to express hopelessness, despair, forgiveness, admiration, amusement, and a variety of other emotions.

'Watch out for this one, lads, or he'll squeeze the juice out of you as neatly as any riverbank whore,' laughed Montbazon, scratching his crotch.

Richelieu looked as glum as if he had gone down several tricks. He realized he had misplayed it badly! At Trick 2 he should not been distracted by his own arrogant appraisal of Montbazon's bidding practices, but should have made a proper analysis of the play options. With favorable splits in clubs and hearts, thirteen tricks were easily available, so he should have made provision for unfavorable splits by playing his top cards in a different order: a second top heart, a spade to the ace, and two top clubs, discovering the bad splits. The diamond finesse is clearly necessary. Finesse in diamonds, play the last heart honor, then the ♠K discarding a heart from this position:

Montbazon
♠ K J
♡ 5
♢ A 8 6
♣ —

Richelieu
♠ —
♡ 7
♢ K 5
♣ Q J 3

The position of the ♠Q is immaterial. If the Dark Lady appears before the King, the remaining tricks may be claimed. If she resides in the East along with three clubs and a heart, Montmorency will be obviously triple squeezed on the play of a diamond to the ♢K. Otherwise, it will be clear that she resides in the West. Now Bassompierre can keep at most one diamond on the play of the top clubs, and Montmorency cannot hold a guard in the suit. When all is revealed in this manner, declarer cannot go wrong. Blindly squeezing the Marquis in diamonds and spades had been a bad mistake despite the favorable outcome. Yes, even a blind chicken sometimes finds grain; all the more reason not to allow oneself to be distracted by a partner's errant bidding which, after all, could prove felicitous.

A second hand was dealt, this time by the graceful hands of Montmorency, so that the cards flew about the table accurately like a rain of arrows. Again Montbazon ignored a 4-4 fit in a major and boldly put Richelieu in a notrump contract that required careful play.

Montbazon
♠ J 7 6 4
♡ 3 2
♢ Q 9 5
♣ K 6 5 2

Bassompierre
♠ K 10 8
♡ 9 6
♢ 10 3 2
♣ Q 10 9 4 3

Montmorency
♠ A 9
♡ A J 8 5 4
♢ J 8 7 6
♣ 8 7

Richelieu
♠ Q 5 3 2
♡ K Q 10 7
♢ A K 4
♣ A J

Bassompierre	Montbazon	Montmorency	Richelieu
		pass	2NT
pass	3NT	all pass	

Bassompierre led the ♣4 with some hope, for he had a possible entry in the spade suit in case partner came up with a helpful club holding. This gave the Bishop a third trick in the suit, but his total had risen only to six tricks in the minors and one in hearts. The defenders held three quick winners in the suits in which he had to develop tricks. This situation matched the one he was facing in politics. There also he would much prefer to wait and see before making a critical, possibly fatal, commitment, but the circumstances were forcing him to take a chance instead of sitting back and awaiting developments. He was never at his best under pressure.

The problem was how to combine the chances for two tricks in the majors without giving the defenders the chance to take five tricks before he had his nine. The best pure chance was to lead twice from dummy towards his ♡KQ, but to go immediately to dummy with the ◇Q would give away the position of the diamond suit. If Bassompierre held the ♡A he would not continue clubs, but switch to an unhelpful diamond. With no further quick entry to dummy, Richelieu would have to play spades from his hand and give the opponents the chance of setting up a diamond trick for themselves. Thus there was a reason for keeping the position of the high cards hidden.

Richelieu steeled himself to the unavoidable task of blindly tackling the spade suit. He would assume the top honors were split between the two defenders, so it was matter of figuring who was more likely to hold a doubleton spade. If Bassompierre held five clubs to justify his lead from a broken suit, it was most likely his shape had been 5332. His doubleton was more likely to be in spades (leaving Montmorency with the common 4432 shape) than in a red suit (leaving Montmorency with the rarer 5422 shape.) Thus blind chance favored the play of a spade to the jack, losing, and thereafter a duck of a second round dropping the presumed singleton honor.

As he was about to make this fatal play, he noticed that the presence of the ♡10 in his hand would yield a second trick in hearts if the jack were onside. He decided to eliminate the inevitable loser in hearts by playing the ♡K from his hand before making his play in spades. Montmorency felt he must take the trick offered in order to play a second round of clubs through declarer before Bassompierre's entry was eliminated. On lead once more with the ♣A, Richelieu had now to play the spade suit from his hand, but his priorities had changed with the circumstances. He could afford to lose two spades to Montmorency, but not to Bassompierre who would be in a position to establish and cash a winning club. Therefore he led not a low spade as previously planned, but the ♠Q. Montmorency won his ace and returned a passive diamond, but Richelieu was fully in command. A spade to the jack won and a third round was surrendered to Bassompierre who returned a futile diamond. Richelieu had won the race, fulfilling his contract unexpectedly by means of two spade tricks and a heart trick to go with his six minor suit winners.

'Heh-Heh. Two hands and that's the rubber,' chortled Montbazon.

At that moment Luynes came through the doorway, apologizing profusely for his tardy arrival.

Maréchal de Bassompierre

It was said of Bassompierre that he would rather lose a friend than an opportunity to be witty. One day the Duc de Vendôme, an illegitimate son of Henri IV, asked for his support in a political cause and was refused. The Duc remarked unpleasantly, 'You support the Guise faction because you make love to his sister.'

Bassompierre replied, 'That doesn't enter into it, sir. I have made love to all six of your aunts, but that doesn't mean I like you any the better for it.'

The Man of

Feathers

Charles d'Albert de Luynes did not look the part of a grand conspirator, which was a great advantage. His features were blandly pleasant. Caesar would have approved of his round contours which gave his clothes the appearance of being stuffed with down. He gave such little outward display of ability that he was greatly underestimated by Concini, himself a man largely of style, who judged mostly by appearances. Approaching the age of forty, Luynes had been acting as a companion to the young King, sharing tirelessly in his adolescent activities, and yet he was known to have engineered several secretive and successful seductions despite a lack of money and a deficiency of wardrobe. So pleasant and affable was his manner that to meet him was to like him, unless, of course, you happened to be Richelieu, who did not judge by appearances and seldom experienced feelings of affection. Like so many popular politicians whose main assets are a pleasing appearance and amiable personality, Luynes knew well enough how to curry favor, but little of how to use power once he had it within his grasp.

Upon recognizing Montbazon, Luyne's handsome face had broken into a broad smile, and as Montbazon pocketed his winnings, Luynes continued to apologize for his lateness. Had he not seen last week in the court Montbazon's beautiful young daughter, Marie-Aimée de Rohan-Montbazon, sixteen years of age, and was he not taken by her beauty and charm? Yes, indeed he was. And was it not wondrous that this lout had sired this witty and charming specimen of French womanhood at its finest? Most suspect, for sure. Luynes bowed low to the man who was soon to become his father-in-law.

'Montbazon, what a great honor and pleasant surprise to find you here. Will you not give us the pleasure of entertaining you at cards?' offered Luynes.

'I'm about to depart for, if not more amiable, then more amorous climes. Thank you nonetheless — some other time. By the way, how was the King after his long day's ride? Did he speak of me?' asked the Duc anxiously. Friend as he had been with the King's father, the Duc was uncertain of Louis' feelings towards him. He knew the young King disapproved strongly of excursions of the type on which he had often accompanied the Old Goat and on which he himself was now about to embark once more.

'He spoke most highly of your part in the day's hunt. He mentioned especially the well-managed crossing of the stream and felt the demonstration of horsemanship well worth the day's effort.' The Duc looked well pleased. 'And, oh, by the by,' added Luynes, trying to sound casual, 'I saw your daughter in the Queen's apartments last week — a charming young lady.'

'Ha,' replied the Duc contemptuously, 'I haven't seen that little bitch for ages. She looked all right to you, Luynes? Not up the stump yet, is she? I wouldn't put it past her. I'm too young, gentlemen, to have some brat calling me grandpa, and I'm too poor to be able to afford a bastard addition to the family who is not of my own making. The sooner she's married off, the happier I'll be. Too bad you're not rich, Luynes, otherwise you might offer to take the extravagant baggage off my hands,' joked the Duc, unaware of the dismay he was generating. 'The man who marries her will be as horny as that ten-point stag we killed today, and in more ways than he bargained for.'

The Duc offered his chair to Luynes. 'My wise investment in the Bishop here has already paid for my night's entertainment, but if I am to take full advantage of my good fortune, the time has come to bid you gentlemen adieu. So pay up and I'll be on my way.'

Soon a happy Montbazon strode out the door with pockets jingling.

'Well,' commented Luynes as he stared at the empty doorway, 'well, well, what a blusterous old fart. I'm sure his daughter is not at all the way he makes her out to be.'

'I'm sure he was just teasing you, Luynes,' soothed Montmorency. 'When you spoke of her, your b-b-blush gave you away.'

'Courage, Luynes,' advised Bassompierre, 'with women beauty and opportunity go hand-in-hand.'

Blush is the symptom, familiarity the cure, mused the Bishop.

Richelieu waited patiently for the meeting to get down to business. He surmised that he had been invited here to join in some move against Concini, whose unpopularity increased daily on the streets of Paris. Richelieu had decided that it was in the Regent's interests, as well as his own, to begin to dissociate from the Florentine upstart and become more accommodating to the wishes of the maturing King. At this meeting he was ready to convey this change of mood, and offer more, if approached properly. However, Luynes suggested that they play cards, so Richelieu would have to wait to hear their offer.

Montmorency
♠ A Q 9 5
♡ K 4 2
◇ J 6 3
♣ 10 9 5

Richelieu
♠ 8 7
♡ Q 10 8 7
◇ K Q 7 5
♣ Q 8 4

Bassompierre
♠ K 10 6 4
♡ 9 3
◇ 9 4 2
♣ 7 6 3 2

```
      N
  W       E
      S
```

Luynes
♠ J 3 2
♡ A J 6 5
◇ A 10 8
♣ A K J

Richelieu	Montmorency	Bassompierre	Luynes
		pass	1♣
pass	1♠	pass	2NT
pass	3NT	all pass	

On the bidding it would be normal to lead the unbid major, but Luynes looked just too complaisant, even for Luynes, almost as if he welcomed a heart lead. In his mind's eye Richelieu could see the ♡J in declarer's hand. Holding length in spades Bassompierre might have that suit well guarded. Thus Luynes would have to play on hearts and clubs to gather enough tricks. Reasoning that he would have to lead diamonds eventually, Richelieu began with the somewhat dangerous attacking lead of the ◇K.

Luynes took this trick and led the ♠J which lost to the king, just as Richelieu had anticipated. A diamond was returned and Richelieu was allowed to clear the suit. Luynes cashed the ♠AQ in dummy and was disappointed to see he had another spade loser. What Luynes did not see was that Richelieu was in trouble. Already he had discarded the ♣4, and a further spade play, albeit a losing one, would apply the pressure of a further discard — either the winning diamond (a dead giveaway to an astute declarer who would construct an endplay in hearts) or an unguarding of hearts. Luynes should have been aware of this situation on the evidence of the potentially dangerous choice of opening lead from a four-card suit, but he opted unawares for two losing finesses. The ♡J lost to the queen, and on the play of the winning diamond declarer discarded from his hand, not a club, but a heart. The heart return was won in dummy and the losing club finesse taken — altogether a pitiful performance from one who would soon lead his country. What made it worse, to Richelieu's way of thinking, was that the fellow appeared not to realize his errors.

'Unlucky, wasn't it?' Luynes commented cheerfully, 'every finesse was wrong. Ah well, that happens. Congratulations on your lead, Bishop — devastating!' Although Luynes was smiling at him, Richelieu caught a look in his eye. Perhaps not anger, but more than respect.

The Bishop was still relatively inexperienced, so he did not realize that those of mediocre mind do not respect so much as envy that which they don't understand. With envy comes jealousy, with ignorance comes fear. A sharp knife may best suit its purpose, yet one fears it most if one has not been taught its proper handling. Thus it was on the very next hand, striving to impress, Richelieu made the political mistake of a brilliant false card.

Montmorency
- ♠ A 9 8
- ♡ K 7 2
- ◇ 8 5 3
- ♣ K J 10 4

Richelieu
- ♠ Q J 6
- ♡ Q 9
- ◇ 9 7
- ♣ A Q 9 7 3 2

```
      N
  W       E
      S
```

Bassompierre
- ♠ K 5 4 3
- ♡ J 10 6
- ◇ J 10 4
- ♣ 8 6 5

Luynes
- ♠ 10 7 2
- ♡ A 8 5 4 3
- ◇ A K Q 6 2
- ♣ —

Richelieu	Montmorency	Bassompierre	Luynes
			1♡
3♣	dbl	pass	3◇
pass	3NT	pass	4◇
pass	4♡	all pass	

Luynes was another of those players who consider only their own cards. With a void in clubs he was not going to allow his partner to play in 3NT — to him that was unthinkable. Of course, a player of Richelieu's ability would have made 3NT on a spade lead by holding up twice, then eliminating the side suits from West's hand before endplaying him in clubs. Even the Princesse de Conti would have succeeded by playing on hearts imaginatively, holding up on the spades then leading the first round of hearts towards the dummy to prevent Richelieu unblocking the ♡Q. However, the contract of four hearts was going to succeed on straightforward play as well, unless...

Richelieu led, not a club, but the ♠Q. Luynes held up the first round of spades, took his ace on the second, and made his plan. There were just three losers if both the red suits split 3-2, so he began to draw trumps by leading the ♡K from dummy. On this Richelieu dropped his queen. Now to Luynes' mind there was the certainty of two spade losers and two hearts. Rather than give up, he decided to make up for his defeat on the previous hand and show this overly clever Bishop that he, Luynes, knew a thing or two. Yes, he could see it now: if he could get rid of a spade on a good diamond before Bassompierre ruffed, he would lose just one spade trick, since the third spade in his hand could be ruffed in dummy.

This was a good plan, but on the third diamond, Richelieu ruffed and played a small spade to Bassompierre's king. A heart trick still had to be lost, so Luynes was down in another cold contract.

Luynes shook his curly head in wonder. 'How do you come up with these plays?' he asked smiling pleasantly. 'I fear I shall never reach your standard. You shine like a diamond in the sand.'

The Man of Feathers fell silent as the cards were being shuffled for the next deal, then suddenly rose from his chair and bowed politely. 'Pardon me, gentlemen, but duty calls me to the King's side. His Majesty suggested the possibility of a late game of billiards so I fear I must bid you a hasty and regretful adieu. Please excuse me, Duc, Bishop, Marquis, we must do this again soon. Good night, my apologies, all.'

After this overly hurried departure the three men remaining looked at each other in puzzlement. It appeared that the time was not yet ripe to formulate plans. Richelieu made one last attempt to provide an opening for negotiations.

'The King has too little to occupy his mind,' he suggested. 'Idleness is the source of all vice.'

'There are those in high p-p-places who would demonstrate for the King's benefit that idleness is a virtue,' said Montmorency.

'Be that as it may, I think the King would do better to accompany Montbazon on his *querouage* than to stay behind with Luynes, playing with his balls,' replied Bassompierre, rising from his chair and stretching lazily for effect. 'Perhaps I should make an early retirement. It is said His Majesty wants to head an expedition against the northern rebels, but that Concini opposes it. What do you think, Bishop? Will the King be allowed to go North with his troops?'

'A King may do what a King wishes, *n'est-ce pas*?' suggested Richelieu. 'I have heard the excuse that Concini is distracted by a land dispute with Montbazon and would have that personal matter resolved before setting his mind to matters of state. Strange that Montbazon didn't mention it.'

This confidence was not reciprocated and the opening that Richelieu had given the two courtiers was not pursued, so Richelieu surmised that Luynes was the key to any forthcoming suggestions of action against Concini. To Richelieu's mind it was intolerable that the two proud courtiers were subjecting themselves to one much inferior to themselves in both status and intelligence. He rose from his seat and bowed deeply with a formal precision that conveyed his disappointment in the outcome.

'I can only say this, *Messieurs*: a fool may have started this latest revolt, but it will take a genius to end it.'

'A genius or a cutthroat,' commented Bassompierre.

Richelieu

in

the

Wilderness

oncini's time in the sun was soon to end. As Richelieu later commented, 'having attained great power, foolishly he chose to flaunt it. Louis became resentful. Upon being warned of the danger of his position by Bassompierre, Concini replied, with the fatalism that is the gambler's drug, that he wanted to see how far his luck would carry him. On April 24, 1617, that luck gave out: he was assassinated with Louis' consent while crossing into the Queen Mother's garden over what was known as The Drawbridge of Love (in the vicinity of St. Germain d'Auxerrois.)

Leonora Galigai was put on trial on various trumped-up charges, none of which could be proved, but no matter, since for her the Drawbridge of Justice had been raised. One who has publicly pronounced others stupid must experience a certain degree of mortification when climbing the stairs of the scaffold in front of thousands of jeering spectators, but the tiny woman made a grand exit with head held high. In front of the block she proclaimed loudly, 'I forgive the King.' A sympathetic hush came over the crowd and a loud, collective sigh was heard as the axe fell.

For seven years thereafter Richelieu was denied the place in government that his proven abilities merited. He was the only Councillor not arrested in the coup, but Louis did not like him and Luynes wasn't inclined to bring into his regime a strong-willed and clever man who might grow to dominate the Council. So Richelieu joined the Queen Mother in exile at Blois, later moving to Avignon with his brother, Henri.

Charles d'Albert was made Duc de Luynes and married Marie-Aimée de Rohan-Montbazon. For four years he was the most powerful man in France. The Court in Paris became the scene of unsurpassed gaiety and high spirits. The royal couple had two years of marital bliss during which Louis wrote love songs and poems to his beautiful wife, but it was not to last. Louis dreamed of leading his country to glory and took to the field with his army on several successful campaigns of siege warfare against the rebellious Huguenots. He proved himself a valiant, cool-headed warrior. Luynes was less successful — he vacillated in times of crisis. Louis became discontented and decided to dismiss his favorite, but Luynes avoided disgrace by a timely death on December 15, 1621 due to scarlet fever contracted at the siege of Montheurt.

Luynes left his widow one of the richest women in France. To avoid banishment from Court she married four months later one of her lovers, the doltish Duc de Chevreuse, brother of the Princesse de Conti. The Duchesse dominated the Queen's court with unmatched wit, irresistible charm, and fulsome sex appeal. She was a marvel of nature, combining the liveliness of a rabbit with the constitution of a horse.

The death of Luynes cleared the path for the return of Marie de Medici. There had gathered about her a group of forceful personages thirsty for power. They constituted a pro-Spanish faction with connections with the old Catholic League once headed by the late Duc de Guise, father of the Princesse de Conti and the Duc de

Chevreuse. Although he was a staunch French Catholic, Louis hated Spaniards and was suspicious of the Pope, attitudes he inherited as a child from his Huguenot father.

Richelieu became the Queen Mother's chief advisor and superintendent of her household. He won favor from both sides by negotiating a reconciliation between mother and son. As his reward he accepted a Cardinal's hat from Louis' hand in December 1622. With courtly good manners he laid the hat at the feet of the Queen Mother and swore his eternal gratitude for her sponsorship. Well… not exactly, for what he said was, 'Madame, this hat, for the receipt of which I am indebted to the goodness of Your Majesty, will forever be a reminder of the solemn vow I have taken to shed my blood in your service.' The Cardinal was to maintain he acted always in the best interests of his patroness, even if that meant, as it often did, acting against her wishes.

BRIDGE AT THE COURT

Bridge reflects the personalities of those who play it. Card games had been a major pastime for Henri IV, but Bridge was not one of his favorite games: ever on the move as a young rebel, he didn't have the spare time to perfect his skills. When his life became sedentary, this king sought more and more the pleasures of the bed and couch rather than those of the card table. Nonetheless, the popularity of Bridge increased among the dour Protestant supporters who had come north with him to Paris. Men of politics and war, they saw much to admire in a contest whose outcome depended largely on merit.

How different it was to become two generations later in the court of Louis XIV at Versailles, where gambling became frantic. Howls of misfortune, shouts of joy, weeping, cursing, hugging, tearing of hair and other emotional outbursts were the norm at the Grand Casino. Cheating became acceptable as 'the means by which to correct the errors of Fortune.' The number of *écus* lost, not the quality of the play, became the yardstick of performance. During one evening at cards Madame de Montespan, the King's mistress, lost the equivalent of ten million dollars out of the tobacco tax the King had granted her. Eventually Bridge was spurned as being too slow; faster ways to lose money were sought and mechanical games of pure chance, like roulette, grew in popularity.

In the Royal Court of Louis XIII, Bridge reached a momentary peak as an intellectual pursuit for ladies and gentlemen of taste. The Catholic King loved the game in the Protestant way and avoided playing for large stakes. To his mind the game was a means of exercising the power of the intellect and the challenge of winning was everything.

At the Bridge table as elsewhere, Louis was a hard taskmaster. Often his sarcastic comments, framed in a dark humor, were aimed at injuring a partner who had failed to live up to the King's high expectations. To compensate for the lack of personal rapport, Louis required that his partners accept a long list of restrictive conventional bids, a list he kept under continuous revision. Woe to the partner who forgot the latest amendments. He wanted to be dominant, but could dominate neither by force of intellect nor personality, so he reverted to a rigid formalism that he could control completely. He resented any unilateral initiative by a partner, which he considered a flagrant abuse of partnership agreement. A thoughtful performer, he spent long hours analyzing results and composing letters to his partners that suggested improvements to their play. His own style was variable, some days highly aggressive, other days passive, so he was nearly impossible to partner with consistent success. It took a Richelieu to control him and develop his full potential.

As a princess, Anne of Austria was accustomed to being served in all matters, so she grew up passive, lazy, and self-centered in her thinking. She possessed an excellent memory and read her opponents well, but she was not an expert declarer, as she often failed to recognize the far-reaching consequences of her early plays. Thus, she was happy to adopt a passive style in accordance with her nature, keeping her values hidden and avoiding risks in competitive situations. However, she was quick to support her partners, sometimes overbidding, if she was not going to declare the hand herself. She did well playing with her ladies-in-waiting, often joking lightheartedly at some misplay or other, but when playing with her husband, she was extremely nervous, the tension often resulting in simple mistakes and angry displays of frustration on both sides. Anne realized her own weaknesses, but hers was an indolent nature, so she was quite content to remain as she was. She spent long hours before the mirror fixing her hair, selecting her wardrobe, chatting inconsequentially, and writing secret letters to her Spanish relatives which bordered on the traitorous.

In Marie-Aimée de Rohan-Montbazon, Queen Anne found her perfect partner. The Duchesse de Chevreuse (as she became) was ever eager to take the initiative and dominate the action, which she did with some grace. The game was never dull when she played; if it threatened to become so, the Duchesse could be counted on to throw in a psychic bid to stir things up.

The Duchesse preferred to play against men, indeed, an invitation to Bridge with the Queen was a convenient way to introduce the gallants of the court to the Queen's entourage and engage in harmless, flirtatious amusement, although with the Queen involved, such behavior could be deemed harmless only by those blind to the political dangers. The table talk was bright, witty, polite and scandalous. The ladies-in-waiting displayed themselves in a splendiferous rainbow of sex appeal at the end of which, always just over the horizon, lay the unattainable pot-of-gold, Anne of Austria. At first the Queen, brought up in the prudish Spanish Court, was shocked by this overt sexuality, but gradually she came to consider it highly amusing. Often after the game Her Majesty recalled the *bon mots* with her ladies and added highly colorful embellishments of her own. In this way she learned of life outside the narrow confines of her Spanish upbringing, besides extending her French vocabulary considerably in the downward direction.

The
Judgement
of
Richelieu

On a warm evening in 1623 Cardinal Richelieu stood in the grand vestibule of the Hôtel de Rambouillet awaiting the arrival of his hostess, Catherine de Vivonne, Marquise de Rambouillet, famous for her establishment five years previously of the famous Blue Salon in which French women and men could meet for the first time as intellectual equals and exchange views in an elegant manner. The Cardinal, smartly attired in his cerise gown and skull cap, hands behind his back, studied the large allegorical painting by Rubens that hung there: a naked Venus (the Marquise) beckons to a helmeted Mars to dismount and join the rustic crowd for a spot of nude bathing in the nearby Lake of Enlightenment, while Aristotle, Archimedes and Hypatia look on approvingly from a distant dark cloud on the considerably foreshortened horizon; Mars, clearly outflanked, capitulates. The Cardinal epitomized the lean and hungry look which so troubled Julius Caesar, yet he gazed with admiration at the ample and pillowy figure of the Marquise thus revealed in her full womanly glory.

His reveries were interrupted by the appearance of the dear lady herself as she called across the hall in a clear voice to draw attention to the arrival of her distinguished guest, 'Ah, Cardinal, how good of you to find the time to come to our little gathering. Please favor us with your opinion of my latest acquisition.'

Not standing on formality, Richelieu bowed gallantly and pressed his lips to the lady's soft hand. 'A work of genius that demonstrates what Man is capable of when he puts his mind to it,' he replied smoothly. 'Rubens' rendering of Venus I find remarkably attractive.'

'You think so? My husband shares that view, but I feel the artist has done me a wrong,' responded the Marquise, allowing the Cardinal to hold her hand longer than the formality required.

'Oh? Where?' asked Richelieu, turning quickly to re-examine the offending figure. Yes, perhaps here and there were excesses of pink which belied the hand of the master.

'Don't you see? It should be Minerva, Goddess of Wisdom, not Venus, who detains Mars on the road to Armageddon,' pointed out the Marquise with a disarming smile.

'Yes, quite so,' agreed the Cardinal, 'but in order that Minerva might bind Mars with her fine words, Venus first must sequester his horse. Consider the goddesses in terms of a bridge hand,' continued Richelieu thoughtfully, 'Minerva represents the content and Venus, the shape. The happiest consequences follow when the two work in harmony.'

The Marquise now whispered in Richelieu's ear, 'Strange you should mention that: I wish to speak to you later confidentially on an important matter concerning Bridge.' Sweet words!

'I am ever at your service, Madame,' replied the Cardinal, much elated that his hunch was proving correct.

A current hot topic in the Blue Salon, second in intensity only to the rediscovery of some dubious verses apparently penned by the Emperor Calendula, was the

Principle of Total Tricks, which proclaimed that in competition Venus (shape) outstrips Minerva (content). Recently a pamphlet on the subject by a bold young card-sharp who signed himself simply 'Des Cartes' had been read to the assemblage: the presumptuous title, *I Bid, Therefore I Win*. As Richelieu had surmised, it was to obtain his views on this startling idea that the Marquise had invited him to this *soirée*, an invitation he was happy to accept, for the Marquise was one of those women with whom he got along well: not too hot, not too cold, not too meek, not too bold. It was the hell-cats who most disturbed his peace of mind — such as the singer Angelique Paulet, nicknamed La Lionne partly on account of her tawny mane but mostly because of her predatory habits with regard to potential lovers. She employed her talents unstintingly in a fervent campaign to stamp out unrequited lust.

After a few agonized arias in the French manner from Mlle Paulet bewailing the aforementioned thorn in the psychic paw, the evening progressed pleasantly enough. However, the Marquise found no opportunity to introduce the Principle of Total Tricks until near the end of the evening at which time Richelieu graciously suggested that they might play a few hands to test out the hypothesis. So it was that three guests remained after the others had left and the cards were dealt for the following hand.

Neither Vul.
Dealer North

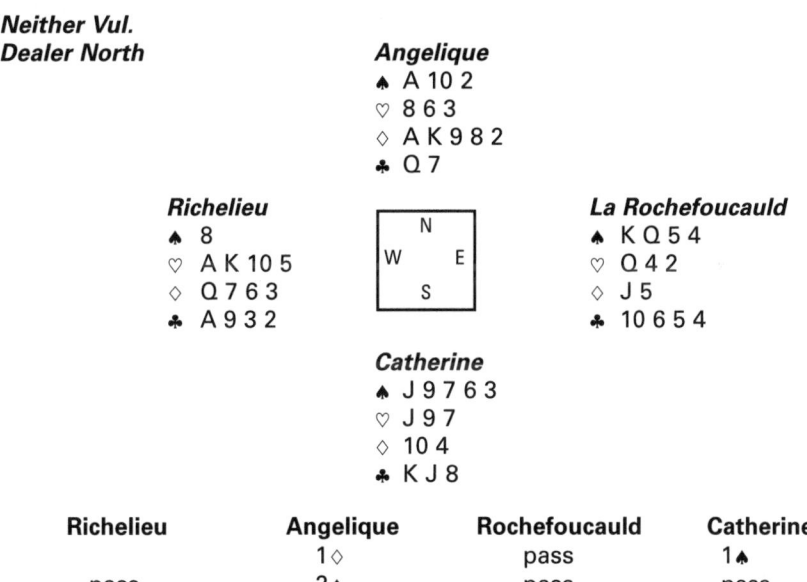

	Angelique		
	♠ A 10 2		
	♡ 8 6 3		
	◇ A K 9 8 2		
	♣ Q 7		

Richelieu		La Rochefoucauld
♠ 8		♠ K Q 5 4
♡ A K 10 5		♡ Q 4 2
◇ Q 7 6 3		◇ J 5
♣ A 9 3 2		♣ 10 6 5 4

	Catherine	
	♠ J 9 7 6 3	
	♡ J 9 7	
	◇ 10 4	
	♣ K J 8	

Richelieu	Angelique	Rochefoucauld	Catherine
	1◇	pass	1♠
pass	2♠	pass	pass
dbl	all pass		

Cardinal de La Rochefoucauld was of the old school, so Richelieu was sure that he would take a direct double at the one level as penalty; thus he bided his time and passed on the first round. In the balancing position he felt that he could now safely take action, so he made a protective double with four-card support for any suit his partner might choose to bid, but the old fellow crossed him up and passed the double for penalty anyway.

Richelieu led the ♡K and received a negative signal. He tried next the ♣A and again received a negative signal. It was difficult to imagine where La Rochefoucauld had found the values to risk a penalty pass. Shrugging resignedly, he continued hearts. This easy defense yielded six tricks, so the contract was set one.

'You didn't have much for your double there,' commented La Rochefoucauld, shaking his grey head, 'but I had the goods to come to the rescue. Rather lucky, I'd say, doubling them into game then finding a passing partner with three defensive tricks.'

The Marquise pondered the result. It wouldn't be so bad if the prelates could make something their way, but it appeared they couldn't.

'Angelique, what would you have led against three clubs?' she inquired.

The buxom singer examined her cards. 'The king of diamonds,' she replied.

'Then I signal encouragement with the ten, I get a ruff and return a spade...'

'Yes, my third diamond would have been the nine,' agreed her partner.

'So, no matter which of us is on lead, we take three club tricks, two diamonds and a spade — they take only seven tricks. The total trick count should be sixteen, but it comes only to a mere fourteen, two short,' concluded the Marquise, a puzzled look crossing her face.

'Ah, yes, the Principle of Total Tricks,' exclaimed Richelieu, politely identifying the topic of discussion for the benefit of La Rochefoucauld who probably had never heard of it, 'I congratulate you, Marquise, on keeping abreast of all the latest developments. I myself have just last week received a learned treatise on it from Rome. It appears the Principle has been found somewhat lacking when the opponents each hold honors in the other's trump suit. In this case we held the king and queen of your spades and you held the king, queen and jack in our clubs, so one can hardly expect that either of us could play successfully with such threadbare trumps.'

'Thank you, Cardinal, for making it clear. I see it now. Do you see, Angelique? We must each possess a good trump suit or it doesn't work.'

'Principle of Total Humbug!' muttered La Rochefoucauld, 'What ever happened to the Principle of Good Judgement?'

The next hand provided more evidence to support his prejudice.

Both Vul.
Dealer East

Angelique
♠ Q 9 8 5 4
♡ Q J 7 2
◇ 3
♣ K 8 7

Richelieu
♠ 7
♡ K 10 9 6
◇ J 9 8 7 4
♣ 10 6 2

```
        N
    W       E
        S
```

La Rochefoucauld
♠ 10 6
♡ A 4 3
◇ A K 10 6 2
♣ A 9 4

Catherine
♠ A K J 3 2
♡ 8 5
◇ Q 5
♣ Q J 5 3

Richelieu	Angelique	La Rochefoucauld	Catherine
		1◇	1♠
2◇	2♠	pass	pass
3◇	3♠	pass	pass
4◇	4♠	dbl	all pass

As his partner treated all jumps as strength-showing, Richelieu had to content himself with a simple raise on the first round. The auction thereafter took on a quaint old-fashioned flavor as the two weaker hands competed defiantly while the stronger hands were silent — until La Rochefoucauld made a resounding double at the four-level. Not for the first time that evening, the soprano had got too high for comfort. The defense had no difficulty taking their four tricks for down one.

'I'm sorry,' apologized Angelique, 'but I thought they might be able to make their four diamonds. I was shapely and I know we have at least a ten-card fit.'

'I'm sure you did the right thing, *chérie*,' answered the Marquise sweetly. 'According to the Principle of Total Tricks, it is right to bid up to the level equal to the number of trumps you hold.'

La Rochefoucauld snorted contemptuously. 'Yes, keep doing it, dear ladies, shapely or not, and I shall double happily every time with four tricks in my own hand and a partner who has raised me three times, no less.' He shuddered to think how much worse the world might become a decade hence in the year 1633.

Richelieu was somewhat puzzled since a recent article in *Spicilegium Bridgium*, by a Jesuit no less, had waxed enthusiastic on the idea of bidding to the four-level when holding ten trumps. 'Yes, we had a ten-card fit as well, so the total tricks should have been twenty, yet, again, it was two fewer. Against four diamonds the ladies take a spade, a heart and two clubs.'

'Each side held very good trump suits this time,' noted La Rochefoucauld smugly, 'so there's no excuse to be had from that quarter.'

'Maybe it is possible to be too good, Messieurs,' commented La Lionne with a sly wink in Richelieu's direction.

'The rule appears less accurate than its author claims. We've played just two hands, simple hands really, and look at the results,' concluded the Marquise sadly. 'I am most disillusioned with that young man,' she added with an indignant sniff.

'Meanwhile, it should be banned, whatever it is,' stated La Rochefoucauld firmly. 'Think of the mess we'd get ourselves into if everybody who thinks he knows something about bidding is allowed to set up his own rules and goes around upsetting the other players who haven't the foggiest idea what he's about.'

'I agree, Monseigneur; new inventions can't make a fool wise, whereas they can make him dangerous; however. . .'

Richelieu stopped abruptly and three pairs of uplifted eyebrows turned in his direction awaiting further enlightenment on this important point. His sudden pause had been caused by someone applying gentle, but insistent, pressure on the toe of his left red slipper — not for the last time was a message being conveyed *sub rosa* under the Bridge table. Initially it had been his irrational fear that the action originated with the upright Monseigneur opposite, but obviously La Lionne was more inclined to this form of communication, tapping out an intimation altogether unrelated to Bridge. Clearly a moment of judgement had arrived. Would it be Venus or Minerva? He cleared his throat.

'However… we need to play at least ten more hands before we can draw any conclusions,' said Richelieu, deftly dealing out the cards.

The
Chevreuse
Cat

It was an unseasonably cold night in early March, 1624. Large flakes of snow were floating gently from the dark sky, covering the dirty streets of Paris with a soft blanket of pure white. Richelieu was in a foul mood. Not only was his carriage stuck in traffic along the Left Bank, making him late for his Bridge game with the Duchesse de Chevreuse, but also that afternoon he had been informed that the King was still blocking his entry into his Council despite the considerable weight the Queen Mother was putting behind the suggestion.

Behind the monogrammed black leather curtains of his stalled carriage the Cardinal cursed under his breath. Although he had advised others that the greatest pleasures are those preceded by the keenest anticipation, he was not himself a man who enjoyed being kept waiting. Was it reasonable that a few snowflakes should cause such havoc? Why didn't ordinary people have enough sense to stay at home and leave the streets clear for important business? But, no! They poured out into the streets as if it were a holiday. He cursed his barber who had taken so long trimming his mustache, his tailor who took so long changing the buttons on his vest from gold to pearl and his hosier who had had to send out three times before getting the right color of silk. It would be faster to get out and walk across the Pont Neuf but even the delightful company awaiting him was not worth risking assassination by exposure on a public thoroughfare. One can never take enough precautions against the irrationality of one's detractors. Richelieu jumped in his seat when a snowball hit the leather curtains and made them flex.

The Hôtel de Chevreuse with its grand entrance off the Rue St. Thomas stood where now is situated the Place du Carousel. It was in the pleasant style of the late Renaissance with an inner courtyard and garden containing a full complement of pilasters, statues and medallions, the nude Greek goddesses giving male guests a pleasant reminder of the competing charms of the lady of the house. The radiant Marie-Aimée, Duchesse de Chevreuse sat in her drawing room entertaining two guests: Henry Rich, Viscount Kensington, said to be one of the handsomest men in the court of James I of England, and her sister-in-law, the Princesse de Conti.

The Princesse had acted as the younger woman's mentor when first she arrived at Court and had promoted some of her early love affairs. She had the reputation of being clever but not wise, decent but not moralistic, respectable but not virtuous, loving but not faithful. She often traveled in the royal carriage with Queen Anne whose virtue was to some extent in her care as Matron-of-Honor. This was a dangerous way to travel. Louise-Marguerite de Lorraine was known to have borne at least two bastards, one a daughter by Henri IV, the other, a son by Bassompierre.

The Viscount had come to Paris with an introduction to the Duc de Chevreuse, a cousin of James I by way of the Guise relatives of Mary, Queen of Scots. His purpose was to initiate negotiations for a marriage between Charles, the Prince of Wales, and Henrietta-Maria, sister of Louis XIII.

'So, Kensington,' said the Princesse, warming herself with her back to the fire, 'I think you brought this cold weather with you from England. Imagine, snow in March!'

'I apologize sincerely, Your Highness,' replied the tall Englishman with a bow. 'However, I cannot be accused of bringing a cold heart,' he added, throwing a hopeful look in his hostess's direction.

'At least it appears you haven't come with cold feet,' remarked the Duchesse warmly, 'but speaking of a cold heart, I think I hear Richelieu arriving.'

When he made his entrance the ladies were surprised to see the Cardinal wearing an outfit of light green silk with a black ribbon above the left knee. The Viscount merely assumed he was celebrating St. Patrick's Day early in a gesture of goodwill towards the British Isles. His hair was curled in the latest style and it was obvious that dark dye had been applied to his beard and mustaches. The thin, intelligent face was almost handsome in a Gallic sort of way, and from the attire one might conclude the heart was not so cold after all. But no makeup could disguise the sharp, sad eyes. Gallantly he kissed the hand of the Princesse and lingered long over the hand of the Duchesse, enjoying the soft warmth that allowed itself to remain pressed against his dry lips.

'You look more beautiful with each passing year,' he said sincerely, 'What is it that gives your cheeks such a radiant glow tonight? Can it be this frigid weather brings with it consolations?'

'Perhaps we can thank the English for something, after all,' said the Princesse gaily. The Duchesse threw a sharp look across the room in her direction.

'Ha, Viscount Kensington I presume,' said Richelieu jovially, 'we meet for the first time. What pleasure! My English is rusty but let me try. 'Ow do you do, Old 'Ound?'

'Unlike the English weather I am fine, Your Eminence,' replied Henry Rich, bowing.

'Ah. And 'ow is your King and the Pranze ov Vales?'

'Both are in excellent health. They send their personal regards to a true friend of England,' replied Kensington, lying in all aspects at once, as ambassadors are trained to do. 'Happily you are in good health, I see.'

'Do not be deceived, I am thinking seriously of retirement from politics,' lied Richelieu right back in return, 'But 'ow is your fraind, Le Duke ov Fuckingham?'

'Ahh... errr... It's spelled with a B actually.'

'Pardon. Fucking-bum?' asked the Cardinal straight-faced.

'In Engleesh, you can nevair says in publeek, 'Fuck,'' explained the Duchesse who had some knowledge of the English tongue. 'Fuck' is, you know...' She made a universally understood gesture with her fingers.

'Oh, pardon a thousand times, I must go back to French for the sake of propriety. So 'Buck' as in 'Buck Rabbit'. I have it. We must call him in French *Bouquin* meaning Buck Rabbit. Buckingham translates to *Bouquinquant*. King James loves him, no?'

'The King loves all his loyal subjects,' replied the Viscount mildly.

'Of course. Now can you please explain to me your Engleesh money?' said the Cardinal, expressing his interest in an important aspect of international negotiations. 'It is so hard to understand these twelves and eights.'

'With pleasure. In fact, let me relate to you a story about the currency that might amuse the ladies and at the same time serve to inform Your Eminence.'

The English Pound

A young English blade secretly courted a pawnbroker's daughter who was as innocent to the degree that her father was greedy – that is to say, eminently. He decided to explain the ways of love in terms her naive mind could easily understand. First he moved a few paces away and blew her a kiss, telling her that he was giving to her that which was the equivalent in lover's terms of a farthing.

'Indeed,' she commented readily, 'it does to me appear to be that a 'farthing' is of little worth.'

Seeing his advantage the swain approached and gave her a brotherly peck on the cheek, calling that a penny.

'Indeed,' she commented, 'a penny does not raise a great deal of interest.'

The swain then took her in his arms and kissed her fervently on the mouth, calling that a shilling.

'Indeed,' she said, catching her breath, 'a shilling is fully worth twelve pence.'

Pressing his advantage the swain undid her bodice and covered her bare breasts with his hot kisses.

'Well, then, I call those half-crowns. A pound is worth eight half-crowns. What do you think so far of the currency of love?'

'Indeed, ' she replied, 'I can hardly wait for you to give me a pound.'

The French ladies exchanged puzzled glances before giving this joke a polite flutter of applause; with regard to English humor even their low expectations had not been met.

'Money and Love alike seek a fair exchange,' mused the Princesse wistfully. In her heyday she had made many bad investments.

'How is having good sex like saving money?' asked the more prosaic Duchesse. 'I'll tell you: with both the trick is to postpone spending.'

'Surely the greatest pleasure comes with liberal spending,' asserted Kensington, a dubious thesis that was greeted with Gallic shrugs.

Richelieu was about to launch into the unexpurgated version of the Abbess's tale when the hostess suggested they cease discussing economics and proceed to the

Bridge table for the business at hand. He was overjoyed when he cut the Duchesse for his partner.

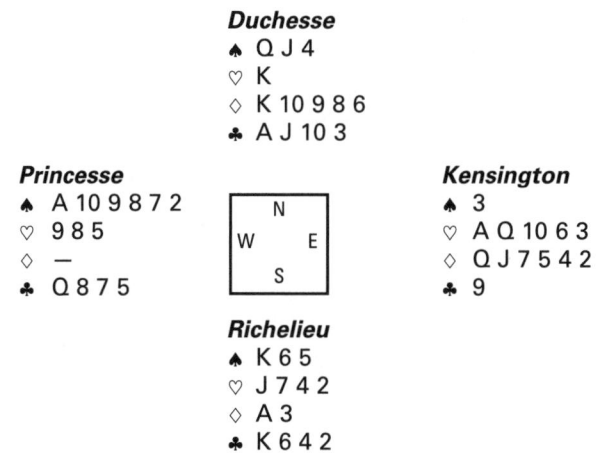

Duchesse
- ♠ Q J 4
- ♡ K
- ◇ K 10 9 8 6
- ♣ A J 10 3

Princesse
- ♠ A 10 9 8 7 2
- ♡ 9 8 5
- ◇ —
- ♣ Q 8 7 5

Kensington
- ♠ 3
- ♡ A Q 10 6 3
- ◇ Q J 7 5 4 2
- ♣ 9

Richelieu
- ♠ K 6 5
- ♡ J 7 4 2
- ◇ A 3
- ♣ K 6 4 2

Princesse	Duchesse	Kensington	Richelieu
			pass
pass	1◇	1♡	1NT
2♡	3◇	dbl	3NT
dbl	all pass		

Even though they had agreed to play a popular Big Club system named *Folies Légères*, the Cardinal could not bring himself to open with the South hand. The Duchesse opened with 1◇, holding a maximum in high-card points under the system without promising length in the suit. The Viscount introduced his suit, planning to bid diamonds later if the situation warranted it. Richelieu knew of the Duchesse's proclivity for light actions and he was reluctant to make a show of strength with a poor holding in the opponent's suit, so he contented himself with an underbid of 1NT. The Princesse raised her male partner in competition as she had been taught to do by those who in her youth had instructed her on courteous behavior.

Marie-Aimée had not been taught in her youth to defer to others and certainly it was not in her nature to let the opponents play at the two-level after a raise in competition. If she were playing a natural system, she could now bid 3♣, giving Richelieu a choice of minor-suit contracts, but this approach was not available to her now: a bid of 3♣ would show longer clubs, possibly even 6-4 in the minors. As Richelieu's 1NT bid must contain some diamond support, she opted for a straightforward 3◇ bid on a suit with good spot cards.

Kensington was delighted to double this bid and Richelieu at last committed himself to game. The Princesse de Conti could not see whence nine tricks would materialize. One of her faults was that she must always frankly express an opinion, (and what could be more frank than a resounding double?) but as had unhappily too often proved the case in the past, her fanciful opinions were based more on passionate prejudice than on sober assessment. Richelieu's subdued approach had combined well with the Duchesse's over-aggressiveness.

The Princesse led the ♡5 to the ♡K and the ♡A. The Cardinal covered the ♡6 with the ♡7 and the Princesse cleared the suit hoping that Kensington held the ♠K. This sequence of plays only served to set up the ♡J as a winner in the Cardinal's hand.

The Viscount also hoped that Richelieu did not hold a top spade, so he returned the ♠3. The ♠A was taken and a spade returned to dummy's queen. It was now only a matter of getting the clubs right. The Cardinal cashed the ◇K in dummy and when the Princesse showed out, the count of the East hand was disclosed. Richelieu led the ♣3 to his ♣K in hand, finessed in clubs and claimed his nine tricks.

Richelieu noted the Englishman appeared to have too great an inclination towards the obvious. The doubling of the Duchesse's bid did reveal a greedy disposition, but for the upcoming negotiations on the marriage the indications were that foresight and subtlety would lie hugely in favor of the French side. Having obtained the information he was looking for, the Cardinal decided to relax for the remainder of the evening and concentrate his efforts on those little attentions and vapid pleasantries that further the cause of seduction. Wasn't it lucky that the Duc would be otherwise engaged that night…

Several hands later the Viscount was again put to the test and was again found wanting. Richelieu was happily relegated to being the dummy.

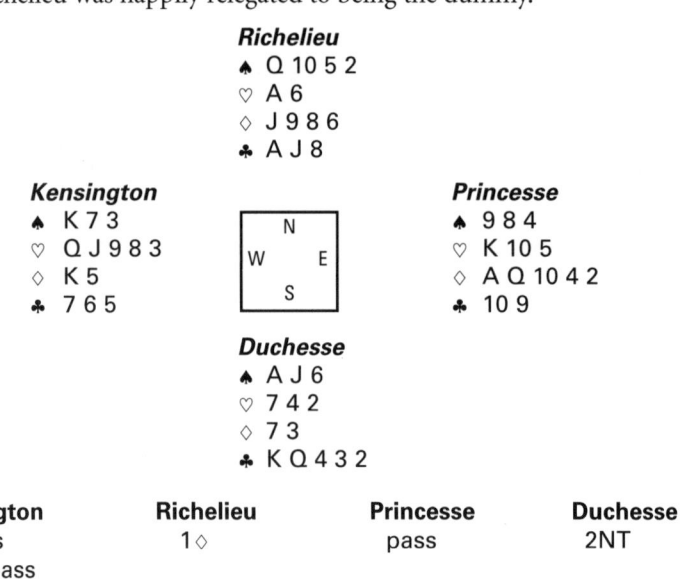

Richelieu
♠ Q 10 5 2
♡ A 6
◇ J 9 8 6
♣ A J 8

Kensington
♠ K 7 3
♡ Q J 9 8 3
◇ K 5
♣ 7 6 5

Princesse
♠ 9 8 4
♡ K 10 5
◇ A Q 10 4 2
♣ 10 9

Duchesse
♠ A J 6
♡ 7 4 2
◇ 7 3
♣ K Q 4 3 2

Kensington	Richelieu	Princesse	Duchesse
pass	1◇	pass	2NT
all pass			

Several overbids had given evidence that the Duchesse was in her accustomed high spirits, so Richelieu continued to make allowances; her light 2NT invitation to game was not accepted. Kensington led his ♡8, the Princesse won with the ♡K and unblocked her ♡10, the second trick being won with dummy's ace. The Duchesse was disappointed with Richelieu's faint-heartedness as nine tricks depended only on a spade finesse. However, when the ♠K turned out to be in the West, it appeared the defenders were poised to take ten tricks, for an embarrassing but not costly five down, undoubled.

On the last two hearts from Kensington the Princesse signaled high-low encouragement with the ◇4 followed by the ◇2, but the Duchesse knew well how to tempt a man into doing her will. In the dummy she bared down to the singleton ace in clubs, giving the Englishman an attractive exit in the suit. He fell for it and now the Duchesse could claim her contract as she had discarded her two losing diamonds and kept all her black cards.

'Simply marvelous,' commented the Englishman, 'I know of no English woman capable of such keen misdirection.'

'Have not your English ladies learned that stolen tricks, like stolen kisses, taste the sweetest?' asked the Duchesse with a gay laugh.

'You arouse my desire for enlightenment, Madame,' replied Kensington.

The Princesse was happy to contribute from her wide experience. 'We French know that a long and happy marriage positively depends upon those sweet, stolen kisses.'

'When a lover regularly returns to her husband's bed, Princesse, surely her caresses are to be thought more borrowed than stolen,' commented Richelieu. 'Love affairs, like duels, can be excused when great passions are aroused, but both activities have taken on the quality of the commonplace. Too many gentlemen have become renowned and admired merely for the large number of their cold-hearted conquests.'

In the heat of the argument he had completely forgotten his resolution to be seductive.

The Duchesse was not one to settle for what she thought she could get easily when with a little more effort she might get what to the ordinary mind was beyond hope. Near midnight she put the Princesse in a game in which most players would fail.

```
                        Duchesse
                        ♠ K 5 4 2
                        ♡ Q 9
                        ◇ K J 9 8 7 4
                        ♣ J

        Kensington                          Richelieu
        ♠ 7 3                               ♠ A Q
        ♡ K 10 2            N                ♡ J 8 7 4 3
        ◇ Q 10 5        W       E            ◇ 6 3 2
        ♣ K 9 8 4 2         S                ♣ A 10 7

                        Princesse
                        ♠ J 10 9 8 6
                        ♡ A 6 5
                        ◇ A
                        ♣ Q 6 5 3
```

Kensington	Duchesse	Richelieu	Princesse
pass	pass	pass	1♠
pass	4♣	dbl	4♠
all pass			

When the Princesse opened in fourth position, vulnerable, with a bid that promised five cards in the major, the Duchesse evaluated her hand upwards on the basis of four-card support. As she would never be content with a contract below game, she made a splinter bid of 4♣, just in case there was a slam in the offing.

Richelieu had accurately gauged Kensington's abilities — they were slight. Hoping to avoid a disastrous lead in a red suit, the Cardinal doubled for a club lead. Why not, for he would always play his ace on the first round regardless? However, as he had reflected in his carriage earlier that evening, one can never have enough insurance against the incompetence of one's allies: Kensington obediently led the ♣K. After considerable time badly spent in faulty analysis he made the error of continuing clubs.

Many a competent declarer would discard a heart from dummy, establishing the ♣Q in hand, planning to finesse for the ♠Q on the left, but the Princesse devised a more inspired plan. Her frequent partner was the not-so-bright but always buoyant Queen Mother and her favorite game was an afternoon session at the Palais de Luxembourg where, although the stakes were high, gossip and laughter came first and declarers had often to be reminded of their contracts. It could be said with fairness that she played the players much more astutely than she played the cards.

Why had the Cardinal, always devious and so seldom wrong, doubled clubs holding such a poor suit? It appeared he had something to hide, and it was her hunch that he held the ♠Q. When an opponent you respect is playing in a strange manner, then the normal line of play is going to fail — so reasoned the Princesse. How sweet it would be to get some revenge for earlier failures by adopting a line of play that would maximally embarrass the Cardinal.

The Princesse decided quickly on a straightforward, albeit hazardous, line of play. She ruffed the second club in dummy, came to her ◇A, and returned to dummy with another club ruff, dropping the Cardinal's ace. The diamond king and a diamond ruff put her in her hand in this position:

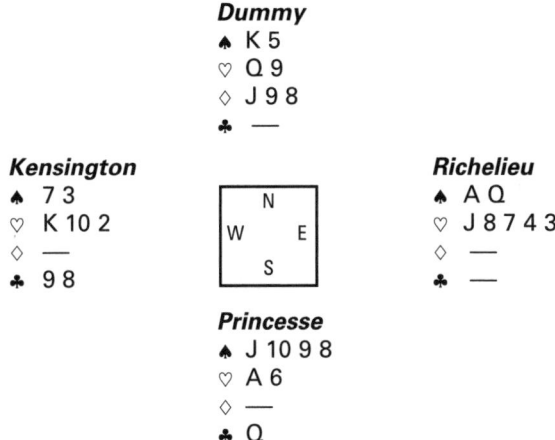

Dummy
♠ K 5
♡ Q 9
♢ J 9 8
♣ —

Kensington
♠ 7 3
♡ K 10 2
♢ —
♣ 9 8

Richelieu
♠ A Q
♡ J 8 7 4 3
♢ —
♣ —

Princesse
♠ J 10 9 8
♡ A 6
♢ —
♣ Q

She played the established ♣Q, discarding a heart from dummy. Richelieu could ruff or not, the defense was rendered hopeless. Resignedly he conceded the contract.

'Oh, well done!' congratulated the Duchesse, clapping her hands excitedly. 'I always bid close games especially when we're vulnerable.'

'There was nothing we could do, Cardinal,' observed the Viscount cheerily.

'Yes, excellently played, Princesse, as the cards lie,' said Richelieu, striving mightily to be generous in defeat. 'In fact, your line succeeds even if my partner holds the ace of trumps. It was a safety play of sorts.' Now that was stretching it to be sure, and as far as winning the ladies' favor was concerned, it was far too little, far too late.

They were about to cut for partners when a handsome footman entered the room and announced the Maréchal de Bassompierre.

'Excuse my intrusion,' said the Maréchal, 'but I was sent by the Duc to present his apologies to the Duchesse that he cannot make his way home tonight because of the snow.' A certain thickness of speech and unevenness of gait indicated that he and the Duc may have been lifting a few in some disreputable establishment in the Marais.

'Although the excuse is feeble, the apology is welcome, as are you, dear Maréchal,' said the Duchesse. 'That is to say *welcome*, not *feeble*.'

'No woman has ever accused me of being feeble,' claimed the Maréchal, proudly puffing out his chest.

'I was about to suggest to my guests that they spend the night here rather than risk the storm. Unlike the inn at Bethlehem, here we can easily accommodate three wise men without doubling up, but if you prefer, you can sleep with me,' she said, holding the Viscount's eye for a pregnant instant before sliding her gaze over to the Princesse and raising an eyebrow.

'Thank you, dear Marie-Aimée, but my inclinations tonight lie elsewhere,' replied Louise-Marguerite in her sexy, low voice, turning her most languid gaze onto the handsome Maréchal.

'For my part, I would gladly sleep in your room with you, Duchesse,' replied that gallant boldly, 'if in that way I should guard the honor of the House of Lorraine.'

The Princesse and the Duchesse laughed at the very idea.

'Indeed, you are a gallant of Lorraine,' said the Duchesse, 'and if I felt my honor were in imminent danger, your face would be the first to come to mind and your name the first to my lips, but tonight it is perhaps your greater duty to protect the honor of a Princess of France. I shall arrange a room next to hers.'

'Yes, and if I feel my honor about to slip, it will probably be Bassompierre's name that comes to my mind and Bassompierre's face that comes to my lips,' replied the Princesse.

'A humble cot in the Chapel is all I need,' suggested Richelieu modestly, glad that he had had the foresight to pack his Cardinal's outfit for the next morning.

'Then you shall have the bedroom at the far end nearest the Chapel. As for the Viscount, something fitting can be arranged for him as well,' said the Duchesse without a blush. 'To fill in the time while the rooms are being heated, perhaps the Princesse will read us a story from her latest collection of fantasies, *Moonlight on the Oasis*.'

Louise-Marguerite gave the obligatory polite refusal, but soon enough she was rummaging through her bulky portmanteau. Richelieu's sharp eye caught a glimpse of, among other miscellaneous items, eyeglasses, a sopranino recorder, half-finished embroidery, and a pretty pink nightdress with a *fleur de lys* trim. This is the story she chose to read.

A Tale of Old Persia

Once upon a time in Persia there were three infidel princes who had no love of women. One day when hunting together they stopped for lunch at an inn run by a devout Christian. Hoping to please his guests and avoid decapitation, the good man sent to serve Their Highnesses his three beautiful daughters, covered in veils as was the custom in the land.

The chief eunuch, Cinnamon by name, was extremely jealous and shouted in a rage, 'Off with them!'

Misunderstanding his command, the three daughters, the dazzling Goldie, the sensuous Frankincentia, and the sweet Myrtle, immediately dropped their veils to the floor, revealing in their full glory three different aspects of womanly beauty.

Seeing what they saw, the three princes of Persia were converted on the spot. They went off to Holy Church to marry the daughters, leaving Cinnamon alone in his room with nothing to do but play solo with his recorder.

'Poor Cinnamon,' commented the Duchesse, 'must he remain a eunuch? Why not in your story have a holy miracle occur that restores his manhood?'

'Indeed, that would produce a happy climax,' agreed the Viscount.

'Not so,' said Richelieu. 'St. Augustine tells us abstinence is a virtue. Sometimes it is to one's benefit to have virtue imposed. That is why we have prisons,' added the Cardinal as a grim afterthought. 'Walls of stone are reminders of the limits to the power of Reason over Man's mind.'

'I didn't know that Augustine advocated prisons as well as marriage,' remarked Kensington. 'I must read him some day.'

'Wait twenty years,' suggested Bassompierre, 'Augustine is like a venerable and miserable host — having himself enjoyed a brief frolic early on, he tires and bids the musicians depart.'

As any good hostess knows, talk of St. Augustine douses the party fires. Who had started it? Richelieu, of course.

'Do you English then learn Latin only for the love of Caesar?' asked the Princesse.

'No, Ma'am, I myself am devoted to Ovid.'

'My footman signals me the rooms are prepared, so I suggest we retire for the night,' said the Duchesse testily. 'Recorders can be provided to those who feel the need to make beautiful music.'

'I can assure you, Madame, that I for one will not be the cause of strange blowing noises in the night,' joked Richelieu. A wise captain awaits a favorable wind.

'I cannot give the same assurance,' said the Maréchal boldly, offering the Princesse his arm.

'Yes, this looks like yours,' said the Princesse, reaching into her portmanteau and handing him her short sopranino.

Richelieu joined his hostess in merry laughter at the sight of the chagrin that appeared on Bassompierre's red face. The Princesse laughed, too, then offered her arm good-naturedly to her lover, ending the Bridge party on a happy note.

Later as Richelieu knelt in the cold Chapel, consoling himself with the notion that of the four guests he was the one least likely to be committing a sin overnight, there emerged from behind the altar a gray cat. Somehow sensing that here was a kindred spirit, the cat padded over to the night visitor and rubbed herself against his thigh. Richelieu opened his eyes and smilingly welcomed the proffered companionship. The feline allowed herself to be placed in his lap and purred contentedly as he gently stroked her thick, soft coat that smelled of straw. After several moments spent happily sharing each other's warmth, the Cardinal spoke. 'So, Little Mother, what do you think of us humans? Are we not indeed mad to deem fools and puppies lovable?'

Louise-Marguerite de Lorraine, Princesse de Conti

When still Mlle. de Guise she granted a rendezvous to the handsome Seigneur de Givry, giving directions to a private house she sometimes used. She arrived early disguised as a nun, threw down a rope, lit a candle and seated herself with a book to await the arrival of her gallant. Soon the eager Givry arrived, found the rope, climbed up and peered in through the window. Imagine his surprise to see not the voluptuous beauty he had expected but a member of a strict religious order bent over a book of devotions. Sheepishly he quietly descended whence he had come.

On the street he met the Duc de Bellegarde and proceeded to describe bitterly what he thought was a heartless prank. The knowledgeable Duc guessed the truth and soon after it was he who climbed the rope and achieved success. Mlle de Guise learned her lesson and never again disguised herself as a religieuse

A Matter of Delicate Timing

When Henry Rich first met with Marie-Aimée de Rohan-Montbazon to seek her assistance in arranging a marriage between the Prince of Wales and Princess Henrietta-Maria, it was like Nitro contacting Glycerine. Attribute it to Fate, attribute it to Chemistry, the combustible Kensington and the explosive Duchesse were soon enjoying the full privileges of the marriage bed well in advance of the royal pair in whose interests they were laboring so diligently.

The ladies of the Court were drawn irresistibly to any intrigue likely to end in a marriage or a disgrace, so the Duchesse easily inveigled them into lending assistance to finding the answers to the many important questions. Was Charles as handsome as his portrait? Was he still madly in love with the Infanta Maria? Would he later in life be in danger of losing his hair? What secret instructions did Lord Cherbury receive from London? Who approved, who opposed? Why?

It is an established rule of fair play between the sexes that one good service deserves another. Thus, the easiest and most reliable way to uncover state secrets is to lift the sheets to the man who knows them. Savoy, Sweden, Bohemia, Holland, every night brought revelations from these and other territories. The Venetian Ambassador, indifference personified by day, stood firmly in favor at night. The Papal Nuncio, thought not to be a backer, happily proved otherwise on three separate occasions. Every morning new rumors were wafted like bursting soap bubbles on the warm spring breezes.

Throughout, Louis XIII remained lukewarm to the match, content to stand aside and let his mother direct the official proceedings. Impatient for a rapid consummation that would make her mother-in-law to two kings, she assigned to Richelieu the task of seeing that the negotiations proceeded expeditiously. Detractors wryly noted that thin of face, sharp of tongue, keen of perception, here was as unlikely a Cupid as ever stretched a bow.

Daily the Duchesse fed her handsome Englishman fresh information on the French positions. Under such happy circumstances, that gallant was in no rush to forsake the pleasures of Paris; forewarned, he was able to counter each new French proposal even before it was presented, religious scruples often serving as the snag of convenience. Cardinal Richelieu was blamed privately for the delay and was unable to present publicly a plausible excuse for his abject failure.

On Sunday, April 28, 1624 behind the thick walls of the ancient royal chateau at Compiègne, rumor was spreading like a contagious rash that Richelieu was about to be replaced as chief marriage negotiator by the King's choice, the Marquis d'Effiat. It was the custom of the melancholy King to draw near to him those he was about to dismiss, and when late in the afternoon Louis summoned the Cardinal to his side for a stroll along the dark corridor that served as a picture gallery, the betting odds in favor of disgrace rose. Louis was a great dissimulator and his performances often ended with a nasty surprise.

'This is my favorite,' said Louis, stopping in front of a gigantic painting depicting the gory martyrdom of St. Denys. 'The decapitated corpse is that of Saint Eleutherius, the first to go, and that is St. Denys, of course, with his eyes uplifted towards Heaven. I think the artist has captured well the spurting of blood from the neck of St. Rusticus at the moment of impact. I doubt Christendom contains its equal.'

'Very fine,' agreed the queasy Cardinal, 'Just as one might imagine it.'

'It troubles me that someday I may have to order the similar execution of an unruly saint for reasons of state,' said the morose monarch.

'Most unlikely, Your Majesty,' replied Richelieu, 'as the Lord has placed at our disposal a society much more in need of improvement than our own to serve as a depository for saints with a mind for martyrdom — I refer to Canada, of course.'

Slowly, engulfed in a miasma of misery, they proceeded down the hall, taking in the various depictions of diverse martyrdoms. It seemed the King was going through a catalog of nasty punishments with an eye to selecting the one most suitable to his escort, so the Cardinal was relieved when they finally reached the far end without incident. The final picture was an inapposite depiction of a contented St. Bernard dog standing knee-deep in snow with a cask of brandy about its neck.

'Ah, these agonies have put me very much in the mood for a game of Bridge,' remarked Louis brightly, rubbing his hands, 'Come tonight and be my partner.' Lucrezia Borgia could not have been gayer when inviting a victim over for dinner and a drink.

That evening courtiers vied for places near the Bridge table where sat the King, the Duc de Chevreuse, Cardinal Richelieu, and the Marquis d'Effiat. Richelieu guessed that a reservation had been made in his name for a quiet room at the back of some remote alpine monastery, so he still hoped for an opportunity to make His Majesty regret his decision to cast a great talent upon the snowbank of history.

```
                          Louis XIII
                          ♠ 9 8 6 2
                          ♡ Q 9 4
                          ◇ K J 10
                          ♣ Q 8 2

        d'Effiat                               Chevreuse
        ♠ A K 3            ┌─────────┐         ♠ J 10 7 4
        ♡ 8 7 6           │    N    │         ♡ K 3 2
        ◇ 6 4 3           │ W     E │         ◇ Q 9 5 2
        ♣ J 9 5 3         │    S    │         ♣ K 7
                          └─────────┘
                          Richelieu
                          ♠ Q 5
                          ♡ A J 10 5
                          ◇ A 8 7
                          ♣ A 10 5 4
```

d'Effiat	Louis	Chevreuse	Richelieu
			1NT
pass	2♣	pass	2♡
pass	2NT	pass	3NT
all pass			

After the Cardinal had opened the hand with a strong 1NT, Louis invited game on meager values; a King's invitation no matter how feeble cannot be refused. D'Effiat led a fourth-highest ♣3 and Richelieu saw that four spade losers were inevitable unless he could take nine tricks before the opponents became aware of the situation. A safety hold-up in clubs would most unsafe, so the Cardinal confidently made the assumption that the lead had been a normal one from a suit headed by the king rather than a poor one from a suit headed by the jack. He called for the ♣Q from the dummy. If the ♣J and the ♣K had been exchanged between the defenders, this play would be the only hope, but as the cards lay the play of the ♣Q snatched defeat from the jaws of victory. The appearance of the ♣K from Chevreuse was an exceedingly nasty surprise, as now there were five unavoidable losers in the black suits.

The frosty friary of his worst fears beckoned, but with nothing further to lose the Cardinal hastily formed a desperate plan. He took the ♣K with his ♣A and led the ♠Q attacking his own weakness, as it were. D'Effiat took the trick and puzzled over what to do next. Hoping that his opening lead had been effective, he cashed the ♣J and continued with the ♣6, setting up his ♣9 with the ♠A as an unassailable entry. Or so he thought. Winning a second club trick in his hand with his ♣10, Richelieu proceeded to finesse Chevreuse in the red suits for the seven additional tricks needed to fulfill his contract.

It was obvious to all that the Marquis had suffered a serious setback, as the King could not fail but notice the ease with which he had been misled. At the back of the room the odds had shifted dramatically in Richelieu's favor, so it was a surprise when Louis said with a rare show of sympathy, 'Unlucky there in the club suit, d'Effiat. I hope you have better luck in discerning the weakness of the English position, for I have decided to ask you to take on the heavy responsibility of being my personal representative in the current marriage negotiations. Your experience with the Protestants in Flanders should prove very useful in moving the process along.'

'Thank you, Your Majesty. I hope I can live up to whatever onerous tasks you bestow on this your humble servant,' replied d'Effiat, falling to his knees in order to kiss the hem of the King's robe.

'Also, I have decided with great reluctance…,' began Louis, pausing for effect as everyone, especially Richelieu, held his breath waiting for the axe to fall, 'ah… not to proceed with the commission of Rubens to produce a set of paintings on the life of my late father. In these times of austerity, one must make sacrifices to set an example.'

The King said no more, but motioned to d'Effiat to rise and deal the cards. The cards lay well for the Marquis, but Richelieu initiated one of those insidious defenses for which he and Louis were to become justly famous.

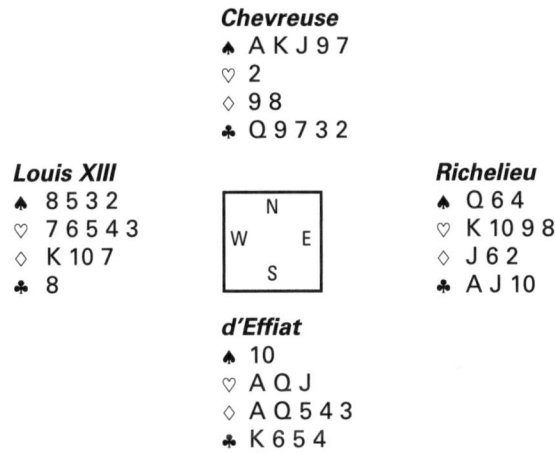

Chevreuse
- ♠ A K J 9 7
- ♡ 2
- ◇ 9 8
- ♣ Q 9 7 3 2

Louis XIII
- ♠ 8 5 3 2
- ♡ 7 6 5 4 3
- ◇ K 10 7
- ♣ 8

Richelieu
- ♠ Q 6 4
- ♡ K 10 9 8
- ◇ J 6 2
- ♣ A J 10

d'Effiat
- ♠ 10
- ♡ A Q J
- ◇ A Q 5 4 3
- ♣ K 6 5 4

Louis	Chevreuse	Richelieu	d'Effiat
			1◇
pass	1♠	pass	2♣
pass	3♡	dbl	3NT
all pass			

Chevreuse's jump bid to 3♡ asked his partner if he had that suit well stopped. Richelieu doubled for the lead and d'Effiat showed his three stoppers with a confident 3NT. In this way the easy contract of five clubs was missed.

Against 3NT Louis led a top-of-nothing ♡7 to which trick Richelieu contributed the ♡8, holding declarer to just two tricks in the suit. D'Effiat winning with the ♡J had the opportunity of making nine tricks by establishing sufficient tricks in the minors with the loss of two tricks in each of the minor suits. However, the spade suit offered the bright prospect of four immediate tricks combined with a sure entry in clubs, so a dummy reversal was superficially attractive. D'Effiat ran the ♠10 without due fear of the return from East should it lose. On lead with the ♠Q, the scarlet-robed prelate switched to declarer's proclaimed long suit, choosing the ◇2 as a subtle indication of suit preference. The King upon winning the ten made the fine return of a club, the suit in which the opponents held nine cards. He was ever assiduous in following a partner's signal for this reason: if the defense proved unsuccessful, there would be no doubt as to where the blame lay. This time the timing had turned in favor of the defense. Richelieu could take a club and return a second diamond, with another club trick to come. The unfavorable club position had come as a nasty surprise to the unlucky Marquis.

'Well defended, Your Majesty! The club return was brilliant!' exclaimed the Cardinal, quickly pressing his advantage. 'A passive spade return and I end up being squeezed unmercifully. Here would be the position on the play of the last spade from dummy:

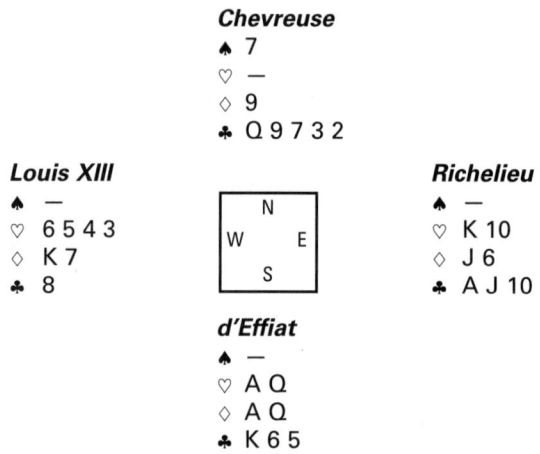

```
                    Chevreuse
                    ♠ 7
                    ♡ —
                    ◇ 9
                    ♣ Q 9 7 3 2

Louis XIII                             Richelieu
♠ —           ┌─────────┐             ♠ —
♡ 6 5 4 3     │   N     │             ♡ K 10
◇ K 7         │ W     E │             ◇ J 6
♣ 8           │   S     │             ♣ A J 10
              └─────────┘
                    d'Effiat
                    ♠ —
                    ♡ A Q
                    ◇ A Q
                    ♣ K 6 5
```

'Declarer has four spade tricks and a heart already, eight tricks are assured, so he needs to develop just one extra. A club or heart discard by me is immediately fatal and should I let go a diamond I am sure the Marquis is astute enough to realize he can discard the ◇Q on the spade, play a club to the king, cash the ◇A and endplay me in clubs to lead away from the ♡K which I had so foolishly disclosed with my double.'

What a fabrication upon the facts! What a show-off! Yet... 'tis true enough! So ran the thoughts of the Duc de Chevreuse. As for the Marquis, he was grateful for Richelieu's high evaluation of his ability and at the same time happy it had not been put to the test in the manner described.

Louis' pale cheek took on an unaccustomed glow. Nothing warmed him as much as a good defense and the general approbation that followed was most welcome as well. He rose from his chair to speak.

'This defense should serve to remind us all that in worldly affairs as in Bridge, timing is of the essence. That being so, it is timely that I announce now after full consideration of the circumstances,' here Louis paused once more, 'that it is my wish the Cardinal withdraw from the wedding negotiations forthwith (another long pause), so that he can devote himself full time to being my Councillor on all matters of state.' The applause of the courtiers was restrained except from those few happy gamblers who held long-shot bets on the Cardinal's survival.

'I shall be honored to assist Your Majesty in that capacity as long as my health permits,' replied the Cardinal with a low bow and a quiet cough.

'That's settled, then,' said the King cheerily, 'but let's keep it our secret for tonight. First thing tomorrow morning I wish to surprise the Queen Mother with the news.'

Through the good offices of his sister, the Princesse de Conti, the Duc managed to slip word to the Queen Mother to expect a visit from Louis at the crack of dawn. In his opinion there had already been too many nasty surprises in the month to risk another.

Henry Rich, Earl of Holland

His residence was at Holland Park, Kensington. As a handsome young courtier he was on the receiving end of one of James's slobbering kisses, but he had the audacity to turn his head and spit upon the ground. Nevertheless he was sent several times to Paris on diplomatic missions, the first time being in 1615 in the retinue of the Earl of Carlyle. French gentlemen thought him effeminate, but French ladies judged him better. Pleasant but incompetent, his life ended on the scaffold a few months after the execution of Charles I.

Louis Appraises Richelieu

Dearest Christine:

Sad news — no longer will old Léon come running in answer to my whistle. I had him put down and shall miss him greatly. There is a certain spot here in the orchards of St. Germain that always recalls to my mind the sunny image of you as a little girl gleefully riding on patient Léon's sturdy shoulders. At that spot, between the plums and the pears, I shall raise a stone in his memory.

Regarding our brother Gaston, the sooner he marries the better. The Princesse de Conti has been giving parties in order to expose him to the wholesome charms of La Montpensier, but he continues to take a greater interest in the less innocent ladies present. Neither age nor honorable reputation has proved a barrier to his advances with the result that attendance has dwindled as one by one the distractions are excluded by the sharp-eyed Princesse. Although I love Gaston as a brother should, I must confess that I would not freely choose him for a life-long companion. As I have been blessed with three wonderful sisters, it is only to be expected that I be deprived in other directions.

Now the good news; Mother, Anne and I have won the prestigious Earrings-of-Pearl Mixed Teams. This year I played with Cardinal Richelieu, who contrary to my earlier misgivings is turning out to be companionable. He plays his cards with great refinement, always anticipating several moves ahead with a view to maneuvering his opponents into an awkward situation, so it is all the more surprising that his bidding is so atrociously ill-conceived.

A bidding system must be designed to be like a fine cabinet with many smoothly functioning drawers fitting neatly in place. My motto is: there must be a compartment for every bid and a bid for every compartment. But the Cardinal constructs his bidding system as a simple rustic builds his *château* — adding a piece here and a piece there as he goes along. He thinks to begin frugally with the bare essentials, but then expands uneconomically as his mood dictates. The first extension may be in the English style, thick and dim; the second, Italianate, thin and suspect. In time a bedroom is made to serve as a passageway and a fine, large window comes to face a bare wall. The end product is found to be extensive yet cramped, gross but not grand, complex yet inadequate. Imagine the effect if, Heaven forbid, I were to take it in my head to add a block of apartments to my neat, little, hunting lodge at Versailles and there you have it.

In addition, the Cardinal's intention is not always clear, nor is it meant to be. Disorder provides the best camouflage for advantageous deceit and Richelieu, politician that he is, cultivates the fields of uncertainty. But a king must serve his subjects as a model of consistency and fine judgment, so I curb his natural tendency by insisting we employ a favorite device of mine: explicit transfer bids over interference, as described in my last letter. The following board from the first half of the final demonstrates their efficacy.

Both Vul.
Dealer North

Richelieu
♠ 5
♡ Q 10 9 5 4
◇ 7 3 2
♣ A 9 8 2

de Condé
♠ K Q 4 3
♡ J 8 7
◇ K J 9 6 5
♣ 3

```
     N
 W       E
     S
```

de Conti
♠ A 9 8 2
♡ K 6 3 2
◇ Q 10
♣ J 5 4

Louis
♠ J 10 7 6
♡ A
◇ A 8 4
♣ K Q 10 7 6

de Condé	Richelieu	de Conti	Louis
	pass	pass	1♣
1◇	dbl[1]	redbl	1♠
pass	2♣	dbl	pass
2◇	pass	pass	3♣
pass	pass	3◇	dbl
all pass			

1.   Shows hearts.

The Princesse de Condé felt her hand merited an overcall of 1◇ over my third hand opening bid. This is safe enough under normal circumstances, but the overcall only helped our cause, for it enabled us to employ my transfer system. The Cardinal's double showed hearts. The Princesse de Conti revealed her points with a space-saving redouble. Now came the brilliancy: I was able to make a free bid of 1♠. Think of what that implied before you read on.

I had these options: bid 1♡ with three-card support; bid 2♡ with four-card support; pass or bid 1NT with two-card support; return to 2♣ with a six-card suit. Thus, the fact I chose to bid 1♠ informed Richelieu I was short in hearts. When I later passed, and then bid 3♣ in the balancing seat, my distribution and strength were certainties. The Princesse de Conti made one move too many with a balance of 3◇ that normally would escape a double, but I could act in the knowledge that I had bid my hand with full accuracy.

After the lead of the Cardinal's solitary spade we collected three aces, two heart ruffs and two spade ruffs, off two doubled, for a useful score of 500. The Princesse de Conti apologized for her last bid, but her greater error was her redouble. She would have done much better to bid one spade, but she rejected my suggestion claiming this bid would have promised a five-card suit, while apparently no conclusion about spades could be drawn from the redouble. One doubts the usefulness of this treatment. At the other table the opponents played successfully in three clubs without a peep from the two Queens. How they expected to win with such passivity is beyond my comprehension.

In all fairness to Richelieu I must say it is satisfying to have an able partner who discerns one's wishes and acts accordingly with good effect in the interests of the partnership.

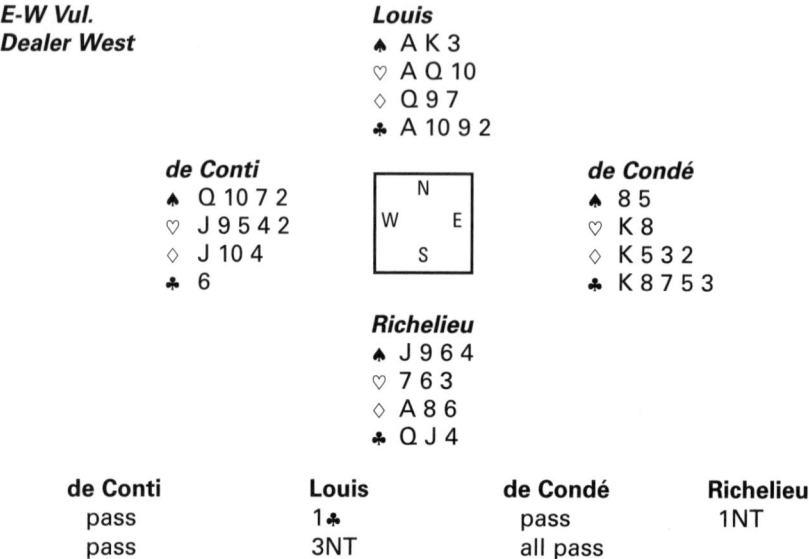

E-W Vul.
Dealer West

Louis
♠ A K 3
♡ A Q 10
◇ Q 9 7
♣ A 10 9 2

de Conti
♠ Q 10 7 2
♡ J 9 5 4 2
◇ J 10 4
♣ 6

de Condé
♠ 8 5
♡ K 8
◇ K 5 3 2
♣ K 8 7 5 3

Richelieu
♠ J 9 6 4
♡ 7 6 3
◇ A 8 6
♣ Q J 4

de Conti	Louis	de Condé	Richelieu
pass	1♣	pass	1NT
pass	3NT	all pass	

As he held the ominous 4-3-3-3 shape, the Cardinal can be forgiven for bidding 1NT at his first opportunity. The ♡K took the first trick, a heart then being returned to the ♡Q upon which trick the Princesse de Conti played the ♡2, revealing that her lead was a normal one from a five-card major suit. Clubs, spades, and even diamonds presented the Cardinal with good prospects for the one extra trick needed for his game.

As you can see, with the minor kings badly located, the natural play of the ♠AK and a low one towards the ♠J will lead to defeat, but Richelieu did not follow that fatal course. Instead he played a club from dummy.

The Princesse de Condé took her ♣K and returned a passive club, as is her wont. On the play of the clubs, the Princesse de Conti discarded her remaining hearts; clearly she was protecting useful cards in spades and diamonds. This was the position in which, having preserved all his chances in the spade suit, Richelieu needed an extra trick in addition to his aces:

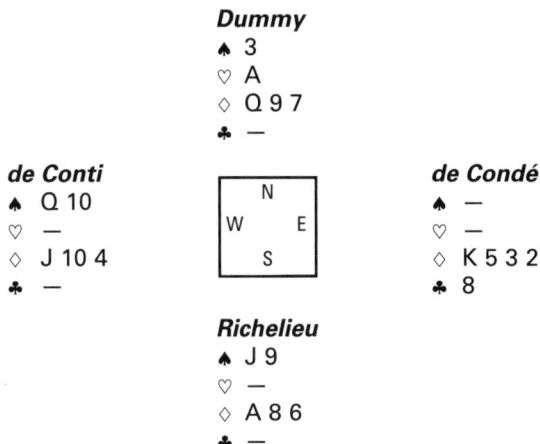

Dummy
♠ 3
♡ A
♦ Q 9 7
♣ —

de Conti
♠ Q 10
♡ —
♦ J 10 4
♣ —

de Condé
♠ —
♡ —
♦ K 5 3 2
♣ 8

Richelieu
♠ J 9
♡ —
♦ A 8 6
♣ —

On the play of the ♡A the Princesse de Conti felt some pressure. After considerable thought, she discarded the ♠10, so the contract was made without further ado.

When later I asked the Cardinal for the reasoning behind his unusual approach, he replied with a thin smile, 'Your Majesty, my critics say it is a flaw of character that compels me ever to look askance at gifts that do not bear the seal of an established affection. The play of the ♡2 struck me as being in the manner of a hollow gift, an unworthy attitude, perhaps, but one subsequently justified by the lie of the cards. If the ♠10 had not appeared I intended to continue with a diamond to my ace and a diamond towards the queen, making my ninth trick in either diamonds or spades.'

'So that ♡2 told you that the Princesse held four spades?' I asked.

'Let's say that was the premise on which I based my investigations. One must act according to what one finds to be true rather than what one wishes were true.'

I think that is rather good. Sister, we must treat the Spaniards in this same manner. They voice worthy sentiments framed in holy references, yet they do nothing that does not promote their own self-interest.

Currently I am at work on my next ballet, *The Dance of the Dinners*, in which I myself will portray the noble wines of France that accompany each course. I was thus able after the results were announced to offer the Queens an opportunity to repeat in dance their impressions of a greater and a lesser *blancmange*. They were not amused. As for the other dancers, although he lacks substance, Bassompierre has warmed many hearts, so let him appear as *The Broth*; The Cardinal, having many parts, fits admirably the role of *The Mixed Salad*; the silly Princesse de Condé, *The Goose*; the censorious Princesse de Conti, *The Carp*; none better than that old ass, Montbazon, as *The Rump Steak*. Mother, resplendent in her rubies, emeralds and pearls, would make the perfect *Glazed Fruit Cake*, don't you agree? Finally, how I wish you, my dear Christine, could be here to dance for me as none can match your creamy sweetness so appropriate to *La Parfaite*.

I must now end this letter regretfully, and remain, forever, your loving brother,

Louis

A Masked Lady

Often ladies of the French Court went about the streets of Paris beautifully dressed but masked hoping to escape the disrespectful taunts of the notorious fishwives who kept abreast of all the latest scandals. Masks were employed not only to avoid recognition but also to protect against the sun's harsh rays. Paleness of skin was regarded a characteristic of refined beauty, a concept that originated in racially divided Spain. Certainly Anne of Austria was proud of her pale complexion and white hands. The second Duchesse de Monbazon, young wife to an aging husband and the last mistress of the founder of the Trappist order, was famous for her amply displayed alabaster bosom as well as her cool disregard of morality.

The

Great

Masked

Duplicate

of

1625

If you could go back and live for one month in the past, which place and which month would you choose? For many the choice is easy: Paris in May, 1625. First, there came the preparations for the royal marriage, always an exciting time, then the splendid pageantry of the marriage on Sunday, May 11, on a pavilion outside the west door of Notre Dame. Royalty was out in full regalia with the Duke of Chevreuse standing proxy for the bridegroom, King Charles I. Then on May 21, Cardinal Francesco Barberini arrived from Rome on a white donkey with the papal dispensation papers — better late than never. Finally the ceremonies were topped off with the arrival on May 24 of the Duke of Buckingham and his 700-man entourage come to escort Queen Henrietta-Maria to her new homeland.

All Paris was dazzled by the magnificent Duke, then thirty-two years old, a man of refined manners and splendid gestures, handsome, exuberant, brave, but somewhat lacking in judgement, to say the least. Buckingham had begun his career as a pageboy to James I, one of those who 'laid themselves open to the King's caresses,' as they expressed it in those days. His continuing dominance of the English Court was living proof that self-confidence, not reason, is the Great Persuader.

The last week of May saw a round of parties the like of which have not been seen since in Europe. The Duke was entertained by the great hosts of their day: Cardinal Richelieu, Madame de Rambouillet, Marie de Medici, and the Duc de Chevreuse. He smelled the fresh paint on Rubens' twenty-one masterpieces at the Palais de Luxembourg, listened to the songs of Angelique Paulet, and gazed upon the unsurpassed beauty of the French ladies, each of whom was eager to please this famous gallant.

He had come with two equally strong desires: to obtain France's military support in a war to recover the Palatinate from the Spaniards, and to seduce the Queen of France. That the accomplishment of the second objective might impede that of the first may not have occurred to him. If it did cross his mind, he brushed the thought aside with minor annoyance, as a fat man brushes away a fly buzzing about a cream puff.

Richelieu judged him unpredictable and incompetent, being totally lacking in foresight and all the more dangerous for that. Consider this. One afternoon as the Duke sat for his portrait before the great Peter Paul Rubens, he chatted absent-mindedly of Richelieu's coolness to his plans for re-conquest of the Rhineland. It never occurred to him that the artist so calmly sketching away might be reporting every word to the Spanish ambassador.

The ladies of the Court adored him, he who subscribed to the widely held beliefs that passion rightly overrides reason and love conquers all. The Duke's familiarity towards Anne of Austria was outrageous even according to standards of the day. His behavior could not be excused as merely impolite as his intentions were all too obvious. Louis XIII was angered by the Duke's amorous advances, but more so by Anne's passive acceptance of the passionate outpourings as no more than the just tributes due her beauty and status, an idea promoted principally by the Duchesse de Chevreuse, a lady who had a fondness for fireworks. The flirtation had begun in earnest at the Great Masked Duplicate.

In the court of Louis XIII the masked duplicate was an infrequent but delightful diversion. The event was always an occasion for the display of gaiety, charm, wit, and high fashion. It combined the strenuous mental calisthenics of matchpoint Bridge with the easy dalliances of a masked ball, without a commitment to physical exertions which might tax some of the more senior members of the royal household. However, smacking as it does of egalitarianism, matchpoint duplicate was not highly considered. Was it Voltaire, or Mark Twain, who later declared, 'Matchpoints, like democracy itself, is a tragedy without pathos, a farce without wit, a carnival without joy, in short, a sideshow of deceptions devised for the gullible'? Whoever said it, he was correct about matchpoints, at least.

The Duchesse de Chevreuse had arranged a rare masked duplicate at her home. Ostensibly this was on behalf of the House of Stuart of which her husband, as proxy to Charles I, was the personal representative, but actually it was in order that Queen Anne might have an opportunity to see the handsome visitor, the Duke of Buckingham, informally close at hand. Perhaps, hidden behind the conventional anonymity of a mask, she might even engage in a bit of sexy persiflage in the spirit of good fun.

The game was arranged so that twelve pairs of ladies sat North-South opposing twelve pairs of gentlemen. The ladies were allowed the privilege of moving between rounds in order to demonstrate their grace and display their finery. It was a slowly paced event. Sometimes unauthorized information was picked up along the way, Cardinal Richelieu being a favored victim, but this was all part of the fun. On the first round the Duchesse faced a partnership that had been thrown together at game time: the Duc de Chevreuse and his father-in-law, the Duc de Montbazon. The latter thoroughly disliked playing Bridge and playing it with his son-in-law in particular, but had to act as a replacement for Louis XIII who was indisposed. It was unlucky for the ladies to face such a pair before their dissension had time to come to fruition.

Both Vul.
Dealer West

Queen Anne
♠ A 4
♡ 7 3
♢ J 9 8 4
♣ A J 9 7 3

Chevreuse
♠ 5 3 2
♡ A Q 8 6 4
♢ Q
♣ K 5 4 2

```
      N
  W       E
      S
```

Montbazon
♠ K 10 9 7 6
♡ 10 2
♢ 10 7 2
♣ Q 8 6

La Duchesse
♠ Q J 8
♡ K J 9 5
♢ A K 6 5 3
♣ 10

Chevreuse	Anne	Montbazon	Duchesse
pass	pass	pass	1♢
1♡	2♣	pass	2♢
pass	3♢	pass	3NT
all pass			

The Duchesse bid every hand for effect, not accuracy. Since she knew that the pair she was facing was one of the weaker partnerships in the field, she pushed on to game, expecting a helpful defense. However, her husband knew her all too well: he led the top-of-nothing ♠5, ducked in dummy. Montbazon won the ♠K and returned the ♡10 without thought. He, too, was familiar with his daughter's penchant for thin 3NT games with fragile stoppers, so he expected her hearts to be vulnerable to attack. Marie-Aimée covered with the ♡J, won by Chevreuse's ♡Q. In desperation her husband returned a spade to dummy's ace, but it was now too late to defeat the contract: the Duchesse could establish another heart trick safely, making five diamond tricks, two spades, a heart and a club. The ♠5 had been the killing lead all right, but Montbazon had missed the winning defense.

'What kind of overcall was that?' demanded Montbazon, costumed as Zeus hurling lightning bolts. 'I led an honor through her hand and you can't set up your suit?'

'Fool!' replied Chevreuse hotly. (He was a noted swordsman.) 'Why can't you see to duck the first spade? A second spade will clear off the ace, then I can reach your hand with the king on the third round. You can score three tricks in spades.'

So much for gaiety, wit, charm, and sexy persiflage.

'You, Sir, are a lout as well as a fool,' replied Montbazon, who as Governor of Paris had many secret assassins in his employ willing to risk their lives for a public appointment and the respectability it brought. 'What is the meaning of that ♠5? Surely it is an attitude lead showing no interest in the suit.'

'If I had no interest in the suit, why did I lead it in the first place?' demanded the Duc. Although dressed as Atlas, he showed no inclination to shoulder the full burden of guilt.

'Gentlemen, please,' admonished the Queen, who was not as amused as the Duchesse by the acrimonious exchanges, 'We love you both and entreat you both to love each other on this happy occasion. Let us pause, however prematurely, for refreshment.'

Chevreuse beckoned to one of the handsome footmen who brought to the table cooled wine in souvenir silver goblets bearing the emblems of the houses of Stuart and Bourbon so recently joined in marriage. Throughout the Great Ballroom of the Hôtel de Chevreuse the spectacle was dazzling, the playing conditions ideal. The Duke of Buckingham had donated for door prizes diamonds from the English royal treasury. The Queen and the Duchesse had dressed in coordination in full pearl-embroidered satin dresses featuring the extremely low-cut bodices then happily in fashion. Their frizzy wigs were meant to indicate shepherdesses, but one would be hard put to take them for wool-gatherers — never were shepherdesses more lively or better endowed. To return to the serious business of card play, this was the second hand to be played by the shepherdesses.

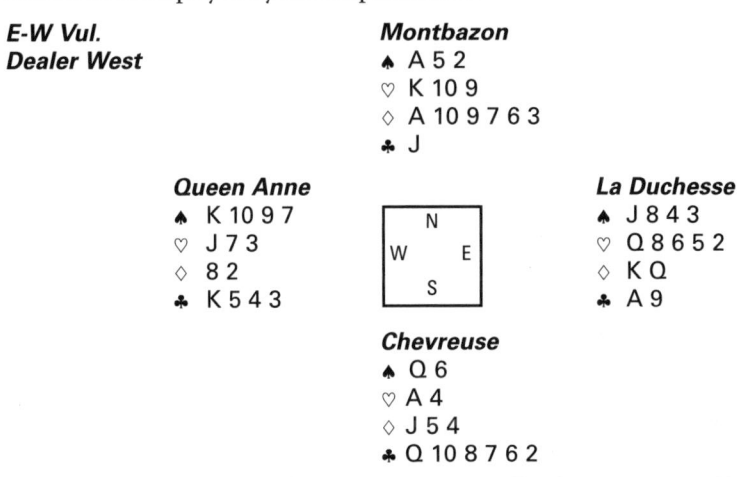

E-W Vul.
Dealer West

Montbazon
♠ A 5 2
♡ K 10 9
◇ A 10 9 7 6 3
♣ J

Queen Anne
♠ K 10 9 7
♡ J 7 3
◇ 8 2
♣ K 5 4 3

La Duchesse
♠ J 8 4 3
♡ Q 8 6 5 2
◇ K Q
♣ A 9

Chevreuse
♠ Q 6
♡ A 4
◇ J 5 4
♣ Q 10 8 7 6 2

Anne	Montbazon	Duchesse	Chevreuse
pass	1◇	1♡	2♣
pass	2◇	pass	pass
2♡	dbl[1]	pass	3NT
all pass			

1. Optional.

(The directions have been changed for convenience of presentation.)

It was typical of the timid Anne that she passed up an opportunity to raise her partner's overcall immediately, then chose to re-enter a dead misfit auction, vulnerable, an action she mistakenly felt to be the safer course facing an overly aggressive partner. Montbazon expressed his opinion of this bad style with an aggressive optional double. With honors in every suit and three-card support for partner's six-card suit, Chevreuse felt his hand was now worth an unusual jump to game in notrump — he feared no lead from the Queen, who was considered by the male courtiers to be first-rate in appearance but second-rate in performance, a view encouraged by her husband. The women of the court rated her game more highly, for they had seen more evidence of her true mettle which she was at pains to hide from men.

Confused as she often was in the swirling dynamics of card play, Anne enjoyed most the lull before the storm when she could dreamily ruminate over her opening lead, holding the rapt attention of all those at table. Indeed, opening leads were her specialty and she took nearly as much pains over them as with the arrangement of her hair. As Montbazon had shown good hearts and Chevreuse appeared to have a safety feature in the suit as well, that typically left very little for the Duchesse in a suit in which she had overcalled. As the opponents had not shown length in spades but found notrump attractive, each must hold an honor there. Thinking along these lines, the Queen looked to the minors for a safe lead.

On the normal lead of the ♡3, Chevreuse would have made his contract, whereas on the actual club lead, he had no hope. The Duchesse won the ♣A and quickly switched to the ♠J, an informative card meant to avoid taxing the Queen's reasoning processes. The defense took no tricks in the suit they had bid, but took two clubs, a diamond, and three spades to set the contract by two, thus assuring an excellent score against the many pluses which would be recorded by North-South pairs playing in diamonds or successfully defending against hearts or spades at the three-level. The Duchesse and the Queen were off to a great start.

Lest you think these courtly players were overly ambitious in their quest for top scores, may we remind you of the words of the immortal Dr. Samuel Johnson who, after a particularly bad session, penned the lines which gave rise to the expression 'Matchpoint Madness':

> *In Matchpoint's strife, what Prodigies abound!*
> *With Madness rife, 'tis Folly to be sound.*

For months the Duchesse had been filling the ears of Queen Anne with words of praise of the gallant and handsome Buckingham, while Kensington's dispatches to London had contained many references to the beautiful and *much-neglected* Queen of France. Thus did the Duchesse and her English lover conspire dangerously to promote a flirtation which might fan the Queen's smoldering passions beyond her control. It was not until a late round of the duplicate that this long-anticipated meeting took place.

Women who found Richelieu infuriating, that is to say most women under sixty or so, also found Buckingham irresistible. He and his partner, Henry Rich, recently promoted to the rank of Lord Holland, came dressed as British pirates with appropriate eye patches and flowing false, red beards. Queen Anne and the Duchesse de Chevreuse approached their table each carrying a long white crook topped with a lilac ribbon, which in those pre-Freudian days immediately suggested to everyone the occupation of shepherdess and nothing more. Even when masked this pair was matched female perfection: the Queen, tall, blonde, and aristocratic; the Duchesse, petite, auburn, and nimble.

Buckingham rose from the table and took the liberty of kissing the hand of the

Queen without being given leave, but without its being withdrawn, either. 'You blondes should know we pirates have a unquenchable lust for gold,' he stated in a gravelly voice, boldly raising his gaze to lock upon bright eyes peeping at him from behind a velvet mask. Inspired, he waxed poetic: 'Roses are red, violets are blue,' he recited in English, 'We like to sport, How about you?'

'Good Lord, Old Boy, think of the ramifications...' spurted out an astonished Holland. Years of quiet English diplomacy were being put at grave risk, or so he thought.

'Bear with me, Rich; pirates prefer rough waters,' interrupted Buckingham, brazenly undressing the Queen with his eyes. 'Trust me, a mask gives leave to boldness.' He then continued in his eloquent French, 'Fair fosterer of fleecy flocks, speak, I pray you, that I may keep the sound of your sweet voice forever locked in my heart.'

Holland relaxed; that was more like it — but really, some men, just because it's Paris in the Spring...

'Roving Jolly Roger,' interposed the Duchesse, 'my sister has not the gift of speech but needs must communicate through sign language that only I can translate.' Anne played her part by moving her fingers in rapid gestures, giggling merrily all the while.

'What the deuce does she say?' asked Buckingham, much amused by this ruse.

'She says you were too bold to kiss her hand in such a manner, but she would know your name so that she might write you a severe letter of chastisement.' The Queen nodded vigorous approval of her friend's inventive device which would excuse an exchange of letters — Accusation, Apology, Forgiveness, Gratitude, Curiosity, and so on and on.

'Tell her I am an Englishman, my title being Duke of Buckingham, but I would be honored if she were to address me simply as George.'

'No, no, I think we shall not call you Georges,' answered the Duchesse, firmly denying his impudent request, 'Not Georges, but *Jacques, Jacques Rab-bit.* It fits you, does it not, bold English pirate?'

Eventually the bidding got underway with the Queen drawing her bids in the air with her fingers.

E-W Vul.
Dealer South

Queen Anne
♠ J 10 8
♡ A K 10 4 3
♢ Q 5
♣ Q 7 4

Holland
♠ K 6
♡ J 5
♢ J 10 9 7 2
♣ A 9 8 3

```
      N
   W     E
      S
```

Buckingham
♠ 3
♡ 9 8 6 2
♢ 6 4 3
♣ K J 10 6 2

La Duchesse
♠ A Q 9 7 5 4 2
♡ Q 7
♢ A K 8
♣ 5

Holland	Anne	Buckingham	Duchesse
			1♠
pass	2♡	pass	3♠
pass	4♠	all pass	

Marie-Aimée bid in her usual exuberant style with an unjustifiable jump rebid in her own suit, then guessed to stop on a *centime* at game. Holland made a safe lead from his diamond sequence. The Duchesse won in dummy with the ♢Q and led the top spade. When Buckingham played a low spade with gentlemanly grace and style, she easily rose with the ♠A and played the three top hearts, discarding her losing ♣5, making 480.

When the traveling score slip was examined it was discovered that every other declarer to that point had been held to eleven tricks, many exuberant pairs even going down in slam, a lamentable state of affairs as far as the English guests were concerned since they had been doing rather well to that point. Imagine the Duchesse's inconsistency — not trying for slam in the bidding then gambling to make thirteen tricks by dropping the trump king singleton! It was apparent she did not play for average scores.

'Odds Bodkins,' said Buckingham, then without further comment he glumly drew out the cards for the next deal.

Both Vul.
Dealer West

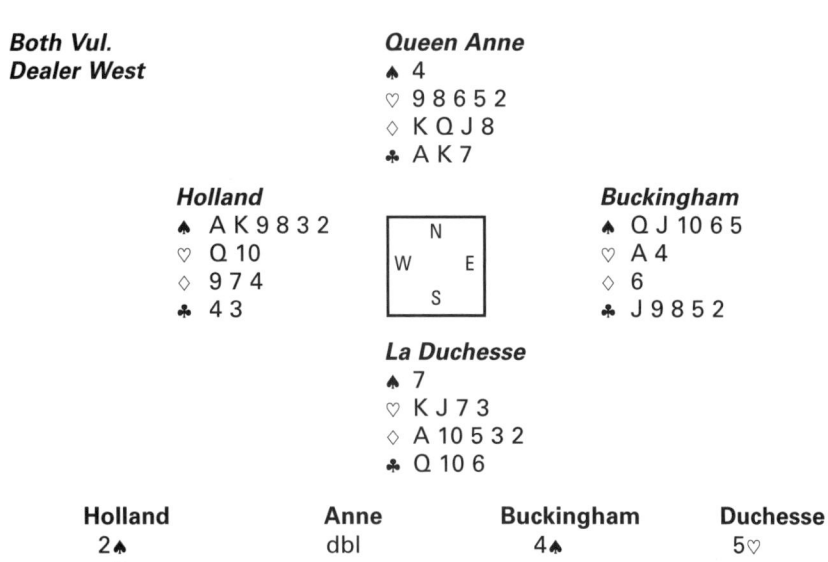

Queen Anne
♠ 4
♡ 9 8 6 5 2
◇ K Q J 8
♣ A K 7

Holland
♠ A K 9 8 3 2
♡ Q 10
◇ 9 7 4
♣ 4 3

Buckingham
♠ Q J 10 6 5
♡ A 4
◇ 6
♣ J 9 8 5 2

La Duchesse
♠ 7
♡ K J 7 3
◇ A 10 5 3 2
♣ Q 10 6

Holland	Anne	Buckingham	Duchesse
2♠	dbl	4♠	5♡
all pass			

The Weak Two was an invention brought by King James to England from Scotland, a land in which the inhabitants had always had to make do with much, much less. Holland was well-stocked for the bid and Buckingham applied maximum pressure, but the Duchesse was one who seldom shied away from danger. Holland led the top spade, to which Buckingham followed with the queen. When Holland continued with the ◇4, the lowest outstanding diamond, the Duchesse called for the king in dummy. When Buckingham did not ruff this, the Duchesse was much relieved, for the Duke had clearly asked for a diamond switch.

On a low heart from dummy, Buckingham played low. Since he was marked with the ace, he might have risen with it and tried to give a diamond ruff to Holland. As he didn't, his signal for a diamond switch could be read a passive one, indicating a safe continuation in that suit, rather than a suggestion for a killing defense. With shortness in clubs Holland might have ignored the signal, so he could be counted on for at least two cards in each minor. To lose a trump trick to a singleton or doubleton queen in Holland's hand would be fatal, so the Duchesse went up with the ♡K, thus making eleven tricks for another top score.

'We was scuppered,' lamented Buckingham nautically.

'Your signal flag caused us to run aground, matey,' grumbled his partner mutinously. 'Jump bid in diamonds and I can find the killing lead.'

'Oh, du vee du sum-zing clev-air?' asked a smiling Marie-Aimée in her charming English. Of course, she dominated the subsequent conversation to the growing frustration of the Queen, who had not foreseen this unhappy consequence of her pretended loss of voice. But whatever pain she caused in the achievement of her aims, the Duchesse was prepared to compensate with the pleasures of her company.

Anne and Marie-Aimée in their role of shepherdesses had done much fleecing on the previous rounds, but on the last round of the Great Masked Duplicate they faced formidable opposition: Cardinal Richelieu and Bertrand de Chaux, the aged

Archbishop of Tours, who was much enamored of the Duchesse, although nearly half a century her senior. He had presided at her first marriage and a decade later he would save her life, but that is another story. Richelieu was dressed as a gypsy dancer with a red kerchief around his head, a disguise which suited his slim figure if not his unruffled demeanor. For the subject of his disguise the Archbishop had targeted Saint Sebastian, incommodiously so, for the decorative arrows that projected from his chest somewhat inconvenienced the play of the cards. He had also suffered some arrows of outrageous fortune but their system, the Strong Canonical Club, often had proved advantageous, and the Archbishop still entertained hopes of a top ranking in their direction when the following hand was played.

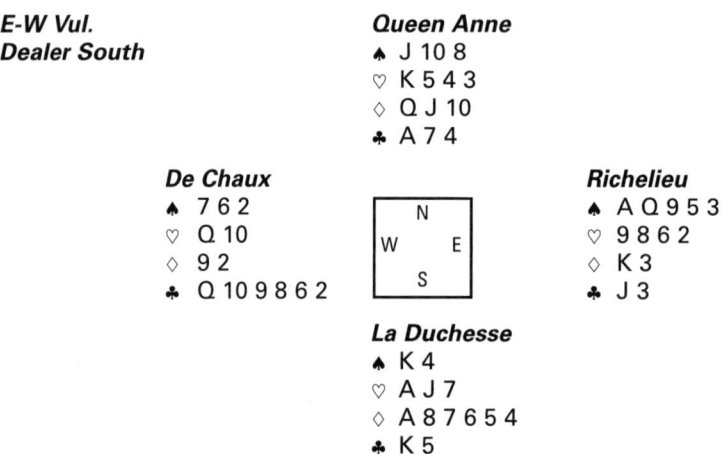

E-W Vul.
Dealer South

Queen Anne
♠ J 10 8
♡ K 5 4 3
♢ Q J 10
♣ A 7 4

De Chaux
♠ 7 6 2
♡ Q 10
♢ 9 2
♣ Q 10 9 8 6 2

Richelieu
♠ A Q 9 5 3
♡ 9 8 6 2
♢ K 3
♣ J 3

La Duchesse
♠ K 4
♡ A J 7
♢ A 8 7 6 5 4
♣ K 5

The Duchesse opened the bidding with 1NT and was raised directly to 3NT. De Chaux saw no problem leading the ♣10, a standard lead at that time. Marie-Aimée won the ♣A in the dummy, under which Richelieu unblocked his ♣J. When declarer next led the ◊Q, Richelieu covered with the ◊K. Now it was just a matter of overtricks, and the Duchesse was ever on the alert for possibilities of a top score. She returned to the dummy to unblock the diamond honors. Noting De Chaux's discard of the ♠2, she saw what others did not see — it was advantageous to play on spades at this point and leave the play in the heart suit until later. Even if the spade finesse were to lose, it was most unlikely the suit would be returned by the Archbishop.

She chose to lead the ♠J from dummy, planning to rise with the king if Richelieu did not cover. Dangerous? Perhaps, but unlikely to prove suicidal and possibly informative. Richelieu rose with the ♠A, keeping full control of that suit, and cleared the clubs for his partner, but this made the subsequent play easy for someone of the ability of the Duchesse de Chevreuse. She ran her winning diamonds to reach this point:

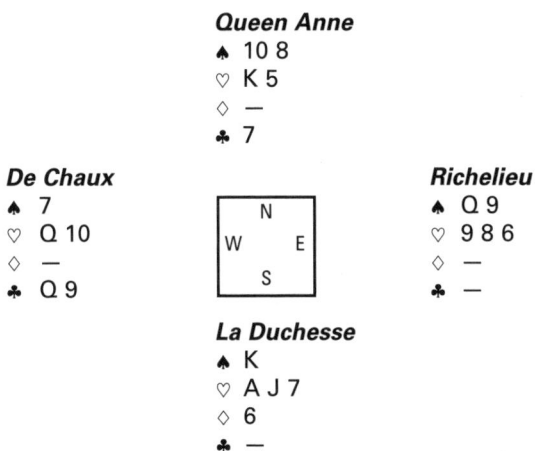

Queen Anne
♠ 10 8
♡ K 5
◇ —
♣ 7

De Chaux
♠ 7
♡ Q 10
◇ —
♣ Q 9

Richelieu
♠ Q 9
♡ 9 8 6
◇ —
♣ —

La Duchesse
♠ K
♡ A J 7
◇ 6
♣ —

On the ◇6 De Chaux judiciously discarded a club and Richelieu had to part with a heart. The ♠K was cashed and all followed, leaving some doubt as to the full count. The Duchesse crossed to the ♡K and led the ♡5 from dummy. When Richelieu followed with the ♡8, she judged from his early play in the spade suit that he was in possession of the ♠Q, so she went up with the ♡A, dropping the ♡Q. Others had finessed in hearts and held themselves to a paltry 430 or a mediocre 460, but the Duchesse scored 490, a clear top and deservedly so.

'Ah, my dear,' exclaimed the Archbishop as he squeezed her knee under the table, 'Why is it you can so easily resist my attacks?'

'Dear friend, you have only your costume to blame,' replied the Duchesse with a smile. 'To more readily exploit our womanly weaknesses, you should show us more of the stallion and less of the porcupine.'

'Alas, I have been mistaken for a prickly creature of quills, when these arrows are Cupid's handiwork. Your harsh treatment has dashed any hope I had of conquest.'

'Take heart, my dear Archbishop,' encouraged the Queen, 'we've just come from giving two bottoms to *Les Bouquins*, so you can still prevail.'

'Ah, at their age the generosity of being presented with your two lovely bottoms, one hard upon the other, can be accommodated with grace and ease, but at my age one has lost the facility of turning the other cheek,' jested the Archbishop, regaining his spirits in the gay laughter that flattered his humor.

Much as he would have liked to play the gallant to these charmers, Richelieu did not participate in the raillery. It had been a long afternoon as wave after wave of worldly womanhood had made his head swim with their unfathomable bids and plays to the point that now he had one of his splitting headaches; the chattering of this last pair thundered within his skull like the sound of a thousand castanets inside an empty wine cask. He had slipped up badly on the previous hand and now it would take his full powers of concentration to perform well on the last hand of the tournament.

The Cardinal was lucky that the final deal provided him the opportunity of playing against the field through the employment of a strong club opening bid.

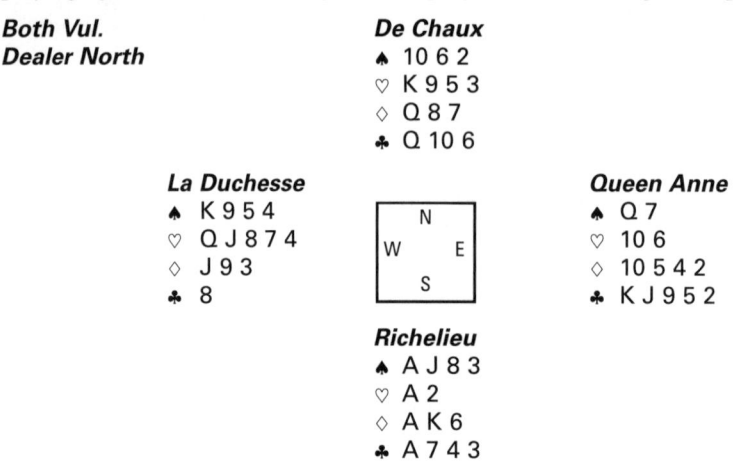

Both Vul.
Dealer North

De Chaux
♠ 10 6 2
♡ K 9 5 3
◊ Q 8 7
♣ Q 10 6

La Duchesse
♠ K 9 5 4
♡ Q J 8 7 4
◊ J 9 3
♣ 8

Queen Anne
♠ Q 7
♡ 10 6
◊ 10 5 4 2
♣ K J 9 5 2

Richelieu
♠ A J 8 3
♡ A 2
◊ A K 6
♣ A 7 4 3

Duchesse	De Chaux	Anne	Richelieu
	pass	pass	1♣[1]
pass	1◊[2]	pass	1♠[3]
pass	2♣[4]	pass	4♣
pass	4♠	all pass	

1. Strong.
2. 0-7 HCP.
3. Promises 4+ spades, forcing.
4. 6-7 HCP.

(The directions have been changed for convenience of presentation.)

Having carried De Chaux to this point in the game with a decent score, the Cardinal was willing on the last hand to abandon his careful approach and to take a flyer in the hopes of a first-place finish. After the automatic start of 1♣ - 1◊, the systemic rebid with 20 HCP would be 2NT, but four aces and a king represented prime values. Might not slam be made on an elimination play opposite as bad a hand as

♠ Q x x   ♡ K x x   ◊ x x   ♣ Q x x x x

One thing was certain, 6♣ would not be given much consideration by most standard bidders.

His slam exploration began with a forcing rebid of 1♠, promising four or more, usually in a distributional hand with a longer minor. When De Chaux rebid an artificial 2♣, showing 6-7 HCP while denying a five-card red suit and four-card spade support, Richelieu continued with a hopeful jump in clubs. Unhappily the Archbishop could only manage a raise to game in spades, leaving Richelieu with the hope of a favorable swing in the known Moyesian fit against the normal contract of 3NT.

The opening lead of the ♣8 was read by Richelieu as a singleton, so he took his ace immediately. To test the distribution he cashed the ace of hearts, then played the ◇K, hoping to look like a man who sought an entry to the dummy with the ◇Q. When Marie-Aimée played the ◇9 (which he did not trust) and Anne the ◇5 (which he did), he had double confirmation that the suit was dividing 4-3. Richelieu played to the ♡K and led a heart from dummy, ruffed by Anne with the ♠Q. Strangely, this worked advantageously by reducing the trumps in the opponents' short-trump hand. The Cardinal overruffed with the ♠A, went to dummy with the ◇Q and led a fourth heart, on which Anne discarded a club. As he had assumed initially that West had led a singleton club, he was not about to change his assumption in mid-stream without evidence to the contrary. His inferential count placed East with a bare spade remaining, but which spade?

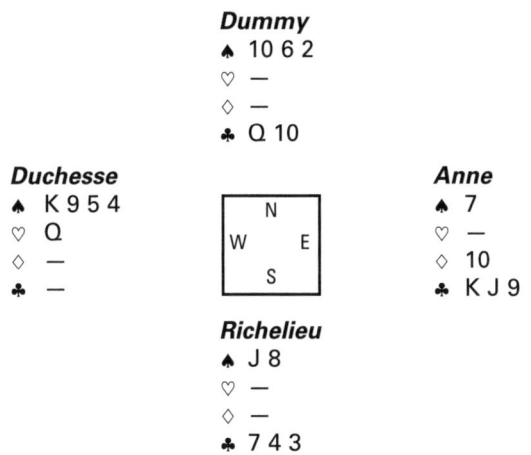

Dummy
♠ 10 6 2
♡ —
◇ —
♣ Q 10

Duchesse
♠ K 9 5 4
♡ Q
◇ —
♣ —

Anne
♠ 7
♡ —
◇ 10
♣ K J 9

Richelieu
♠ J 8
♡ —
◇ —
♣ 7 4 3

Needing just two more tricks, the Cardinal saw an advantage to playing the ♠J from his hand, luckily pinning Anne's ♠7. That put the Duchesse in an impossible situation. If she made the 'natural' play of taking the king and returning a low trump, the Cardinal could win in hand with the ♠8, with the ♠10 remaining in dummy as the tenth trick. The return of the ♠9 would serve only to promote the ♠6 in dummy.

Richelieu's score of 420 was a clear top, as those in three notrump contracts made only nine tricks after playing on clubs. Overall the Duchesse and the Queen were easy winners North-South at 74%. That final board against them gave Richelieu and De Chaux a respectable score of 57%, tops for the men sitting East-West.

The official report of the tournament that heaped praise on Richelieu's play of the last hand eventually made its way with Cardinal Barberini to Rome where it became the subject of much discussion within the sepulchral splendors of the *Sanctum Santorum Bridgium*. Laying aside the account with obvious distaste, Urban VIII observed, 'I perceive here Folly being masqueraded as Brilliancy.'

'As Mankind is forever getting into a muddle, I suppose the ability to extract oneself from a mess of one's own making must be considered a virtue, ergo in that sense Richelieu can claim to be virtuous,' remarked Francesco Barberini, his strong words reverberating off the marble interior.

To which the recently elected Pope replied dryly, 'Virtuous or not, Nephew, he was victorious and that's what counts at matchpoints... and elections.'

The
Conspiracy
of the
Dames

After her satisfying victory at the Masked Pairs, the indefatigable Duchesse de Chevreuse despite her advanced state of pregnancy, celebrated long into the night with the two English pirates until finally it was time for them to go to bed and rest up for the next day's festivities. As she sat before her boudoir mirror a wide smile of satisfaction crossed her lips. The candlelight added sparkle to her eyes and glow to her rosy cheeks; she could see nothing to complain about in the image smiling back at her.

Everything was going her way. The marriage of Henrietta-Maria would not have occurred but for her guidance during the negotiations. It was she who had introduced Henry Rich to his future queen and it was she who behind the scenes had guided the tricky negotiations to their successful conclusion. Rightfully, she was beside her husband when he stood proxy for Charles I before Notre Dame. Soon they would be going to London with the royal bride to meet and win over the young king. *Oui!* she exclaimed gleefully as she gave herself a congratulatory love pat on the cheek before blowing out the candle.

But as she lay alone in her big bed in the dark, her optimism subsided. There was one problem remaining: Louis XIII, who was proving less of a man than befitted a French monarch. Recently he had forsaken the marriage bed on the excuse that Anne had given offense for some unfathomable reason that remained locked within his Majesty's secretive mind. Imagine that! Absenting oneself from the most beautiful queen in Christendom over some imagined slight. Chevreuse would never do that. She formed an amusing plan to recall Louis to his duty.

What of Richelieu? The Cardinal bears watching, she told herself, but he is little more than the clever servant one puts in charge of the gold plate. Too clever, perhaps, but he is obviously smitten, so, as always, she would cultivate the fertile field of fervent feelings until the time came in the not-too-distant future to discard him like a stained glove.

It is right for women to have a hand in the affairs of state, she concluded sleepily. Unlike men, we always work for peace and prosperity, not war and devastation. Resolve the conflict with Madrid, keep England at bay, restore full and friendly relations with Lorraine, and above all, keep Paris the gayest capital in the whole, wide world.

The next morning the Duchesse visited the Queen Mother and set her plan in motion. It was the first step in what has gone down in history as the infamous Conspiracy of the Dames. And of course, it involved Bridge.

The Challenge of the Dames

arly one morning a few days after the Great Masked Duplicate, Cardinal Richelieu was called to the Louvre. The royal messenger had emphasized it was urgent. As he hurried past a quartet of handsome King's Musketeers and entered the King's chambers, his mind was in a turmoil. What calamity could have called him out at this early hour? News from outside Paris always reached his ears before those of his monarch, so most probably it involved the Duke of Buckingham's mission. So far the visit had gone smoothly; what could have gone wrong at this late date?

'Thank you for coming so promptly, Cousin,' said the sad-eyed Louis in a rare display of gratitude. One could never tell from his face how bad the news was, for the King's expression always conveyed the message that 'being born is bad enough, now this has had to happen.' On the other hand he was extremely even-tempered, neither deeply upset by adversity nor overjoyed with success. There was even a remote possibility that this time it would be good news!

'Read this and tell me what you think,' the King said as he handed his Chief Councillor a strongly perfumed letter bearing the signature of the Queen Mother. It was marked 'personal'.

Dearest Louis:

My son, now that your young sister is married off my thoughts return once more to your problems. To put it bluntly, it's time to stop these delays and get down to the business of producing an heir to the throne of France. Although I see the fault is not entirely on your side alone, your neglect of poor Anne has become an embarrassment to Frenchmen. Did your father neglect me? I should say not. Quite the contrary — for which you of all people should be grateful.

Don't tell me again that thirteen is an unlucky number. My astrologers have assured me that a very important event is due to occur in nine months' time. That should tell you something. To miss this opportunity would only add to the suffering of a mother who loves you dearly. Yes, even though you had poor Concini shot without my permission I understand why you did it and I have forgiven you long ago.

As my past entreaties have gone for naught, let me this time make an appeal to your sporting nature. Three rubbers of Bridge, total scoring; you and your partner of choice against Anne and the Duchesse de Chevreuse. If you win, I tell you everything I know, and it is considerable, about the Duke of Buckingham and the English plot to support La Rochelle. If the ladies win, you must spend the night in Anne's bed-chamber and yield entirely to her wishes until dawn. Then I may tell all I know, etc., which is, as we say, considerable. Either way you can't lose, my son.

I hope your answer will demonstrate to an anxious mother that at least your sporting blood can be aroused. Remember, whatever happens, you'll always be my son. Why can't you make me happy just this once?

Your loving Mother and former Regent,
M de M

P.S. Don't show this letter to Cardinal Richelieu.

'Well, Cousin?' asked Louis with an upraised eyebrow.

'Ah, Your Majesty, we all have mothers, God knows, and my dear mother, now dead these eight years...' waffled Richelieu.

'Yes, some are more fortunate than others in that regard,' interrupted the King ambiguously, 'but if you'll excuse me, I am impatient for your advice.'

'I hesitate to interfere with the relationship between man and wife even when the interests of the state are at stake. Wives are to life as details to a project: one should not neglect them altogether, but neither should one spend too much time on them.'

'Exactly! I need only tell you, which I do to keep you informed insofar as necessary, that I have not slept in the Queen's bed for several months. It is her punishment concerning a personal matter that I shall keep private.'

'I commend your restraint, Your Majesty, and will comment only that a monarch if he is to rule to greatest effect must set aside his personal feelings and forever keep the interest of the Crown foremost in his thoughts. Having said that, I can only advise you to take the counsel of Bassompierre, a man better qualified than me to deal with matters of the heart.'

'Bassompierre! That heartless stomper on the holy bonds of matrimony? Why, he is even less qualified than you to advise me on marriage. But I didn't call you here for marriage advice, I called you here for your thoughts on the proposed Bridge match. That matter should lie well within your realm of competence,' said Louis angrily.

'Your Majesty, this is so sudden. Perhaps we should think about this from all angles, and tomorrow...'

'What is the reason for delay? The terms are clearly expressed.'

'Your Majesty is certainly the best player France has ever known,' lied the Cardinal to gain time in his accustomed flattering style, for he knew full well that he, Armand-Jean du Plessis, was that player. Still, three rubbers? There was an element of risk, especially when playing with an unsound bidder who would insist on playing more contracts than was good for him; the Duchesse de Chevreuse was not to be taken lightly as an opponent, what with her lightning thrusts at all vulnerabilities. 'But if we should lose...'

The King slapped his thigh in annoyance. 'Lose! What a defeatist attitude! I can't lose playing against a pair of women; besides which, I have already accepted and added a wager of one hundred crowns. I called you here to have your advice on whom I should select as my partner. Your suggestion of Bassompierre might be appropriate after all.'

The Cardinal was taken aback by this unexpected turn. He had assumed, naturally that he... Well!

'Truly a great player against other men, Your Majesty, but, alas, a man who might be overly excited in the presence of a lady of the excessive feminine charms of the Duchesse de Chevreuse. You can't afford a minus 1100 in so short a match.'

'Cardinal de La Rochefoucauld, then. He cannot be accused of being susceptible to female charms.'

'At his advanced age a most appropriate comment, to be sure, but I see you with a younger man like yourself whose great deeds lie before him.'

'Montmorency?'

'A capable man, but you need a selfless soul, who would make sure you played the difficult 3NT contracts.'

'Chevreuse?'

'He overbids crudely.'

'D'Effiat?'

'He underbids too delicately.'

'Dammit! Who then? Give me a name.'

'Your Majesty, if my health permits...' replied the Cardinal with a slight cough, bowing humbly before his partner-to-be.

Louis could barely suppress a smile. 'I had you down for the arbiter of disputes, but as this is a friendly game *en famille,* I suppose we can dispense with that functionary in the cause of showing these ladies how Bridge should be played at the highest level.'

Richelieu Misplays a Slam

he afternoon was spent at a garden party in honor of the Duke of Buckingham and the successful 'wooing ambassador', Lord Holland. The Duke, outfitted in presumptuously purple satin festooned with a myriad of pearls, had several opportunities to speak with Anne, who grew friendlier with each encounter. In the evening there was a banquet followed by a *soirée intime* at the Hôtel de Rambouillet during which Mlle Paulet's fine voice was wasted on several long and dull songs on themes mythological. Sitting like a prisoner between Cardinals Barberini and Richelieu, Buckingham's only amusement was in watching the singer's ample bosom heaving up and down, which performance served only to add to the Duke's growing restlessness. After the concert the Duke was invited to watch the royal family at Bridge, which event would give him additional opportunities to communicate further with the Queen, whom he was now thoroughly convinced would yield easily to his considerable charm.

In the seventeenth century there was royal privilege, but not royal privacy. In a palace of closely linked rooms with multitudinous keyholes, there was no need for the telephoto lens or the electronic bug, so the secret terms of the King's wager were well known by the time the royal personages gathered in the packed card room for the fateful three rubbers. Even the foreigner Buckingham had been informed of it by Lord Holland, who had got the information directly from the Duchesse de Chevreuse.

The walls of the card room were richly decorated with the finest tapestries whilst the interior was sparkling with the jewelry of the kibitzers who had done their utmost to outshine each other in the magnificence of their costumes. It was warm and the Ladies fluttered their fans to disperse the smell of burning wax emanating from the overhead chandeliers. Bassompierre was there wearing his famous sword with scabbard and hilt encrusted in precious stones. The Queen Mother made her grand entrance nobly bearing up under the excessive burden of her heavy gold ornaments. The Princesse de Conti, walking a step behind, gave off sparks of blue and green from the sapphires encrusted in her magnificent gown. They seated themselves beside Queen Anne.

As was the custom, the King took the North seat. Louis looked appropriately kingly — handsome, well groomed, austere. He had even bathed — a nice touch, thought the Ladies of the Court, as it indicated he gave some consideration to the possibility he might lose. Richelieu was attired in his cerise robes and skull cap. Suspended from his neck by a blue silk and silver cord was the ornate Maltese Cross of the Order of the Holy Ghost. Behind the Cardinal sat the King's fidgety brother, Gaston, accompanied by his disreputable favorite, the Marquis de Puylaurens, while on the other side stood the King's Master of Wardrobe, the immature Comte de Chalais, a deadly swordsman.

Seated East was the ravishing Duchesse de Chevreuse wearing pearls and a pale yellow silk gown, extremely low cut, which did little to hide her charms and much to draw attention to them. In the West seat Anne of Austria was looking more radiant than usual in a red dress ornamented with silver, a coronet of diamonds resting lightly upon her blonde head. The Duke of Buckingham stood with his hands placed familiarly on the back of the Duchesse's chair. His newly donned scarlet costume was bedecked with diamonds and pearls in a profusion of sparkles and colors that matched the Queen's. Richelieu noted that the handsome Buckingham was staring directly across the table at Anne, causing her to blush and drop her eyes. A dangerous, presumptuous man, this English peacock.

A decade of indulgence as the favorite of an aging king had imparted to the Duke's features a dreamy, pampered look. Certainly there was an element of danger to be seen there as well, for his whole aspect conveyed the impression of a man who could not for long tolerate having his desires thwarted. Perhaps it was this danger transmitted by his intense gaze from under hooded eyelids that made feminine hearts beat faster.

To a fanfare of *hautbois* the pre-dealt hands arrived and the game began with the Cardinal being put to the test by the Duchesse.

Neither Vul.		Louis XIII	Score	
Dealer South		♠ K J 5 2	Ladies	0
		♡ A J 10	Men	0
		◇ A K Q J 10		
		♣ J		

Queen Anne		La Duchesse
♠ Q 10 9 6		♠ 4
♡ K 8 4 3	N	♡ 9 7 5
◇ 9 6 3	W E	◇ 8 7 5
♣ K 5	S	♣ Q 10 7 6 4 2

Richelieu
♠ A 8 7 3
♡ Q 6 2
◇ 4 2
♣ A 9 8 3

Anne	Louis	Duchesse	Richelieu
			pass
pass	1◇	pass	1♠
pass	4♣[1]	dbl	redbl[2]
pass	4♡	pass	4♠
pass	5◇	pass	5♠
pass	6♠	dbl[3]	all pass

1.	Shortness.
2.	Shows the ace.
3.	Asks for an unusual lead.

After a complex auction in which the Duchesse participated far beyond the merits of her holding, the ♡8 glided to the table from the lily-white hand of the Queen.

'The double of 4♣ indicated a desire for the lead of a club, did it not, Your Majesty?' inquired Richelieu politely.

Anne of Austria laughed nervously. 'Yes, but the double of 6♠ asked for an unusual lead, not clubs. It is called Guildenstern, a new English convention taught us by Bucking- ga-ham. I suppose I should have alerted it.'

'Cardinal, are you surprised that a lady may both want something and not want it at the same time?' asked the Duchesse, her teeth gleaming with all the luster of Buckingham's pearls.

'Not at all. My only surprise is that you ladies have embraced Guildenstern but not, it seems, Rosencranz.'

Before playing from dummy Richelieu tried to imagine a situation in which the Duchesse would see the benefits of an immediate heart lead through the ace, marked in the dummy by the bidding. His quick mind responded to the challenge; with

♠ 4 ♡ K 9 7 ◇ 8 7 ♣ K Q 7 6 5 4 2

a player might fear the possibility of an elimination and endplay in clubs to force a costly return into a heart tenace in dummy. But if East held such a hand, a trump loser was inevitable, in which case Richelieu could not afford the loss of a heart as well. Luckily the ♡J10 were well-placed for the plan he had in mind, an eventuality the Duchesse could not have foreseen.

He called for the heart ace from dummy, came to his hand with the ace of trumps and took the successful finesse only to find that there was a trump loser. He smiled a smile of grim satisfaction; the suit lay as he had expected. He played on diamonds, discarding his last heart on the fourth round. Anne ruffed and returned an ineffective trump to dummy's king. Now for the *coup de grâce*: the ♡J was led for a ruffing finesse… down one! The Cardinal was astounded, but managed to join in the applause that accompanied this disaster.

'Well defended, Anne, carissima,' said Queen Mother, clapping her fat hands delightedly. 'However did you guess to underlead the king of hearts?'

'*Formidable*, Madame,' complimented the Duke of Buckingham gracefully. '*Quelle double!*' he murmured admiringly from his vantage point directly behind and slightly above the Duchesse.

'*Merci*. I hope the Cardinal will forgive *mes petites diversions*,' she added turning to the victim of her stratagem.

'Of course, Madame, but there is nothing to forgive as it is the nature of women to provide diversions.'

It is man's nature not to be in the best of moods after going down in a cold slam because of a deceptive female defense, but the Cardinal's bitter thoughts were not flavored with misogyny. He recognized that to be fooled is not the same as being outwitted and he blamed himself for his bidding, which, like Madame's gown, was altogether too revealing. Her double was no mere whim; she was quite capable of deducing that the ♡K must reside in her partner's hand, and she cleverly took advantage of that knowledge. The Queen also had played her part well.

It was his usual good fortune that kind fate immediately dealt him a hand which enabled him to recover some lost prestige as well as to reap some purely personal revenge from the overly active Duchesse whose normal practice it was to over-call frequently on inadequate values.

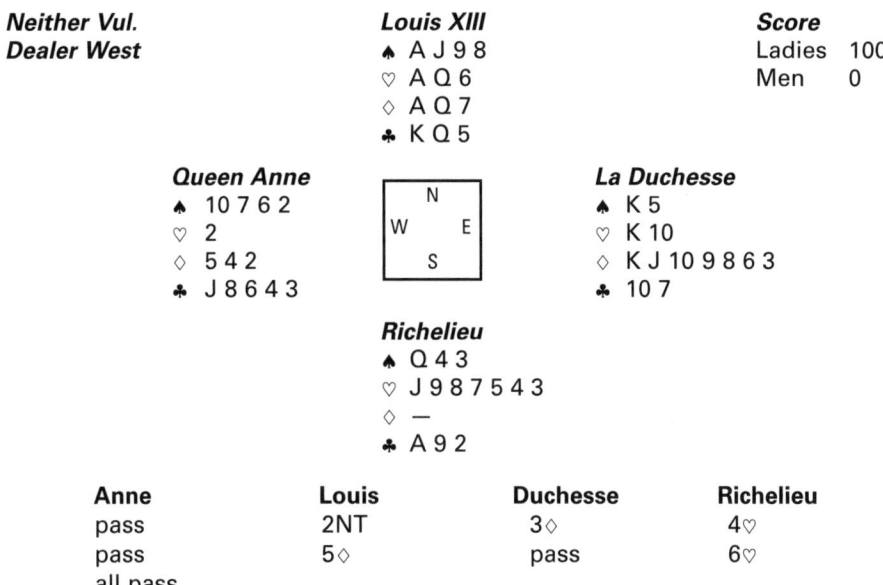

Neither Vul. Dealer West		Louis XIII ♠ A J 9 8 ♡ A Q 6 ◇ A Q 7 ♣ K Q 5		Score Ladies 100 Men 0
	Queen Anne ♠ 10 7 6 2 ♡ 2 ◇ 5 4 2 ♣ J 8 6 4 3		La Duchesse ♠ K 5 ♡ K 10 ◇ K J 10 9 8 6 3 ♣ 10 7	
		Richelieu ♠ Q 4 3 ♡ J 9 8 7 5 4 3 ◇ — ♣ A 9 2		

Anne	Louis	Duchesse	Richelieu
pass	2NT	3◇	4♡
pass	5◇	pass	6♡
all pass			

The interference pushed the men to a slam they might not have bid otherwise. Anne led the ◇2 which Richelieu took with the ace in dummy, throwing a spade from his hand. The contract appeared to depend on the success of one of two finesses in the major suits. However, there was no rush to test his luck in finesses, which had already been proven to be poor, besides which one was usually correct in suspecting Madame of having something up her sleeve besides nicely dimpled elbows. He began by ruffing a diamond in his hand, then leading a trump towards the tenace in the dummy.

The Cardinal was only human. How human it is to seek revenge by attempting to succeed under circumstances where the usual course would fail. The Duchesse's bidding was usually far from normal, so Richelieu decided to play her for both the major-suit kings or neither. Instead of finessing in hearts, he played the ace and was delighted to see the Duchesse follow to the trick with the ♡10; he'd hoped to see the ♡K appear, but the ten was gratifying nonetheless. He ruffed the last diamond from dummy then played off the top clubs. When the Duchesse did not ruff the last club, he exited from his hand with a trump. With the minors eliminated, Marie-Aimée was forced to play into the spade tenace or give up an equally fatal ruff-sluff.

'By not finessing, he played with great finesse,' complimented the perceptive Gaston, not normally an admirer.

'Ah, *mon Dieu*. I haven't been backed into a corner so effectively since I last encountered Maréchal Bassompierre on a dark staircase,' commented the Duchesse, tossing a beguiling look in that gallant's direction.

'But in this instance, the Cardinal, unlike the Maréchal, took only what was rightfully his own,' jested Louis with some truth.

'The Maréchal plays at love like a bad actor who takes more pleasure in an easy success than in a faithful performance,' commented the Princesse de Conti.

'If one wishes to know one's faults, one may always count on a close friend to provide a full recitation,' retorted Bassompierre.

'An active dog will get the stick, at one end or another,' commented the Duke.

'I have observed, Buck-in-ga-ham,' offered Louis XIII, 'that a dog will remain faithful to one master its whole life more often than a wife to her husband.' He had been suspiciously watching the exchange of looks across the table between his wife and the English Duke. Between jealousy and desire, his stronger emotion with regard to Anne was jealousy.

'That's most unjust, Your Majesty,' countered the Princesse. 'At least women are more constant than men, for we love with our heads as well as our hearts.'

'Take my example,' added the Duchesse, 'I was faithful to my first husband until I was well past eighteen years of age. You can't say that of many dogs.'

'But ever since, both the years and the lovers continue to mount up?' suggested Bassompierre.

'Alas, it is quite beyond my power to slow the inevitable progress of either,' answered the Duchesse with good-natured gaiety.

Richelieu sat quietly awaiting resumption of play. Women, he mused, are one of God's more delightful creatures, but one must despair of the chances of ever being able to tame them. The bonds of matrimony, the rules of diplomacy, the precepts of religion, none could prevail against a woman's gay laughter. Well, certainly when that woman was as formidable as Marie-Aimée de Rohan-Montbazon, Duchesse de Chevreuse.

The King
Defends
Himself

n the match against *Les Dames*, Richelieu faced a dilemma. As the Chief Councillor's power derived solely and directly from the King, it was in the Cardinal's interests to maintain Louis on the throne. Yet he wanted the Ladies to win the three-rubber match, for this would have the result that the otherwise reluctant King might produce an heir, thus improving Richelieu's chances of holding on to his power, perhaps during a regency of Queen Anne. God forbid, of course, but it is best to be prepared. On the other hand it is always prudent to hold on to what you have, so he had to be seen to play spectacularly well in order to keep the confidence of the King over the short term, while somehow managing to lose in order to protect himself over the long term. What a challenge even for a great player!

The match continued to go in favor of the King, who defended well on this hand (rotated for convenience).

E-W Vul.	*La Duchesse*	*Score*
Dealer West	♠ A 6 4	Ladies 100
	♡ 6 4	Men 680
	◇ A Q 6 4	
	♣ Q 8 7 5	

Louis XIII		*Richelieu*
♠ Q 10 5 2		♠ 8 3
♡ A 8 5	N	♡ J 7 3 2
◇ J 3	W E	◇ K 10 9 7 5
♣ 9 6 4 2	S	♣ J 3

Queen Anne
♠ K J 9 7
♡ K Q 10 9
◇ 8 2
♣ A K 10

Louis	Duchesse	Richelieu	Anne
pass	1◇	pass	2NT
pass	3♣	pass	3♡
pass	3NT	all pass	

Playing a strong (15-17) notrump, the Duchesse opened the North hand 1◇ and Anne jumped to 2NT to show a flat hand with 16+ HCPs. An exploration for a 4-4 fit ensued, ending in 3NT, and Louis was left to find the best lead after Anne had indicated she might hold both major suits. On a spade lead declarer has an easy time of it after she drops the ♣J doubleton, but on Louis' choice, the ♣2, a careless declarer may bring bad luck down on her own head. Anne of Austria was that type of declarer; Hapsburgs were not bred for their intelligence and she was doubly a Hapsburg.

Richelieu's ♣J was taken with the ♣K and Anne could count eight sure tricks: four clubs, a diamond, two spades and a heart by force. She could see three possible ways to make a ninth: a diamond finesse, a spade finesse, or two leads towards the hearts in her hand with something good happening. Louis' passive lead was an indication that he might have some top cards from which he was fearful to lead, so

Anne unblocked her clubs and took the diamond finesse with high hopes of immediate success.

Richelieu won the king and considered how he might aid the Queen without arousing suspicion. Already he had weakened his hearts by discarding the seven and had retained all his diamonds, a futile defense as he had no entry to his hand, yet a course many a lesser player would automatically follow. A second diamond at this point would surely not cause a problem for the Queen, just the opposite. Diamonds would be removed from the King's hand and later he might be endplayed with no safe exit card, the usual consequence of an overly passive lead from a hand containing most of the defensive assets. Satisfied that his plan could not fail to hand over the contract, the Cardinal returned the ◇5.

The Queen did not like this turn of events. She took the ◇A and played a heart from the dummy, hoping Richelieu would take his ace and she would lose just three diamonds and the ace of hearts. When the ♡K held she returned to dummy with the ♠A, cashed the ♣Q and repeated the heart play with high hopes, but Louis pounced on the ♡Q and returned a heart to Richelieu's now bare jack that Anne had turned into an entry for the long diamonds. Down two.

'A most excellent lead, Your Majesty,' commented the Cardinal, trying to soften the blow for the dejected opponents. If the Queen continued to play her cards that way, he would have to defend even worse, or the King's position would become impregnable.

After this successful defense Louis went to check personally on the arrangements he had made for the entertainment during the break in play. Buckingham took the opportunity to walk over to the West position to engage the Queen Mother in a conversation so banal that Cardinal allowed himself to fall into a reverie in which he recalled his nightly dream of the delicious Marie de Rohan-Montbazon, now seated so close to him he could inhale her intoxicating perfume. In his dream she came to his chamber dressed in the lightest of nightgowns, she approached his bed, she smothered his protests with hot kisses... These fantasies were interrupted inconveniently by the voice of the object of his desire, the lady herself in the flesh. And what flesh!

'Cardinal Richelieu, may I have your opinion on my decolletage. Do you think His Majesty has been offended by our display of fashion?' (On one occasion Louis had rudely spat wine down the front of a lady's dress he had found displeasingly revealing.) She leaned forward to expose to the cardinal's gaze a full view down her bodice of the creamy orbs that haunted the churchman's dreams. He closed his eyes, but not before quickly registering the lustrous view for dreamy recall. The King's holdup of the heart ace had been in its way a welcome sight, but it could not rival that provided now by Madame's gown. However, it was questionable whether the King would choose to continue to overlook such open effrontery.

'The consensus of the Ladies-in-waiting,' continued the Duchesse, 'is that tonight we do not greatly risk being drenched in the royal fluids.'

'His Majesty admires beauty in all its forms, Madame, as do I,' said Richelieu, taking a sip of wine to wet his dry throat, 'although his greatest admiration is reserved for the statues of Michelangelo, whose beauty will not fade even in a hundred years and whose aspect is subject neither to decay nor loathsome diseases.'

'You speak reverently of Michelangelo but I find his representation of female beauty somewhat lacking — he never gets the bosoms right. Look, compare mine to his Virgin's.'

'I must defer to your judgement in this matter, Madame, for neither have I the experience to verify nor the inclination to argue this claim further. It is perhaps unfortunate that Michelangelo didn't have access to a body such as yours for his sculptures. On the other hand, in your present delicate state you would make an unlikely Virgin, *n'est-ce pas?*'

'How perceptive, Cardinal. It has never been my wish to be cast in the role of a holy virgin; I am not cut out for it. Virtue, not beauty, is a heavenly characteristic, but ephemeral beauty, which is offered today and denied tomorrow, does that not excite, if not the greatest admiration, at least the greatest desire for possession before the grandeur fades?'

'Undue haste and precipitate action are wasteful as well as dangerous. The greatest rewards are obtained at the least cost by those who can wait,' said the Cardinal with a smile.

'But he who waits too long risks being unable to enjoy the ripe fruits of his cultivation. They say a hungry man dreams of food, but a starving man is sickened by the sight of it.'

'Ideally one consumes neither too little nor too much, only that which is necessary — a nibble here, a nibble there. No, we must direct our desires towards what is lasting and true. Ten years? Twenty years? A long time in a man's life and a longer one still in a woman's, but what is that compared to the centuries of glory that stretch before us? Women provide the world with the future generations who will embody that glory.'

'That is a man's view, but to women motherhood is a condition imposed by nature, an obligation expected by society, an honor thrust upon us rather than sought. Our female pleasures, although at times *très, très agréable*, are infrequent and momentary, scant recompense for the inconveniences we subsequently endure.'

'That may be just as well, as too much pleasure leads to grief. Publicly I would have to say that your view is not endorsed by the teachings of the Saints. Privately, I must agree that each of us in our own way is promoting the future of France; I, in the ways of Moses, a guide from the wilderness, you, through your influence on Her Majesty, in the ways of Eve.' Then, leaning over to breathe in the spicy, erotic scent of her warm cheek, he whispered, 'In this matter our interests may coincide.'

'I am so glad we can work together towards the same happy end. Let me whisper in your ear a confidence that would ruin my reputation if it were to be revealed. It is this: like yourself, my true passion is for politics. Now then, can I sway you to my view of Michelangelo's works?' asked the Duchesse, tapping him playfully on the point of his nose.

'Count me your slave, Madame,' conceded Richelieu gracefully, his long, aristocratic nose a-tingle.

Armand-Jean du Plessis de Richelieu

Richelieu lived before the age of science, yet there was in Paris a true genius who much in advance of Watts invented a steam engine that could move water to great heights. Salomon de Caus, a Huguenot, had the misfortune to fall in love with the courtesan Marion Delorme and took to following her about, causing such annoyance that she called upon Richelieu (with whom she was on intimate terms) to rid her of her stalker.

Richelieu interviewed the unfortunate man, who was overjoyed at the opportunity to describe his invention complete with diagrams and predictions of other useful applications. The Cardinal listened politely, thanked him profusely, then ordered the great genius be arrested and sent to the lunatic asylum at Bicêtre. Two years later Marion Delorme paid a visit to that horrible institution but would not acknowledge the cries for mercy from the prisoner who loved her madly still.

Louis Gains an Advantage

he King returned to the table to play well and bring in a vulnerable game and end the first rubber when the Duchesse's active style worked to her disadvantage once more.

N-S Vul.
Dealer South

	Richelieu		Score
	♠ A 9 7 2		Ladies 100
	♡ 10 2		Men 780
	◇ 4 2		
	♣ K Q 9 7 5		

La Duchesse		Queen Anne
♠ Q 10 3		♠ 8 6 5 4
♡ A 9 3		♡ Q J 8 5
◇ A Q J 10 8		◇ 7 3
♣ 8 2		♣ J 6 4

```
        N
    W       E
        S
```

	Louis XIII	
	♠ K J	
	♡ K 7 6 4	
	◇ K 9 6 5	
	♣ A 10 3	

Duchesse	Richelieu	Anne	Louis
			1NT
2◇	3♣	pass	3NT
all pass			

The Duchesse's overcall would seem pointless to some purists, but in fairness it must be said that this action gave Richelieu a problem in deciding how to react. Without the interference he would have explored game in spades, but now it appeared he had to take an undefined action. His political experiences had taught him that those who support aggression are seldom criticized for their stand and, even after everything goes horribly wrong, seldom are punished for their culpability. On the other hand, those who advocate caution are often accused of disloyalty, and, even after disaster is avoided, seldom are they rewarded for their good advice, but must forever bear the label of cowardly compromiser. Richelieu found the happy bid of 3♣, leaving the next, possibly fatal, decision safely in the hands of his partner. At this vulnerability Louis did not hesitate to bid game in notrump despite his underweight opening bid.

Madame de Chevreuse, as expected, did the unexpected and led the ♡3 to the ♡10. This was the killing lead. The contract of 3NT was Louis' favorite, so, unlike the Queen who more often than not was relegated to playing in the minor suits, the King had had lots of practice in the art of taking nine tricks with only eight on view. The overcall had given him a good idea of how the cards must lie, so he held up on this trick. Good things happened if you let Anne hold the lead.

So it proved. In deference to her partner's overcall, the Queen returned the ◇7 to the ◇J. With the ♡A as a sure entry and the spades well guarded, it appeared obvious to set up the diamonds, so Madame played ◇A and a low diamond to Louis' ◇K, a process we shall term the '*wreckification* of the defense' for reasons that will become apparent. Perhaps if she spent more time thinking about Bridge and less about, well, other things, the Duchesse might have perceived the danger and exited passively with a club. But is it not the case that those women who are most attractive to men are just those young ladies who act impetuously and give little thought to the consequences?

Louis was pleased with her but for other reasons. He ran off the club tricks to this position where he could afford to lose just one more trick:

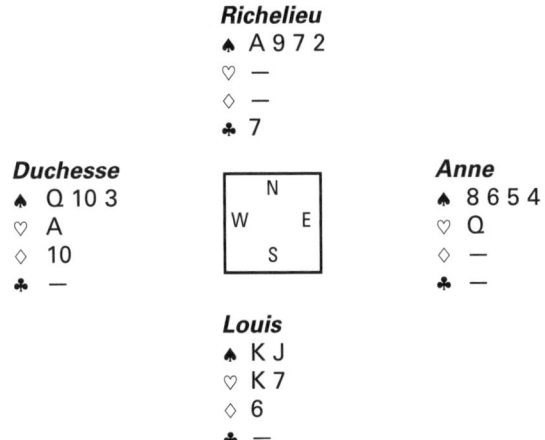

Richelieu
♠ A 9 7 2
♡ —
♢ —
♣ 7

Duchesse
♠ Q 10 3
♡ A
♢ 10
♣ —

Anne
♠ 8 6 5 4
♡ Q
♢ —
♣ —

Louis
♠ K J
♡ K 7
♢ 6
♣ —

Technically, Anne's discard on the last club was irrelevant with regard to the making of the game, but the appearance of the silly ♠6 assured her husband he was on the right track. He discarded the ♡7 and Marie-Aimée, who could not discard a red suit winner, had to part with the ♠3, unguarding the spades. In the end Louis made all four spades in the dummy, ten tricks in all.

'On the heart lead, Your Majesty did well not to play the king,' commented Gaston.

'*Naturellement.* Learn from that, dear Brother. I need not *play* the King, for I *am* the King,' boasted Louis.

'Oh, my dear,' said the Queen Mother to the Duchesse, much distressed, 'you parted too easily with your ace of diamonds. Think of your aces as lovers and do not part with one until you can be sure of the other.'

'But, Your Majesty,' responded the Duchesse, 'I do not cling to my lovers; an old lover is an old joke that grows stale with repetition.'

'Yet a familiar lover, like a familiar joke, can still bring a smile to your lips, even if you are well-acquainted with the outcome,' countered the Queen Mother.

'Lovers are unlike jokes in this respect: the less amusing they are, the more one feels the urge to pass them along,' added the Princesse de Conti.

'The best lovers, like the best jokes, are true,' said Buckingham, catching the Queen's eye.

'It is appropriate that love be treated as a comedy,' commented Louis sourly. 'What many call love is no more than a self-delusion resulting from an imbalance of the humors. The afflicted unconcernedly overstep the bounds of good sense, in the way that an inmate of the Bicêtre asylum might step over a parapet, either unmindful of the consequences or hopeful of a quick release. Cardinal, you are silent. Give us your opinion on love.'

'Your Majesty, I am the last person here who should be asked, for I believe an observer should not comment on a game he has never played himself,' apologized Richelieu, a comment that brought smiles to the faces of many who knew otherwise.

'But since you ask, Your Majesty,' he continued, ignoring the titters from his audience, 'it seems to me that mankind has always engaged in love affairs just as it has always engaged in war, although both usually do more harm than good. I go further — love affairs are women's warfare, their opportunity to defy danger, display valor and practice cunning, for women plot their campaigns as carefully as generals.'

'How apt,' agreed Bassompierre, 'but they employ powder puffs, not cannon, gaiety not gunfire, and fly fancy ribbons, not tattered standards, from their breastworks.'

Gaston had something to add. 'Being poorly equipped to withstand a determined siege, their strategy is to sally forth and take prisoners.'

'Women, unlike generals, purposely plot their own downfalls. Isn't that so, Bassompierre?' asked the Princesse sardonically.

'If Your Highness says so, it must be true,' conceded the Maréchal, adding, 'For myself, I've always judged women as I've judged generals, holding in highest regard those who display the greatest eagerness to engage the enemy at close quarters.'

This view was greeted with general approval from East to West.

Les Dames Take Their Chances

The first two hands of the second rubber produced little excitement — only the Ladies had managed a score below the line, a mere 40. Then Queen Anne pushed for game in another partscore and Louis extracted the maximum penalty.

Neither Vul.
Dealer West

Queen Anne
♠ A 10 8 3
♡ Q 6 3 2
◇ Q 5
♣ A J 6

Score
Ladies 190
Men 1610

Richelieu
♠ K 9 4
♡ K 9 5 4
◇ A 6 3 2
♣ K 9

```
      N
  W       E
      S
```

Louis XIII
♠ J 7 2
♡ A J 10 8
◇ 10
♣ Q 10 8 7 3

La Duchesse
♠ Q 6 5
♡ 7
◇ K J 9 8 7 4
♣ 5 4 2

Richelieu	Anne	Louis	Duchesse
1◇	dbl	pass	1♠
pass	pass	2♣	pass
pass	2♠	dbl	all pass

After Richelieu opened his four-card minor, the Queen entered the auction with a questionable takeout double on an eight-loser hand. If Louis had bid 1♡, his side might have reached the makable game in hearts, but he preferred to pass and await developments. The Duchesse now had an awkward bid, since 2◇ was used by the ladies as an artificial forcing bid. She decided to settle for a weak bid in her three-card spade suit, rather than trying a penalty pass.

In the balancing seat, Louis bid his five-card minor. Since he had not redoubled, this showed some values, but less than 10 HCP. He felt he had the heart suit in reserve, just in case the Cardinal corrected to diamonds with shortness in clubs. When 2♣ came around again to Anne, she made the mistake of bidding her values again, something she would have thought about twice if she herself were to be the declarer. She counted points at face value and failed to discount the value of her ◇Q and the club honors. She trapped her partners at the bridge table the same way she ensnared her supporters in real life — by pushing them forward into danger while she remained free of personal risk.

Louis doubled the 2♠ re-entry somewhat speculatively, but he asked himself where the tricks for the offense would come from when it appeared that he and the Cardinal had the side suits tied up. If the Queen made her contract it would give her enough below the line for a game regardless. The ladies had an eight-card fit in diamonds, but the Cardinal's opening bid had the consequence that it was impossible for them to play in that suit.

Richelieu began with the lead of the king in his partner's suit. Fearing an ensuing crossruff, the Duchesse was quick to take the ace in dummy and play the ♠A and a spade to her queen. Unfortunately for her the Cardinal could win and play a second club to Louis' ♣10. Louis took some time to reflect on his next play. He deduced that Richelieu, with the ◇AK, would have led out the ◇K as an informative card before continuing the clubs. The fact that he had not done so placed him with the ♡K instead for his opening bid.

Louis made a spectacular return, not of a club, but of a heart to the king. Richelieu returned a heart to his partner's ♡10, forcing the Duchesse to ruff with the last trump in her hand. She exited a diamond won by Richelieu's ace. The Cardinal played a third heart, won by the ♡J. When the Duchesse could not ruff this card, the full distribution was revealed. Louis cashed the fourth heart, representing the third defensive trick in the suit, then, instead of cashing his club winner, returned a low club, giving Richelieu a ruff. Now the enforced diamond exit gave Louis a ruff with his ♠J. The defense had taken three spade tricks, three heart tricks, a diamond and a club, down three for 500.

The King was happy with this result, so much so that he shook off his moroseness momentarily and initiated a conversation with the English envoy.

'So, Bucking-ga-ham, tell us of your King Charles. Will he make my little sister a happy bride?' inquired Louis with stiff joviality.

'Henrietta-Maria, *mia cara bambina*, come forward — don't be shy. Oh, where is she?' asked the Queen Mother in her loud voice and thick Italian accent.

'She is at the Luxembourg, Madame,' reminded Richelieu, 'taking last-minute instruction from Père Bérulle.'

'I am glad religious issues have not proved an impediment to the marriage,' said Buckingham, addressing the Cardinal.

'I agree,' said Richelieu lightly. 'Why should we become enemies over matters on which even saints have disagreed?'

The Princesse de Conti made an effort to steer the conversation away from dangerous waters. Her next remark caused some French chuckles.

'I trust Henrietta-Maria has been taught the ways of the French kiss. Lord Holland has demonstrated for us the favorite English way of kissing which is most peculiar. To show affection, the English stand far apart and each person kisses his own hand, then waves it in the air to dry off the spittle.'

The Duke bowed graciously. 'Yes, Princesse, I must admit that you French have much to teach us in the ways of showing affection in public. In private I assure you we Englishmen have most effective means at our disposal.' Again his look was directed at the blushing Queen.

'The giving and receiving of affection is woman's study,' stated Anne. 'While in musty libraries the professors' beards grow long as they pore over their dusty books, we women spend happy hours in sunny pursuit of higher learning in our own chosen field. A woman's library is her circle of friends.'

'Next she will tell us that when the Duchesse dons a mask and takes to the streets at night she is like unto Galileo searching with his telescope for the Man in the Moon,' loudly whispered the mischievous Gaston.

The Princesse de Conti was greatly annoyed at this show of male contempt, especially as it came from a youth. She spoke with conviction on a favorite topic. 'I suggest that the Queen Mother should call a conference of the three Estates on the topic of Love, at which women would be allowed to speak. We of high birth would discourse on the more noble aspects of love while those of lower birth would speak on what for lack of a better phrase I call 'Ways and Means'. Those in religious orders would lecture on love as described in the Scriptures: how Bathsheba conquered the brave David, how the Queen of Sheba outwitted wise Solomon. Abbots and Abbesses could debate publicly on how to apportion blame between foolish Lot and his two innocent daughters.'

'Ah, Princesse, you have intelligence in the way a rose has a thorn,' said Louis. 'But as regard to books, I dare say the Duchesse would lend the Duke one of her learned and illustrated texts on the topic of lust.'

'The Duke during his brief visit to France has not the need for books,' said Bassompierre, 'but books do have this advantage, Sir, that you can take them back to England with you and enjoy them at your leisure.'

'Also you are at liberty to shut them up when you so desire,' observed Louis.

'Ah, speaking of books reminds me of an obligation I have undertaken with Montmorency to speak to Your Majesty on behalf of this scoundrel, Théophile de Viau,' said Buckingham boldly. 'As Your Majesty may not be aware, he has been sentenced to death by the *Parlement* for some ill-conceived verses. Montmorency told me there was hope that Your Majesty might commute the sentence as a gesture of forgiveness and grace on the happy occasion of my visit to your fair city. As you have noted, one is always at liberty to close a book if it displeases and thus avoid corruption by the text.'

'Oh, please, Your Majesty,' pleaded the Duchesse, 'show mercy and save the life of a poor poet.' Other ladies added to this request, but, significantly, not Queen Anne who leaned too far towards orthodoxy.

Louis looked very solemn. 'Forgiveness creates exceptions to the law and injustice prevails when too many exceptions are allowed; however, if you could somehow show me the sentence is unjust...'

'I can,' offered the Princesse de Conti quickly. 'If he were a better poet, he would deserve death and there would be no question of lightening the sentence of the courts. However, since his poetry is so abominably bad, the danger to the minds of the readers is considerably lessened, and therefore, so should his sentence be lessened.'

The assemblage applauded this delightful reasoning, and as the game was going well, Louis gave the order that the sentence be commuted to life in prison. Richelieu voiced no opinion, although he felt the argument of the Princesse was totally wrong: public opinion is *most* greatly influenced by bad writers. The unaccustomed thinker, like the infrequent swimmer, takes most readily to that which is shallow. But he was content with the King's decision as the order for execution was largely the doing of the King's confessor, a Jesuit rival. Here was an opportunity to demonstrate where the real authority lay. (The Cardinal appreciated men of letters — four months later he managed a full pardon.)

The next hand gave Richelieu a chance to make what he hoped to be an unobtrusive defensive error to the advantage of the Duchesse that kept the ladies' slim chances alive.

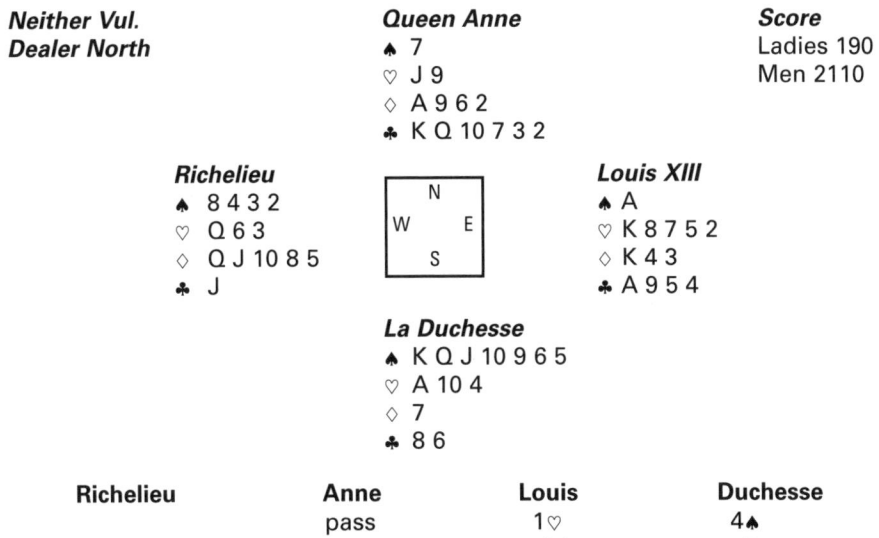

Neither Vul.	Queen Anne		Score
Dealer North	♠ 7		Ladies 190
	♡ J 9		Men 2110
	◇ A 9 6 2		
	♣ K Q 10 7 3 2		

Richelieu
♠ 8 4 3 2
♡ Q 6 3
◇ Q J 10 8 5
♣ J

Louis XIII
♠ A
♡ K 8 7 5 2
◇ K 4 3
♣ A 9 5 4

La Duchesse
♠ K Q J 10 9 6 5
♡ A 10 4
◇ 7
♣ 8 6

Richelieu	Anne	Louis	Duchesse
	pass	1♡	4♠
pass	pass	dbl	all pass

Having suffered a disaster on the previous hand, the Duchesse attempted an instant recovery by overbidding to a game that should be defeated. The Cardinal saw that his four spades represented a minor obstacle for declarer that might be turned into a major obstacle through application of a forcing defense. As the King must have some defensive value in the suit, a diamond lead looked particularly tempting, combining safety with attack. The heart lead might also prove effective, but Madame might be well prepared for that lead.

As he did not wish to defeat the contract, Richelieu looked for a less effective alternative, one which would not arouse suspicion, and he found it in the jack of clubs. This lead had two purposes: to shorten his own trumps and to set up tricks in what looked like declarer's secondary suit, possibly removing a guess along the way. An attacking lead was not likely to be criticized. Why, it might even work, whereas a trump lead would be conspicuously passive and suspect.

Richelieu's deductions were correct. The diamond lead and a diamond continuation would have led easily to the defeat of the hopeless contract. On the club lead Louis took the queen with his ace and gave the Cardinal his ruff. Once more the ◇Q beckoned and once more the Cardinal rejected her advances. What about her sister, the ♡Q? No, from the Cardinal's point of view, the ♡3 was better as it could be construed by an active imagination as a suit preference lead asking for a club return.

The Duchesse took the $\heartsuit$K with her $\heartsuit$A and played the $\spadesuit$K to Louis' ace. As Richelieu had hoped, the King thought the defense pointed towards a trump promotion, but the club continuation caused no trouble as Marie was able to ruff high, draw trumps and enjoy the clubs in dummy with the $\diamond$A as an entry. The Ladies were overjoyed with this unmerited success and hugs were exchanged.

Richelieu apologized profusely in such a way as to cover his tracks.

'I'm sorry, Your Majesty, perhaps I should have returned the queen of hearts instead of the trey. That would have made the situation clearer. When she plays a spade to your ace, you can take your king of hearts as the setting trick and then lead a club for the possible promotion and extra undertrick.'

'No, no,' corrected the King authoritatively, 'low from an honor is the normal play, but it is an ambiguous signaling situation. It is much better if I return the $\diamond$K to extinguish the dummy for that ensures the defeat of the contract whether you have the $\spadesuit$10 or the $\heartsuit$Q.'

'What if the Cardinal leads a diamond initially?' asked the indiscreet Gaston, raising Richelieu's ire — it was improper for a kibitzer to comment adversely on the play.

'A good choice,' stated the Cardinal with a slight bow of acknowledgement. 'It would have worked this time, but I was too greedy. *Mea culpa.*'

'I won't hear of it,' said the King wishing to belittle his brother's suggestion, 'the fault was entirely mine.'

There was something in Richelieu's manner that aroused suspicion in the mind of Louise-Marguerite, Princesse de Conti. Although no expert card player, intuitively she knew something was amiss and refused to be taken in by his show of contrition.

'Tell us, Cardinal, what value do you put upon character and, indeed how may one judge whether or not another possesses it?' asked the Princesse in a haughty manner that indicated all too well her opinion that Richelieu was lacking in this regard.

The Chief Councillor, rather than being put out by this hostile question, welcomed an opportunity to divert the discussion away from his defense of the hand. He smoothly turned the attack into flattery of the entire noble assemblage.

'I wish that character could be measured like a piece of cloth, that one could judge its quality, its texture, its fabric. Alas, the qualities to which you allude are unknown until put to the test. That is why breeding and heritage are so important as guidelines to a person's inner qualities. There are those of ambition who would rise from low rank to positions of authority, and they may have ability, great ability, but what assurance does one have that such people have the character needed to govern wisely and without an excess of self-interest? A rise to power at its inception can be mistakenly attributed to wisdom and virtue whereas at a later date it can be seen easily to have been no more than a consequence of good fortune.' These remarks were to some degree directed against the English guest.

'I have heard you say that to serve the King is to risk your soul. At least you, Cardinal, have freely made that choice,' stated Anne, 'but what of us who have inherited worldly power through accident of birth?'

'Accident of birth? Are you mad?' scolded the King, always quick to find fault with his consort. 'God does not perform *accidents*, He performs miracles. Fools cause accidents. God has chosen us for our tasks and will forgive us our trespasses made in His service. I would be disappointed greatly if I were made to think you felt otherwise.'

The assemblage grew silent at the King's angry display of displeasure, brought on, no doubt, by his own misdirected defense.

George Villiers, Duke of Buckingham

The Duke thought to enlist Cupid to promote a marriage alliance between Spain and England. In 1623 he and Charles traveled incognito as 'the Smith brothers' to Madrid to win the heart of the Infanta with sweet words and loving glances. En route they were allowed to attend a dress rehearsal of a ballet in which Queen Anne and sixteen of her loveliest ladies, including Henrietta-Maria, performed. Cupid would be accused of being a lousy shot, for Buckingham was smitten by the beauty of the Queen to the extent that her image became an obsession that thereafter over-ruled his political judgment, whereas Charles I could never recall having seen his future bride at that time.

In Madrid Cupid's hands were tied. When the fleet sent to fetch Buckingham and Charles returned them safely home, bonfires were lit to celebrate the failure of their hare-brained scheme. Thus Buckingham by pursuing his own agenda against the will of the people, through mismanagement inadvertently satisfied their wishes.

The
Duchesse
Attacks

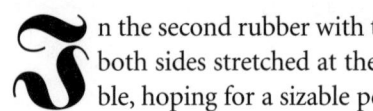n the second rubber with the Ladies vulnerable and forty on towards game, both sides stretched at the three-level and Marie-Aimée made a bold double, hoping for a sizable penalty, but risking an even greater loss.

	Richelieu		Score
E-W Vul.	♠ 10 3		Ladies 520
Dealer East	♡ 4 3		Men 2150
	◊ A 9 4 3 2		
	♣ A 10 3 2		

La Duchesse		Queen Anne
♠ A 9		♠ 8 7 6
♡ A K Q 8	N / W E / S	♡ 9 7 5
◊ Q J 10		◊ 8 6 5
♣ J 7 6 4		♣ K Q 9 8

	Louis XIII
	♠ K Q J 5 4 2
	♡ J 10 6 2
	◊ K 7
	♣ 5

Duchesse	Richelieu	Anne	Louis
		pass	1♠
dbl	1NT	pass	2♠
dbl	pass	3♣	pass
pass	dbl	pass	3♠
dbl	all pass		

Louis opened with primarily offensive values and the Duchesse, rather than bidding 1NT, chose to make a takeout double with good support in the other suits. Richelieu showed some values after which Louis showed the nature of his hand with a weak rebid. Not willing to sell out cheaply, Marie gambled another double for takeout and was glad to hear the Queen bid her four-card minor. Since making three clubs would give the Ladies their vulnerable game in any event, Richelieu felt that there might be an opportunity to extract a penalty at little cost, so he doubled speculatively. This contract had chances of going either way, but Louis felt it was better to not risk it. He bid spades again and was again doubled, this time for penalty.

The Duchesse began her defense with the ♡A. Upon seeing dummy, she decided that Louis might want to ruff a heart in dummy, so she played a trump — not the ace but the nine, keeping the ace as a control card. Louis played three rounds of diamonds, successfully negotiating a ruff and setting up the suit. Now he played the ♡J, taken by the Duchesse who cashed the trump ace, preventing the heart ruff in dummy, before exiting with a club, removing the entry to the good diamonds. The Queen had a trump remaining to ruff a diamond and Louis overruffed, eventually losing four heart tricks and a spade for down one.

'Bless my soul, Ma'am, but that was well done,' congratulated Buckingham.

'Yes, indeed,' added the King grudgingly, 'I can make my contract with an over-trick if you start with the ace and a low spade.'

'Yes, Louis,' intervened the Queen Mother, 'you can see we women are quite capable of making far-sighted decisions just as well as you men. Don't you agree, *mon Cardinal?*'

'Indeed, Your Majesty,' replied Richelieu, 'the intelligence of Woman is the equal of Man; one only wishes She'd not be so shy in demonstrating Her mental abilities.'

The Princesse de Conti now came forward to express her heart-felt opinions, formed from the discussions of the freethinkers who assembled in the *salons* of Madame de Rambouillet.

'The Cardinal thinks to flatter us by attributing to women equal powers of intelligence, but our intelligence is of a different kind. Whereas a man, like a dancer with one leg, hops unevenly from 'yes' to 'no', a woman in her mind can stand easily on 'maybe'.'

This statement received mocking laughter from the male courtiers. The Duchesse blushed angrily at this reception. Although a lover of men, she had always found her woman's subtle mind to be more than a match for theirs.

'Just as God has given Man his strength in order to maintain justice by force, so He has given Woman beauty to be used as a force for Good,' she maintained. 'Beauty, like Strength, is not a quality that can be judged apart from the purposes to which it is put.'

'Beauty may conquer men's hearts but it is Novelty that captures his mind,' contributed Bassompierre.

'Platonic Love is the most enduring form of love, being sustained by its very remoteness,' Louis proclaimed enthusiastically. 'We should all aspire to transcend the physical in our relationships with our fellow humans, male and female equally.'

'I find it odd that despite all the claims of its perfection, Platonic Love engenders the least jealousy,' noted Gaston.

'Well said,' commented Buckingham. 'As you know, Your Highness, gold in its purest form is too soft for common use. A baser element must be added to give it the strength to encase a jewel, to pinch a lady's ear, or to lie to best effect upon a lady's bosom. So, too, love in its purest form is amorphous and needs the addition of earthly proofs of love to give it shape and purpose.'

Anne gasped at the directness of these bold words so clearly directed from across the table to her. It was clear to all that Buckingham was not a believer in disinterested love. The Princesse de Conti spoke up quickly to save the situation, aiming sharp words at her favorite target.

'So, Richelieu, give us your opinions on the proofs of love; as a man, the physical proofs and as a cardinal, the spiritual ones.'

'Indeed, Madame, I have just one idea in this matter. The proof of love in either case lies not in the granting or seeking of favors, but in the keeping to one's vows.'

This answer pleased Louis and caused much fluttering of fans.

The Cardinal now looked for a chance to display his skill so as to allay any suspicions his defensive play may have aroused in the King's mind. The Ladies still had forty towards game when this hand arose:

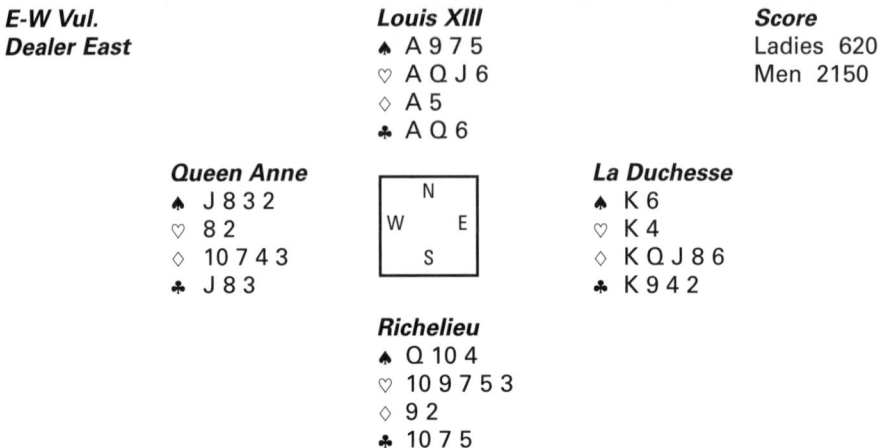

E-W Vul.
Dealer East

Louis XIII
♠ A 9 7 5
♡ A Q J 6
◇ A 5
♣ A Q 6

Score
Ladies 620
Men 2150

Queen Anne
♠ J 8 3 2
♡ 8 2
◇ 10 7 4 3
♣ J 8 3

La Duchesse
♠ K 6
♡ K 4
◇ K Q J 8 6
♣ K 9 4 2

Richelieu
♠ Q 10 4
♡ 10 9 7 5 3
◇ 9 2
♣ 10 7 5

Anne	Louis	Duchesse	Richelieu
		1◇	pass
pass	dbl	pass	1♡
pass	4♡	all pass	

With a very good hand Louis stretched to a game that had only one advantage: most of the defensive values would lie in one hand. At rubber bridge rather than gamble on a dubious game, it is better strategy against vulnerable, weak and impetuous opponents to attain a partscore and try to tempt them into an indiscretion and a large penalty. However, once Richelieu had been thrust into this exposed position, it was too risky for him not to play well as the King would be most displeased to have his bad call given the punishment it deserved. The vulnerability was not fatal to the Ladies' chance of ultimate victory, so if Richelieu were to make this game with skilful play, Louis would be satisfied and all suspicions arising from future doubtful actions in more critical situations might be forestalled.

Anne led her partner's suit, choosing the somewhat ambiguous ◇3. The Cardinal won in dummy and played a second round of diamonds. The Duchesse nervously rose with the ◇Q, and was somewhat annoyed to see declarer follow with the ◇9 and Anne with the ◇4. As Anne might have led from three to the ten, a black-suit return seemed to be more dangerous than possibly yielding a ruff-and-sluff, so she played the ◇K, which Richelieu ruffed in hand, discarding the ♣6 from dummy. Marie-Aimée was now punished for not guessing to switch to a club at Trick 3, as Richelieu played the ♡A, followed by the ♠A and a low heart to put her once more on lead without a safe exit. This time it cost her the game.

This endplay was politely applauded by the courtiers who gave a man they thoroughly disliked his just due. The King was well pleased with this effort, and in turn the courtiers congratulated him fulsomely on his fine bid. Thus, the path had been cleared for future betrayal if necessary.

Young Gaston quickly introduced a topic he had heard discussed amongst his gentlemen-in-waiting. 'Tell me, Buck-ing-ga-ham, is it your opinion that Beauty can only exist in the eye of the one who beholds it?' he asked, smiling at his own cleverness.

'That, Your Highness, sounds like utter nonsense to my ear,' replied Buckingham. 'The woman who lies beside you does not lose her beauty as soon as you have blown out the candle.'

This remark provoked much laughter, but Richelieu saw the King was not amused.

'Yes, it is a foolish concept: one might just as well say that truth exists only in the ear of the listener,' declared Richelieu.

'A lie need only be repeated a sufficient number of times in order for it to be believed,' added the Queen Mother, who had suffered many slanders in her day, most of them more entertaining than truthful.

'On the other hand, too many lies reveal the truth,' recalled the Princesse.

'Often it is sufficient that a lie sound sweet in order that it be willingly accepted,' observed the Queen sweetly smiling at the Duke across the table.

'Some sweet falsehoods are better believed than bitter truths,' said the Duchesse.

'Not only is it not necessary for something to be true in order to be believed, but it is not even necessary that it be remotely possible,' said Gaston, a statement which much displeased Richelieu, not because it was possibly blasphemous or because he didn't agree with it, but because the young man was revealing himself to be the type who, as they say in the countryside, likes to piss in the fireplace.

'Gaston, you understand me well. What I said is true: a lie need only be repeated a sufficient number of times in order for it to be believed,' repeated the Queen Mother emphatically. Richelieu had to admit that the Old Girl wasn't always so far off in what she said.

Louis XIII

A true stoic, he was fond of saying, 'If I had the feelings of a private person, I would not be King.' For all his ill-humor it has been said that he was the last French monarch whose death was met with genuine sorrow by the French people at large.

Once Bassompierre was sent to Madrid as a special ambassador. On reporting back to the King he described how he had entered the capital mounted on a magnificently decorated mule. Louis remarked sourly, 'What a fine spectacle that must have been, an ass riding on a mule.'

'Careful, Sire,' replied the Maréchal, 'I was representing you.'

Richelieu's Rescue

n the very next hand there came an opportunity for a subtle play by Richelieu that acted to the advantage of the Queen, who to this point had not been playing well.

Both Vul.	La Duchesse	Score
Dealer South	♠ Q 10 9 3	Ladies 620
	♡ 7	Men 2270
	◇ A Q J 10 5	
	♣ J 8 4	

Louis XIII		Richelieu
♠ K 7 5		♠ 8 4
♡ J 8 6 5 2	N	♡ Q 10 9 3
◇ 7	W E	◇ 9 6 4 3
♣ A 10 6 5	S	♣ K 3 2

Queen Anne
♠ A J 6 2
♡ A K 4
◇ K 8 2
♣ Q 9 7

Louis	Duchesse	Richelieu	Anne
			1NT
pass	2♣	pass	2♠
pass	4♠	all pass	

The Ladies put themselves at a disadvantage when they reached the wrong contract; 3NT was solid, whereas the King put the spade game in jeopardy with the lead of his singleton diamond. Anne viewed the dummy with foreboding. One often regretted the Duchesse's inclination to dash into contracts without giving partner a chance to express an opinion.

Anne had no trouble reading the lead as a singleton. She herself was very fond of singleton and doubleton leads, but her husband was critical of this propensity. 'Leads from shortness give away the suit,' — how many times had he said it? However, he did allow that one may lead a singleton profitably if one has decent prospects for control in the trump suit. Here was a singleton lead with the ♠K sitting on the left, concluded the Queen. She would not hazard the trump finesse.

The problem was how to avoid a subsequent switch to clubs in order to gain entrance to the East hand and obtain a diamond ruff. Winning in the dummy would give Richelieu an opportunity to signal that his entry lay in clubs, not hearts, by playing a low diamond on the honor from the dummy. This interpretation would be possible as both defenders could easily read the distribution. To prevent any obvious suit-preference implications, Anne called for a low diamond from the dummy and Richelieu, fully aware of the situation in toto, saw his chance for a move that might escape the attention of the King. Instead of playing the ◇3 as a clear indication for a club switch, the Cardinal covered pointlessly with the ◇9.

Anne won in hand with the king and led a low spade towards the ♠Q1093 in dummy, but the King was not deceived by this move. Unlike Richelieu who did not understand women at all, Louis had full, unbiased and instinctive knowledge of their ways. Perhaps this was why he didn't find them particularly intriguing or attractive. At any rate he took his ♠K immediately and played the ♣A, expecting a signal from his Chief Councillor to guide his next move. The ♣3 appeared from East and the ♣9 from the Queen. More deception, thought the King; Anne must have started with ♣K92 and partner with ♣ Q73. There is still room in his hand for the ♡A, so I may yet get my diamond ruff. So thinking, the King played a heart and the contract was made, reviving the Ladies' slim hopes of victory.

Louis was not happy with the result. 'What were your clubs?' he asked Richelieu.

'Why, king-three-two. I tried to signal for a continuation with what poor resources were available,' the Chief Councillor replied with a frown. 'Perhaps we should give consideration to playing upside-down attitude in future.'

'Perhaps,' muttered the King unhappily. 'What trump did you play?' Before he could think further on that fine point of defensive signaling, the musicians were announced. Louis' somber countenance broke into a smile as he greeted two short men lugging large viols and a tall man with a guitar in his hand and lute on his back. 'Come, friends, let's entertain the company,' Louis said as he eagerly accepted his guitar.

'All tuned, Your Majesty,' said the lutenist, much to the relief of the audience.

The King's music was to Buckingham's ears unexpectedly light-fingered and gay. The four musicians played as one. First, Louis' guitar alone introduced a stately melody of his own composition. A viol added an ambling pace, with a saucy sway here and a delightful dip there. The second viol joined in with rich rhythm to force the action. Just when one felt that the piece had reached its climax of excitement, the lute burst in with fast fingering at double the pace of the others, then all four players raced frantically to the end, crossing the finish line simultaneously to much applause and great self-satisfaction on the part of the King.

'And now, for our English guest, a duet of my own variations on a theme by John Dowland,' announced Louis with a happy nod to the taller of the two short violists.

As Louis bent over his guitar in intense concentration, his face, so often flawed by a pinched look of concern, became radiantly handsome. The sad, sweet music softened the hearts of all those who listened. Even Buckingham, briefly, regretted his lecherous intentions towards the Queen of France, but he quickly excused himself with the thought that if a husband is made a cuckold it is largely through his own doing. At the conclusion of this piece the company enjoyed a light collation while Louis went to change his shirt which was soaked with sweat. It was commented that the King himself had supervised the baking of the delicious almond cakes.

Buckingham turned to Bassompierre as one soldier to another and remarked, 'I am enjoying these cakes and I enjoyed the performance, but isn't it said truly, Maréchal, that music makes men's minds womanly?'

Bassompierre was offended by this remark aimed at the king he served. 'I have never observed that effect upon myself,' he replied haughtily, adding pointedly, 'isn't it also said that music merely nourishes whatever inclinations it happens to find?'

'Music makes everything beautiful,' enthused Marie de Medici.

'Ah, Your Majesty quotes Plato, how erudite,' said Richelieu flatteringly.

'Do I really?' asked the Queen Mother, much pleased, 'I must have remembered it from my reading of long ago.'

'Most admirable. You may also recall that Plato says that music is the essence of order and that Man's love of music reflects his need for order,' the Cardinal stated, not entirely accurate in his interpretations.

'He may have been right, but Plato was only a Greek, after all,' said Marie de Medici airily. 'To us Italians, love and music are as one.'

'How very true; I have always considered Italian songs the most civilized of mating calls,' noted the Princesse de Conti.

'Music's the fire that kindles desire,' recalled the Duchesse poetically.

Queen Anne had some thoughts to share. 'In my opinion ballet is the music best suited to women. We can make music with our whole bodies, whereas a man too often is wedded to his instrument.'

'Frantic frolics merely mimic madness,' observed Richelieu severely. 'The beauty of ballet lies in its discipline in that it provides the beauties of geometry to both the eye and the ear. However, to impart a deeper meaning music requires the accompaniment of words. A melody on its own is merely a daydream without substance.'

'I beg to differ, Monseigneur,' said Gaston with ill-concealed hostility. 'False words often fall sweetly on the ear, whereas sweet music never lies to the heart.'

Louis had meanwhile rejoined the group. 'Unfortunately music affects the mind only so long as it lingers in the ear. Joy turns to grief with a change of key,' he noted. 'On the other hand concepts based on reason, once established in the mind, are everlasting. Shall we finish our game?'

Richelieu felt gratified; his little lectures on Logic were finally beginning to pay off.

The
Final
Rubber

or *Les Dames* the situation was desperate but not hopeless as the third rubber began. To give them encouragement, Buckingham offered a large wager that they would win. Louis scowled at this impertinence and no courtier dared to accept the offer for fear of giving further offense to His Majesty by treating the bet seriously. The women in attendance were greatly impressed, and it was said later that both the Queen and the Duchesse fell irrevocably in love with Buckingham at the moment he spoke the words, 'ten thousand on the Ladies.'

To sustain the Duke's faith in their chances, the Ladies had to defend superbly on the first hand when Louis reached a 3NT that would make on normal play.

Neither Vul.	Richelieu	Score
Dealer East	♠ A J 6 5 2	Ladies 1240
	♡ J 7	Men 2270
	◇ K 10	
	♣ K 8 6 3	

La Duchesse		Queen Anne
♠ Q 9 4 3	N	♠ 10 7
♡ A 10 6	W E	♡ K 9 4 3
◇ 6 3 2	S	◇ 9 8 7 5
♣ A 5 4		♣ J 10 7

	Louis XIII	
	♠ K 8	
	♡ Q 8 5 2	
	◇ A Q J 4	
	♣ Q 9 2	

Duchesse	Richelieu	Anne	Louis XIII
		pass	1◇
pass	1♠	pass	1NT
pass	2♣[1]	pass	2♡
pass	3NT	all pass	

1.   Checkback.

The auction took a form much beloved by Louis. 2♣ was artificial and asked if the King held three spades. His 2♡ response denied three spades but promised four hearts. Richelieu delayed no longer in placing the contract. The Duchesse therefore had a good picture of the opponents' holdings. It appeared that a club lead was called for, but she had an aversion to underleading an ace from a short holding — yet nothing else appealed, so the ♣4 it was.

On the club lead, Louis played low from the dummy and Anne contributed a deceptive ♣J. Louis was happy to take the trick with his ♣Q and play on spades: ♠K, then a successful finesse of the ♠J. The ♠A and a spade exit to the ♠Q put in him good shape to take ten tricks. The Duchesse could not be certain of the position of the hearts and clubs, but as she always employed an attacking defense, however foolish she might appear in the post-mortem (she never engaged in post-mortems in any case), she led the ♡A to gauge the reaction of her partner. Was it merely a desire to deceive, or was it rare insight that led Anne to play a discouraging $\heartsuit$3? Perhaps both. When the Duchesse next played the $\clubsuit$5, Louis, holding the nine, played low from the dummy. Winning with the $\clubsuit$10, Anne was quick to cash the $\heartsuit$K and return a club and set the contract, the defense taking two clubs, two hearts and a spade.

'I was deceived into expecting the $\clubsuit$A on my right and the $\clubsuit$10 on my left.' stated the King sourly, addressing himself to Richelieu and pointedly neglecting to compliment the Queen on her fine defensive play. 'What is your opinion on underleading aces from ace-third? Very much against the odds, is it not?'

Although he himself was not averse to such a stratagem, as we have seen, the Cardinal was ready with an answer that would soothe the King's injured pride.

'Yes, it will cost a trick as often as once in nine times, nearly twice as bad as leading the ace. Your Majesty may consider himself unlucky.' This was the sort of analysis on which Louis feasted. Of course, no consideration was given to the fact that the bidding greatly affected the odds, a feature to which Bassompierre now alluded.

'It has been my experience that the club suit lends itself most readily to the unusual lead. I have wondered often whether there is something in our bidding systems which tends to lead one to this action more often in clubs than in other suits,' he conjectured.

'Tell me, Cardinal,' asked the Princesse de Conti, returning to her attack against the man she admired with her head but hated with her heart, 'have you observed many differences between men and women?' This brought smiles to the faces of the worldly company.

'Only what must be obvious to all, which is, a man plays bridge to win, a woman plays to please her partner,' replied Richelieu, avoiding a subject in which he could claim little expertise.

'I think the Cardinal has come up with yet another delightful difference,' observed Bassompierre. 'Tell me, Princesse, is it true that a woman chooses a lover in the same way she chooses a gown, on the advice of a good friend?'

'Only partly true, Maréchal; a woman also judges a man by his reputation. The worse his reputation, the more attractive he appears, which makes you the most desirable man in this room.' (This was probably true, for in order to protect the innocent the Maréchal had to burn over six thousand love letters the night before he was arrested six years later.)

Buckingham gave his view. 'Men and women are not as differently motivated as some philosophers think. An old man likes to see his young mistress publicly displaying the jewels he gave her for the very same reason she likes to display them: pride of possession.'

'There is a difference in the ages of men and women,' noted the Duchesse. 'Old men, like young blades, unsheathe to young mistresses at any time, whereas mistresses, like muskets, are readied for discharge once they're past their prime.'

'A woman's nose, like the soldier's, must be ever sensitive to the scent of the burning fuse,' observed the Princesse.

'Cannot a man love just one woman his whole life through?' asked Anne.

'Yes, if the man is made of stone,' answered Bassompierre.

'And the woman of wood,' added the Princesse.

'What does my wise brother say?' asked Gaston.

'Note well, Brother; to appear wise, I say nothing,' replied Louis with a thin smile.

On the next hand Richelieu was again able to give Marie-Aimée a chance to make game, this time with an overcall of the type that has little to gain and much to lose.

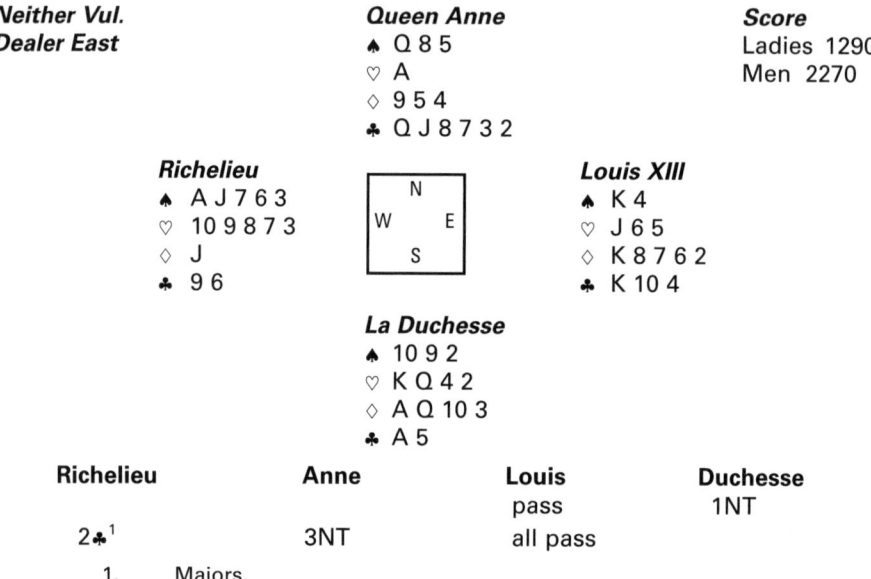

Neither Vul.	**Queen Anne**	**Score**
Dealer East	♠ Q 8 5	Ladies 1290
	♡ A	Men 2270
	◊ 9 5 4	
	♣ Q J 8 7 3 2	

Richelieu
♠ A J 7 6 3
♡ 10 9 8 7 3
◊ J
♣ 9 6

Louis XIII
♠ K 4
♡ J 6 5
◊ K 8 7 6 2
♣ K 10 4

La Duchesse
♠ 10 9 2
♡ K Q 4 2
◊ A Q 10 3
♣ A 5

Richelieu	Anne	Louis	Duchesse
		pass	1NT
2♣[1]	3NT	all pass	

1. Majors.

Marie-Aimée opened her strong hand with 1NT and Richelieu made a two-suited takeout bid for the majors. As Louis could not possibly hold the cards to make game probable for his side, the Cardinal's bid would give the Ladies the maximum amount of information with which to explore the best contract, while 2♣ took up no space whatsoever, so they still had a full range of bids at their disposal. However, Anne took the direct route to 3NT, which was passed out. Giving them all the help he could, Richelieu led the ♡10. If his partner had held the ♠K doubleton and declarer the ♠Q, a spade lead would have defeated the contract off the top, but Richelieu could explain that the heart lead might work better in the long run, since he had preserved an outside entry to cash hearts once they were established. As it happened, a heart lead took away an entry to dummy, so that the club suit could not now be run. Unintentionally, Richelieu had made what appeared to be the killing lead.

But now the Duchesse had one of those lightning flashes of inspiration for which she had become notorious, but this was inspiration based on sheer intellect — none of this nonsense about feminine intuition. First she counted her tricks — three hearts, two, possibly three, diamonds and two clubs — they totaled seven, possibly eight. Of course, she had to assume that the spades would provide another trick, so she tried to place the honors in the spade suit. If Richelieu held ♠AK, he would have led that suit, so she could place Louis with a doubleton ace or king. Also, she needed at least one club trick from the ♣Q or ♣J, but the lead had removed an essential entry. She was going to need a little luck, but the situation was not as hopeless as it seemed, as there was a good chance that Louis held both minor-suit kings. Of course, it meant playing Richelieu for an idiot, but the Duchesse was inclined to see him in that light anyway. She immediately led the ◇4 off dummy and put in the ◇Q, winning as Richelieu dropped the ◇J. This could be a false card, but one sometimes has to give the Devil, and the Cardinal, his due.

In the hope of removing the spade entry from the East hand while also setting up a trick in the suit, the Duchesse next led the ♠10 and passed it to Louis' ♠K. A heart was returned to her ♡K. The Duchesse now led the ♠2 towards the ♠Q8, the ♠Q taking the trick. Playing for an elimination, she led the ♣3 from dummy, took her ace, cashed her ♡Q, and exited with a club to the ♣Q in dummy in this position:

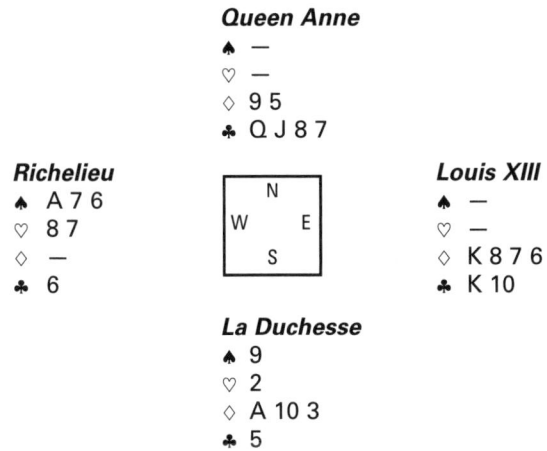

```
                    Queen Anne
                    ♠ —
                    ♡ —
                    ◇ 9 5
                    ♣ Q J 8 7

Richelieu              ┌─────────┐      Louis XIII
♠ A 7 6                │    N    │      ♠ —
♡ 8 7                  │ W     E │      ♡ —
◇ —                    │    S    │      ◇ K 8 7 6
♣ 6                    └─────────┘      ♣ K 10

                    La Duchesse
                    ♠ 9
                    ♡ 2
                    ◇ A 10 3
                    ♣ 5
```

It mattered not whether Louis took his ♣K now or later, the ◇9 would be an entry to the established club suit in dummy. The Duchesse ended up making eleven tricks, losing only the two black kings.

Only the gallant Buckingham saw fit to congratulate the Duchesse on her successful play, one that seemed so lucky to some, so easy and natural to others. The other spectators talked excitedly amongst themselves about the situation that making this game had created. The Ladies now had a fair chance to come from behind and steal the match on the next hand, provided they could bid a slam. Quickly the pre-dealt hands were distributed to the players.

La Duchesse
♠ Q 2
♡ Q 8 4
◊ A Q J 8 7 4
♣ Q 6

Score
Ladies 1400
Men 2270

Louis
♠ K 10 8 3
♡ A J 7 5 2
◊ 10 5 2
♣ 2

	N	
W		E
	S	

Richelieu
♠ J 7 6 5
♡ K 10 9 3
◊ —
♣ J 8 7 5 4

Queen Anne
♠ A 9 4
♡ 6
◊ K 9 6 3
♣ A K 10 9 3

Louis	Duchesse	Richelieu	Anne
			1◊
pass	2◊[1]	pass	3♡[2]
pass	4◊	pass	5◊
pass	6◊	all pass	

1. Forcing with 5+ diamonds.
2. Shortness.

The deficit stood at 870 points, so a mere vulnerable game with its 700 bonus (under the old scoring) would not be enough to win on total. The Duchesse was not a backward young lady. Within her exquisitely shaped head ticked an exquisite brain. True, at times this brain failed to function to its full capacity, a condition, Richelieu surmised, that was due to excessive, uninhibited fornication. But this was not the case at the time of which we write: the entire evening had been given over to playing bridge and the morning, for the most part at least, to regenerative restraint. Thus Marie de Rohan-Montbauzon was quick to realize that her hand would not be worth opening in third seat, for unless her partner could open the bidding, there would be no slam for them on this hand.

For her part, Anne had no such perceptive thoughts. She had opening points, so her only concerns were what she would rebid if she opened one club. Opening in her longer minor would find her badly placed on the next round, since to start with one club, then bid diamonds, would be a reverse, showing a good hand. Judging from past actions, this was a dangerous situation for their partnership: Marie would need little encouragement to blast to some impossible game, she reasoned, failing to take into account the overall situation.

The Duchesse was able to make a forcing raise in diamonds at the two-level and Anne made a splinter jump in hearts. Marie could see that game in diamonds was secure, but she knew that game would not be enough. She might bid 3NT and hope that it would be defeated, giving her another chance at slam, but the opponents could win the match by defending badly. Finally, she decided to bid just 4◊, hoping that Anne would see the need to pass below game if her hand did not possess slam potential.

Alas, the Queen reevaluated her hand on the basis of her good, undisclosed club suit. As Marie-Aimée hadn't bid 3♠ or 3NT she must have the clubs needed to fill out the suit, the Queen reasoned, and so she bid game in diamonds without realizing the full consequences of her bid — even making two overtricks for +840 would not be enough to win the match. Had the attentions of Buckingham subconsciously changed her mind about the desirability of winning the match and spending the night in her husband's arms? If so, that would not be very sporting, thought the Duchesse. She raised to six diamonds, as a two-way shot: if this went off one, the next hand might present another opportunity for slam.

Louis sensed there was a certain desperate quality to the bidding. He himself held what looked like two defensive tricks and the clubs weren't splitting favorably for declarer. Rather than give away the club situation, he prudently led a trump.

The Queen was alarmed to see the sparse dummy and her alarm increased when Richelieu showed out of trumps, playing the deliciously nebulous ♠6, hiding the truth without really violating it. The ♠5 lay hidden in amongst his clubs, as it was his habit to sort his hand in such a manner that the opponents could not easily discern his holdings from the position of the draw of his cards.

Not thinking clearly, Anne drew three rounds of trumps, and immediately tackled the club suit, relying entirely on a favorable split for her twelve tricks. Alas, Louis showed out on the second round after she had played a club to the queen and another to her ace. Her mind froze, not to the extent that the brain of Madame de Chevreuse might seize up temporarily at the sight of a nicely upturned mustache, but pretty well frosted up for all that. Naturally she had wished to impress her English admirer with her card play, and now she was at risk of losing his esteem by her quick play — obviously a finesse for the ♣J would have seen her home. After a few moments during which she had to fight back the tears, her brain thawed and formed a desperate plan in this position:

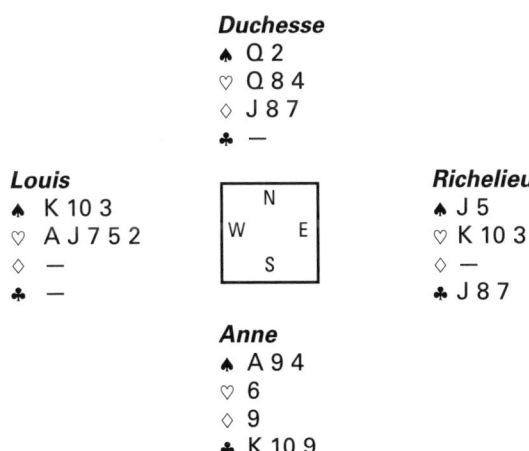

Richelieu had kept all his clubs and discarded a heart. Even a great player has difficulty predicting exactly how an incompetent declarer will misplay the hand.

The Queen led the ♣9 and threw a heart from the dummy, a loser-on-loser play. Richelieu returned the ♡10 in obedience to Louis' strong ♡J discard, but the Queen ruffed it. Now she played the ♠A, followed by the ♣K and the established ♣10, pitching the major-suit losers from dummy.

'The dummy is good,' she proclaimed triumphantly, pointing to the remaining trumps.

'Not so fast,' stormed Louis, 'let us see your cards, Madame.' He was suspicious that such a simple play should have caused so much anxiety.

The crowd of onlookers gasped in shock at this affront to the royal consort. This was the age of Zero Tolerance and even a monarch should not behave disrespectfully to a fellow player, even if she were his wife. The fine clothes, the sparkling jewels, the good grooming, the exalted company, all this would go for naught if foul accusations and disparaging remarks were allowed to fly across the table.

'Louis, mind your manners! Don't you trust your own wife?' exclaimed the Queen Mother.

'Mother, is it too much to ask to see the cards? It is my right.'

Richelieu said nothing, feeling it prudent not to enter into a conflict about which His Majesty felt so strongly. Marie-Aimée crossed the table and embraced her friend who had burst into tears as a last resort.

'Look at this pitiable sight, Your Majesty. You have made your poor wife cry, when all she wants to do is to please you with all her mind and body. Shame, I say.'

As she spoke these words she took up the ♡6 from the Queen's fingers and stuffed it down Her Majesty's bodice. Anne saw fully the wisdom of this maneuver.

'There, Your Majesty, if you wish to see the Queen's cards you must repair to her boudoir and search her for yourself.'

'Yes, Louis,' added the Queen Mother, 'only by disrobing her with your own hands will you satisfy your morbid curiosity.'

'Bassompierre,' Louis pleaded, but there was no accustomed help from that corner, only a Gallic shrug.

'Richelieu, I order you to search the Queen... immediately!'

The Cardinal rose obediently. 'If Your Majesty so orders,' he said resolutely as he approached the trio of women still seated at the table. 'Excuse me,' he said mildly, 'I mustn't touch Her Majesty's person, that would be a great breach of etiquette, but if I might just take a peek.'

Once more the Cardinal found himself gazing on two superb rounded, smooth, forms of female beauty — not quite of the quality of the earlier display by the Duchesse de Chevreuse, but far surpassing Michelangelo's best efforts nonetheless. Between them lurked a card that looked suspiciously like the ♡6.

'Ah, if Your Majesty might just shift the positions of your... er... just jiggle a bit so I could see better.'

'Cardinal, have you lost your mind!' screamed the Queen Mother.

'*Monsieur!*' admonished the Princess de Conti with an amused smile on her face.

'*Mon Cardinal*, step aside,' pleaded the Duchesse, pulling at Richelieu's arm. This gave him the opportunity to slip the ♠5 surreptitiously into her hand without its being noticed by others.

'Oh, very well,' conceded the King, 'To tell the truth I have found that you have aroused my curiosity and I am somewhat looking forward to a search of your person.'

He turned directly to the Englishman who had all evening caused him so much displeasure. 'Good night, Buck-ing-ga-am. Unfortunately I must proceed immediately to the business at hand,' said Louis, taking Anne possessively by the arm. Buckingham might have aroused passions, but it was Louis who would benefit.

'Oh, no, Your Majesty,' protested the Queen, 'You must remember that you have lost the match, so you are honor bound to follow my instructions until dawn. After that you may do what you will with my undergarments... but not until dawn breaks.'

This declaration drew applause, except from Buckingham, and the King surrendered himself to the Queen's tender mercies with good grace thereafter. Of course, being a good loser is not a characteristic one hopes to find displayed repeatedly by one's monarch — a good winner is more to the common taste — but this time all the courtiers were content with the outcome and its consequences. Some felt Louis deserved one more chance at paternity and wished him well, while others felt that this would prove the last straw after which it would become easier to replace Louis with his brother Gaston. None wished to be the first to voice a suspicion of the Queen's play — there would be opportunities for innuendo later.

Later that night Richelieu made his way to St. Germain d'Auxerrois where scribes were hard at work making copies of the official hand records for publication the next morning. He called to the man who was in charge of this operation.

'Fancan,' he said, 'I abhor inaccuracies, so I have noted a couple of hands for which I want you personally to insure the correctness of each card. Check them and make whatever changes are necessary. Bring the proofs to my study as soon as they are ready to go to print. I shall be up all night catching up on my correspondence anyway.'

The next morning a fatigued Richelieu was again called to the King's chambers, where he found Louis calmly looking out the window with his hands clasped behind his back. As he approached, the Cardinal spotted on the King's desk a crumpled playing card lying face down. At that moment he would have paid a considerable sum to know whether that card was of a red suit or a black suit. The King did not turn to face his Councillor, but pointed out the window at a group of fully armed Musketeers standing below.

'Look there, Cousin — that's a strapping big bruiser if I ever saw one. Do you know him?'

The Cardinal looked down on the parade ground and picked out the Musketeer who had caught his master's eye.

'Ah, yes. I believe his name is Porthos and the one beside him is, hmmm… a new one.'

'It doesn't matter. Shall we look at those plans for the siege of La Rochelle now?'

'Very well, Your Majesty. I think I see a role in it for Montmorency.'

Still Louis did not move from the window. He had something on his mind.

'Cousin, women are strange beings,' he said in a faraway voice.

'I agree, Your Majesty. With a void in the suit I would have jumped to four hearts on that last hand.'

'No, no,' explained Louis, 'I meant they are like little boats tossed about on the seas of passion.'

'Very apt, Your Majesty,' agreed Richelieu. 'Look, here comes your mother full sail across the parade dressed in a ten galleon hat.'

It was a beautiful straw hat, broad rimmed, generously decorated with fresh flowers; yet the Cardinal couldn't help thinking that a new lid looks bad on an old pot.

The Aftermath

On June 2, 1625 Queen Henrietta-Maria left Paris under the escort of the Duke of Buckingham. It was the custom to accompany royal brides to the borders of France in full splendor, but Louis XIII, pleading ill health, went only as far as Compiègne. The procession reached Amiens on June 6. It was here that the famous incident in the garden took place.

At Amiens a son had been born to the Governor, the Duc de Chaulnes, so it was doubly a time for festive celebration. No one was in a hurry to leave for England, least of all Buckingham who continued to court the favors of Queen Anne. Although she would never accept any part of the blame for the subsequent scandal, twenty years later the Queen confided to her biographer, Madame de Motteville, that 'his suit was received with a certain degree of satisfaction.' The prevailing liberal attitude towards seduction in the guise of gallantry was expressed in the following words by Madeleine de Souvré, in married life the Marquise de Sablé and one of Madame de Rambouillet's famous *précieuses*:

'I maintain that the desire of pleasing women inspires the noblest actions and that it imparts wit, generosity of spirit, and countless other virtues. Women, being the gems of society and the ornaments of the world, are created to become the recipients of such homage. Therefore, they may accept and, indeed, ought to encourage adoration and service, which they need repay only by innocent condescension.'

There were banquets and balls, a christening, and fireworks along the Somme. The setting promoted romance. The weather was warm and the Queen Mother was put to bed suffering from fatigue, further prolonging the stay. Madame de Chevreuse suggested a stroll at dusk in the Archbishop's garden beside the river. She walked on the arm of Lord Holland, Queen Anne on the arm of Buckingham. Rather than a cooling off, the effect was quite the opposite. The Duchesse stopped to rest and by design engaged the Queen's attendants in a contrived conversation. Buckingham steered the Queen into a dark arbor out of sight of the company. A few minutes later Anne screamed. Her bodyguards ran into the arbor to find Buckingham standing near the Queen in obvious discomfort. Before accusations could be made and swords drawn, the Duke and Holland made a hasty retreat into the dark.

The incident was reported to the Queen Mother who ordered Henrietta-Maria to leave Amiens the next morning. Queen Anne accompanied her partway towards Abbeville. At the point of separation Buckingham rode to the Queen's carriage and bade her a tearful farewell, swearing his eternal love. The Princesse de Conti observed their emotional parting and later reported wryly, "As Matron-of-Honor I can answer for the Queen's fidelity from the waist downward, but not upward."

This ill-conceived attempt at levity served only to raise Louis' ire. The Queen Mother tried to excuse Anne's behavior but the more she gave lame excuses the more incensed the King became. With supporters like these, Queen Anne didn't need detractors. When confronted by an angry husband, Anne replied coolly that it appeared to her strange that a wife should be condemned for protecting her honor, besides which, nothing had happened. She would say no more, but asked that her disgraced attendants be restored to their former services.

Louis stared at her for a long time in silence then said, 'Madame, by saying nothing you condemn yourself.'

Of course, everyone knew the Duchesse de Chevreuse had been the instigator of the whole affair, but she was now in England amusing the Court there and making friends with Charles I whom she delighted with her gay conversation. Charles even wrote a letter to Louis thanking him for the opportunity of meeting this charming lady.

But there was still more mischief afoot. While in London Marie-Aimée received letters from Anne that she passed on to Buckingham. As she had anticipated that her mail might be read by other than the intended receivers, she had devised a code for the names of those mentioned in the letters that she hoped would confuse any unauthorized reader. French courtiers were assigned the names of flowers. The Princesse de Conti always had about her person bits of paper on which to jot down her latest thoughts, so it was natural to name her 'Pansy', in French, *Pensée*. Cardinal Richelieu was known as 'Dogwood', in French, *Punais*, which also connotes 'stinker'. The Duke of Buckingham was called 'Rosebud' as the Queen was allergic to roses and sometimes swooned in their presence.

Anne of Austria went often to the convent of Val de Grâce where the Abbesse operated a drop box for her secret correspondence with her family, all of whom were enemies of France: her brother, Philip IV of Spain, her aunt, Archduchess Isabella of the Spanish Netherlands, her sister Maria, Queen of Hungary. One day in early July she sat in her cool cell and wrote to Buckingham, following the notes that the Princesse de Conti had provided on a Bridge hand they had played together.

From Lily of the Valley to Rosebud

Dear Rosebud:

I have come briefly to P--- for devotions at the V-- -- G---- and so will take the opportunity to fulfill my promise to Tulips *(Madame de Chevreuse)* to write to you something amusing concerning the happenings at Court. The task she set me is difficult, for Nettles *(Louis XIII)* goes hunting every day and we Ladies are left alone to strive mightily to amuse ourselves with silly talk in which a gallant such as yourself would find little of interest. The gaiety of Paris in the spring to which you so greatly contributed seems now but a pleasant dream from which I have just awakened to the overcast grayness of dull company. Of course, there is always Pansy to keep us amused by her shocking stories that she swears are true to the last detail. I dare not repeat them.

Did you know she is working on yet another novel? One has to be careful what one says within her earshot for fear it might appear in her latest installment! Ladies have been known to turn quite pale when they see her reach for her notepaper, but

I wouldn't mind appearing in a novel as long as it were well written. Seriously, we all love her very much and I am sure she would never intentionally write anything to injure one's reputation, she herself having suffered so much in that regard.

Lady's Slippers *(Dona Estefana, her old nurse)* accuses me of indolence, but I feel I was not born so. I have spirit when the occasion demands -- you have seen me dance! If I could change my life, I would have my hair clipped short and become a Sister. Foxglove *(Archduchess Isabella)* likes to dress herself in the coarse habit of the Poor Clares, but my tender skin cannot tolerate rough fabric, besides which, I would become not a recluse but a Nursing Sister who goes out into the world to do charitable deeds. I see myself dressed in a loose, white, satin frock with glorious, large red crosses at front and back, encircled by a blue belt of soft Spanish leather with a diamond buckle. My mission would be to go to battlefields and comfort dying enemy cavaliers, even Moors and Infidels.

We sometimes play Bridge in the evening with Nettles and Dogwood, who take the game so seriously! In his eagerness to excel, the former plays almost exclusively with the latter and, I fear, is becoming more the follower than the leader, a role that ill befits his rank. You would think the world depended on their winning, yet they make plays that would make even Buttercup *(Marie de Medici)* blush. Neither one will ever admit they made a mistake, and each defends the other's actions. Here is an example. *(From this point we drop the transparent ciphers.)*

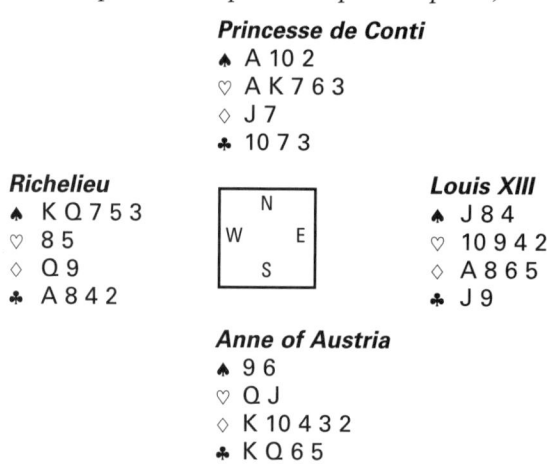

Princesse de Conti
♠ A 10 2
♡ A K 7 6 3
♢ J 7
♣ 10 7 3

Richelieu
♠ K Q 7 5 3
♡ 8 5
♢ Q 9
♣ A 8 4 2

Louis XIII
♠ J 8 4
♡ 10 9 4 2
♢ A 8 6 5
♣ J 9

Anne of Austria
♠ 9 6
♡ Q J
♢ K 10 4 3 2
♣ K Q 6 5

Richelieu	Princesse	Louis	Anne
	1♡	pass	2♢
pass	2♡	pass	3♣
pass	3♠	pass	3NT
all pass			

The Princesse demonstrated the power of her imagination in her bidding on this hand. I showed my two suits, properly I think, but the Princesse forced me to game in 3NT rather than correct to diamonds. If she had done so I could have supported her hearts.

At any rate there we were in a bad 3NT contract again (why does it always happen to me!), and Richelieu leads his fourth highest spade, the ♠5. Imagine my surprise when my ♠9 wins the first trick! I need some tricks from my minor suits, so I lead out my ♣Q which the Cardinal allows to win. I need just one more stolen trick, so I try the effect of the ◇K from my hand. When this also is allowed to win, I cash my ♡QJ and when all follow I can claim my contract. Isn't that amazing?

The men put on long faces and the Princesse is not one to allow such an opportunity pass her by, especially when the Cardinal is involved. She got out her paper and pen.

'Your Majesty played low to the first trick; to guard the ten, no doubt?' she asked.

'Exactly,' replied Louis haughtily, 'the play of my jack would expose my partner's honor to a second round finesse and yield a second entry for plays through my ◇A.'

'Very well reasoned, Sire,' added the Cardinal, 'it is much more likely that the honors are divided than that they are held in one hand.'

'Then, Monseigneur, you allowed the ♣K to hold the third trick?'

'Of course!' exclaimed Louis, defending with belated vigor. 'The bidding has revealed declarer's distribution, so he can clearly see that taking the trick would set up the ♣10 as an extra entry to dummy; he, too, was destroying the communications.'

'Thank you, Your Majesty, for your understanding,' said the Cardinal with a deep bow, 'and your allowing the ◇K to hold the next trick was equally farsighted.'

'Thus it appears no one made an error on the hand,' concluded the Princesse with a vigorous final jab of her pen.

'You may write down that declarer would have done better to play on the clubs exclusively,' said Louis. 'The Queen's line of play was dependent on a favorable lie of cards in both minors.'

'Exactly so, Your Majesty. I would add that the heart honors must be unblocked immediately upon winning the first club trick to ensure that all the heart tricks can be taken,' added Richelieu.

'It is odd to my mind that allowing declarer to make nine tricks when five were her due can be thought of as being correct, whereas...,' began the Princesse hotly.

'Perhaps the Princesse is unaccustomed to the employment of the hold-up,' interrupted Louis, grandly dismissing her protest with a flick of his handkerchief.

'I find Your Majesty's observation most flattering,' replied she with a respectful bow of her head, 'when, as a matter of fact, I am wearing one right now.'

You may ask Tulips to explain that to you.

Lily of the Valley

The Duchesse in middle age

The young Anne had been led by her friend to oppose Richelieu and work for his dismissal. By the time she reached her mid-thirties the Queen had come to realize she could gain nothing by continuing her opposition. In 1637 the rebellious Duchesse was sent in disgrace to her residence near Tours to await the King's pleasure, living there in fear that Richelieu was about to order her arrest. Anne was to send a Book of Hours as a signal of the latest developments: if the cover was green, the danger was past; if the cover was red, flight was imperative. When a red book arrived, the Duchesse raced to safety over the Spanish border and a six-year exile. In fact, the wrong book had been sent as there was no danger of arrest. However, it was most convenient to Richelieu to have this troublesome schemer absent herself from France for awhile. No one suspected that Anne might have sent the wrong book deliberately.

Marie-Aimée's Dangerous Game

On August 25, 1625, as was his custom, Cardinal Richelieu arose early before French roosters had even begun to clear their throats. First priority was given to reading the reports of his agents. There was one from the Bishop of Mende, in London as grand almoner to Queen Henrietta-Maria. He was in charge of a score of priests who were sent to the English Court to promote tolerance for the Roman Catholic faith, an important feature of the marriage treaty. Progress on his mission was slow. His reports had become increasingly critical of the French ladies-in-waiting who had accompanied their royal mistress to her misty kingdom. 'It appears these women have come here to establish brothels rather than to promote religion,' the young man complained bitterly. He then suggested Richelieu have the lot recalled. Always the realist, Richelieu chuckled as he read this. We are content that our Marie-Aimée has returned, he said to himself, those other sluts can stay put in England as we suffer in France from an overabundance of that type.

There was paperwork to be done: the writing of detailed instructions to his officials, then the making of lists of things to do, leaving to the end the pleasant task of reading through the private correspondence intercepted by his spies on the previous evening. Of such letters, the ones he invariably left to the very last were those of the Duchesse de Chevreuse, and on this day there was special bonus: here was one addressed to none other than the Duke of Buckingham. The Cardinal leaned back in his chair, sipped his cup of hot chicken broth, and began to read Madame's scrawl with an anticipation made all the greater by his self-imposed postponement. It was in the Duchesse's strange English.

To my Big, handsomest Jack Rabbit from his fuzzy Bunny Baby

(*Sacré bleu*, thought the Cardinal, is this how English aristocrats address each other these days? Surely not — it must be a coded message. Whatever could it mean?)

The weather here is so hot and my reception at Court has been so cold, that I wish I could journey again to London and be with you English who are always ready for some jolly fun, n'est-ce pas? I miss you how very much, my big Jack Rabbit, I cannot write, but if you were standing here beside me you could put your hand gently on ma poitrine gauche and feel how joyfully my heart goes boum-boum at the thought of your return to France. I hope that will be very, very soon.

(Ho, Ho, chortled Richelieu, a safe offer to be sure — that will be the day the Pope wears kilts. It appears this little vixen has stolen the rabbit from the Queen's snare.)

This afternoon the King and Richelieu played Bridge with Anne et moi. What fools! To think the likes of them are ruling this country makes my French blood boil. How lucky you English are to have a clever king like Charley and how lucky he is to have a brave and gallant advisor like you. Here is a hand that might amuse you and show what bouffons they really are.

(How absurd! My Bridge is impeccable, fumed the Prime Minister. Perfidious imp! If the hot-headed Buckingham actually believed these unfounded allegations, it could start a war, but France would not prove as defenseless to English advances as had her Queen.)

Imagine you open a strong notrump that is passed away. The Cardinal leads the ♣4, his fourth highest, as usual, and this is what you see:

Anne
♠ 7 3 2
♡ 10 5 4
◇ K 5 4
♣ Q 10 7 2

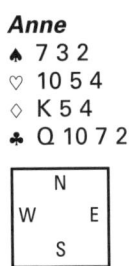

Moi
♠ Q J 4
♡ K J 8 3
◇ A J 7
♣ K 9 3

The ♣4 led, ♣2, and Louis plays the ♣A. Naturellement, you would do as I did and drop the ♣K under it, since you need entries to La Morte for finesses. My dim monarch pretends to think before returning the ♣8 to the ♣9, ♣J and the ♣Q. Quel poseur!

(Yes, recalled Richelieu, that was rather passive, but surely it is not an act of folly to return partner's suit. Indeed, it is commendable for a player of Louis' caliber.)

So now you are in place for your first finesse. In which suit will it be, chéri, a heart, the symbol of true love, or a diamond, the proof of passion? Don't peek.

Anne
♠ 7 3 2
♡ 10 5 4
◇ K 5 4
♣ Q 10 7 2

Richelieu
♠ K 9 8
♡ A Q 6
◇ Q 9 6
♣ J 6 5 4

Louis
♠ A 10 6 5
♡ 9 7 2
◇ 10 8 3 2
♣ A 8

Moi
♠ Q J 4
♡ K J 8 3
◇ A J 7
♣ K 9 3

In the North hand after two rounds of clubs, I see the spade suit is open to attack by the defense, but neither opponent found it attractive to break the suit. Knowing me all too well you may have guessed that I led a spade from dummy, and put in the queen, playing for split honors. There was another reason for this: upon taking his ♠K, the Cardinal returned the ◇6 to my ◇J, concluding naturellement that I held the ♠A so must be weak in diamonds. He is clever but so, how do you say? sallow? that it is easy to lead him by the nose.

(Richelieu slapped his knee in agitation. Here was the muddy puddle daring to call the crystal lake shallow! One could almost begin to feel pity for any man gullible enough to be taken in by this rot.)

Now I play a club to the ♣7 and another spade from La Morte and Louis foolishly flies with the ace to play another diamond. Does he imagine I have just two diamonds? Hou-hou! He does not ask himself why his partner first led clubs, not diamonds. My contract is safe now, so I cash the ♠J, go North with the third diamond, draw the last club, my seventh trick, and endplay Richelieu in hearts ... voila! making eight tricks after starting with four, with all the red suit finesses wrong!

So did all those pretty tricks make me happy? A little bit, yes, but how more happy I would be spending my afternoon being covered with hot kisses from some handsome man. I am thinking of such a man right now. Can you guess who? Did you guess the Cardinal? Ha, Ha - my Dream Boat is not a Frenchman.

(*Mon Dieu*, what a terrible waste of a good brain, thought the Cardinal. An intelligence that is capable of causing such havoc may equally well be employed to do great good.)

From this hand, where I played so successfully on the suit that appeared most dangerous, I conclude as follows: one's greatest hope may reside within one's greatest fear. Sometimes when it grows dark and cold at night, and when I am alone, like tonight, I pray Death, our greatest fear, when it comes will be comme ça.

Adieu, mon brave,

Your Sad M.

How often at night those very same thoughts had invaded the cold darkness of the Cardinal's lonely bedroom. Overcome with emotion, Richelieu quickly stretched out his right hand lest the paper he held be stained with his hasty tears. Yes, he was easily moved, not by the misfortunes of a few, some of whom were his victims, but by a deeper melancholy for Mankind that surfaced at moments of mental fatigue such as these.

'Boisrobert,' called the Cardinal in a husky voice to his new secretary, 'please make a copy of this and send it on its way. Forgive me,' he added, blowing his nose loudly, 'but my tears pay homage to a mind that is worthy of a saint when not clouded by selfish passions and ill-conceived prejudices. Tell me, my son, do you know of a man who can enlighten me on what truly lies on this young woman's mind?'

The little Abbé was of the type not easily taken in by female wiles. 'Perhaps her hairdresser, Monseigneur?' he suggested uncharitably with a shrug.

Suddenly Richelieu came to the realization that this seemingly frivolous letter had been meant for his eyes as well as those of the English Duke. How very clever. To think he had almost allowed himself to be bamboozled by this sly contrivance! What a pity the Duchesse doesn't behave reasonably.

Appendices

The Young Richelieu — 1585-1614

Armand-Jean du Plessis, Duc de Richelieu et Fronsac, Cardinal of the Roman Catholic Church, is acknowledged to be one of the greatest statesmen of all time. During the nineteen years of his ministry (1624 - 1642) he dominated European politics through the strength of his intellect and character and raised France from the status of a weak state beset with internal strife to that of the foremost nation in Europe. His policies were continued for decades after his death with unparalleled success until Louis XIV saw fit to institute his own dictatorial reign, thus bringing France to ruin financially, morally, and intellectually.

Richelieu was born in Paris into a family of the old nobility, du Plessis being a common ancient appendage denoting 'a small fortification'. His mother, Suzanne de la Porte, was not of noble stock, being the daughter of a prominent councilor of the Paris *Parlement*, an advisory organization consisting primarily of lawyers. Armand may have felt some shame at the lowly origins of his maternal side, but later in life he did not hesitate to draw liberally on associates of that side of the family to form his governmental administration.

It is most probable that his superior intellect came more from his mother than his father, Henri de Richelieu. By today's standards Henri would be judged a murderer, and even in his day he felt it prudent to seek asylum in a foreign country, Poland. There he entered the service of the man who would be recalled to France as Henri III, the last Valois king. Finding favor with his master, Henri returned also and achieved the high post of Grand Provost. When the King was assassinated in 1589 it was the Grand Provost who arrested the culprit, Brother Clement, with hands still red with royal blood.

Although he guessed right during the last war of religion by switching his allegiance to the Huguenot warrior who was to become Henri IV, Richelieu *pere* did not prosper. He may have been on the threshold of great success, but he died of typhoid during the siege of Paris, 1590, at a time when his investments were badly placed. As a result the family fortune was in a state of ruin. His widow did not despair. By prudent management and with the help provided by her half-brother, Amador, she was able to provide the funds necessary for the promotion of her three sons in royal favor as well as for the dowry necessary to provide a marriage for her eldest daughter. The youngest daughter married late in 1617 and the middle daughter, Isabelle, eloped at the age of thirty and was disowned by the family.

The oldest son and heir, Henri, became a lowly member of the King's Court and showed promise of rising much higher. The second son, Alphonse, was slated for the clergy, a vocation for which he was well-suited, as he was most devout. The youngest son, Armand, was to become a soldier, and, it was hoped, would win his fortune on the battlefield. He was sent to Paris to attend the famous academy of Antoine de Pluvinel, there to learn the arts of the gentleman: how to dress handsomely, how to act with the greatest politeness, how to handle an *épée* and a horse, how to please a young lady. (It may seem a strange coincidence that another great advocate of the supremacy of the intellect, René Descartes, also took up arms quite happily a decade later. At the time soldiering was the profession of choice for the junior members of noble families.)

Paris in the early 1600's was the place to be for young men of spirit. It teemed with life, being the most populous city of Europe with 400,000 inhabitants crowded into three districts composed mainly of five-story houses. True, Spain was seen to be the most powerful country in the world with all the riches of America in its possession, and Italy had long been the center of Christian civilization, but the vitality of Paris was more exciting than the soft sophistication of Rome or the rigid regulation of Madrid.

The French wars of religion were ended. The tolerance promised to the Huguenots under the Edict of Nantes served to promote political conformity under a wise monarch whose sole aim in life appeared to be to enjoy the fruits and spoils of victory. Many devout Frenchmen thought it just a matter of time before a well-rested France joined Spain and Italy in their military efforts to return the Germanic Protestant states to the Catholic fold. In the meantime they, too, resolved to enjoy life. There was no self-indulgence so great that one's conscience could not bear the burden of it.

Life in Paris was precarious, the language coarse, the style extravagant. The fortunate few were worshiped by the submissive, envied by the ambitious, and hated by the obstinate. The rich lived in filthy magnificence surrounded by bodyguards and never ventured into the streets without their weapons. False doctrines abounded, hygiene in particular being tragically underrated. Kindly doctors with the best intentions killed their patients. The relics of St. Geneviève were paraded yearly through the streets in the hope of alleviating the inevitable ravages of the plague. The smell of Paris carried for miles and overcame some visitors unaccustomed to the stench. Even the royal staircases of the Louvre had to be washed down daily to clear away slippery human excrement. Gourmet cooking was of the future, the simple, common diet being mainly meat with a few vegetables judiciously washed down by copious quantities of wine. Forks were so uncommon that fastidious nobles carried about their own set of cutlery.

One could get used to the noisome conditions in the same way today one may learn to cope with the noxious environment of New York City. There was excitement in the air as well as bad smells. Perhaps the highly dangerous and unsanitary atmosphere served to add a dash of fatalism that heightened the elation. Fortunes were spent on clothes and elaborate entertainment. Men as well as women wore the finest silks and laces and placed on their heads broad brimmed hats decorated with the feathers of exotic birds. Precious stones and pearls were on display from head to toe: in hair ornaments, on shoe buckles, in earrings, on buttons.

Dancing was a great passion of the affluent. A favorite dance was the vigorous volte during which the male dancer lifted his female partner by the waist, twirled, and tossed her in the air so as to cause her skirts to billow out on descent, sometimes revealing sweet attractions that normally remain hidden beneath. A height of five feet was tall for women in those days. It was a sign of the times that one dancing master felt obliged to advise young gallants, 'Wear clean shoes and use a handkerchief. Never spit directly onto the dancing surface.' Yes, that could result in a nasty fall during the volte.

Intellectual life centered around libertine poets who were always in danger of being sent to an ecclesiastical prison. They were protected to some degree by their noble patrons who hired them to compose love verses in aid of seduction. Poets could also provide the nobleman with exquisitely crude insults in verse with which to revenge a rejection or to provoke a hated rival. Dueling was endemic, causing hundreds of deaths each year. However, there was very little in the way of what we recognize as freedom of expression. Death by execution or cruel neglect was a real risk to those free-thinkers who had clearly overstepped the boundaries of conventional thought.

The teenage Armand was looking forward with some degree of favorable anticipation to his life as a soldier when all his mother's plans were upset by the refusal of brother Alphonse to accept the Bishopric of Luçon; he wanted to become a reclusive monk. This precipitated a financial crisis as the family commitments could not be met without the meager but steady income the post provided. At his mother's behest Armand obediently gave up his military career in 1602 and prepared to join the clergy as a full-fledged priest.

The oath of celibacy would not present a problem. At the time celibacy was required in theory but not expected in practice, so frequent were the transgressions. As with dieting today, authorities agreed that as a general scheme it was most commendable, but that if carried to extremes it might prove injurious to one's health and general well-being. The most important aspect was not whether one had indulged but that one felt guilty about it afterward. Understood.

In the future many women's names would be linked with that of Cardinal Richelieu, but his sexual liaisons were brief and shallow. By and large his mistresses were from the lower social orders. One prominent nighttime visitor to his house was the infamous courtesan Marion Delorme. The lady claimed in her memoirs to have thrown the Cardinal's money in his face, but that seems unlikely as prostitutes never offer refunds. Certainly he did not feel a deep need to share his life with one of the opposite gender. There was an exception...

The daughter of Richelieu's eldest sister had married into a prominent family, but her husband was killed in battle. The young widow, Marie-Madeleine de Combalet, resolved to end her days in a convent, but Cardinal Richelieu did have a need for feminine companionship outside the priestly orders. He persuaded his niece instead to join him in Paris and manage his household affairs. Many nasty rumors were circulated concerning their intimacy, but it is very unlikely there was any foundation to them. Richelieu preferred his sex without complications. His niece, as the Duchesse d'Aiguillon, became a prominent figure in Parisian society and a frequenter of the salon of Madame de Rambouillet. She was kind-hearted, generous, and perhaps just a little pretentious at times, no great fault among the French, surely.

Insanity ran in the Richelieu blood. The history of the youngest sister, Nicole, was a most unhappy one. She ended her days in confinement at the fortress of Saumur under the delusion that her buttocks were made of glass so fragile that the touch of another human would shatter them. There are stories that the Cardinal suffered mental breakdowns sometimes lasting two weeks, during which periods he imagined himself to be a horse. There were mysterious days when he remained locked up in his bedroom attended by only a selected few servants.

Ironically, Richelieu was a great advocate of the power of Reason. To him, to act reasonably was to act in accordance with the natural laws of the Almighty, the giver of Reason to Man. Only in the possession of reason was Man different from animals. Emotion was seen as the great enemy. He wrote the following: 'Often one regrets at leisure what emotion has hastily wrought, but such regrets never occur when an action springs from a well-reasoned plan.' Could it be that he covered his fears of the onset of insanity by placing too great a reliance on reason at the cost of emotion?

To return to Armand's early life, we find that after leaving Pluvinel's academy in 1602 he entered a provincial seminary and engaged himself fully in the study of theology and administration. By the time he reached twenty-one years of age he felt that he was sufficiently qualified for the duties of a bishop. Impatiently he traveled to Rome to push for his early consecration, which he received in 1607 from the hands of Pope Paul V himself despite the fact that he was under the canonical age. Once he had the appointment securely in his grasp he admitted that on his application he had fibbed about his birth date, at which Paul V laughed forgivingly for the young man had impressed the Curia with his fervor and quick intelligence. It was then the pontiff made his famous prediction, 'He will prove a great rascal!'

He returned to Paris to give the Easter sermon at court in 1608. Henri IV even put an arm about his shoulders and called him affectionately 'my Bishop', but no high post was forthcoming. Without rich patrons for support he was in for a long apprenticeship far from the glamour and excitement of Paris. Luçon was a dull town with a damp climate due to its location at the edge of the Vendée marshes. One may feel some sympathy for a bright, young man who had once dreamed of glory on the battlefield, who had won the approval of a king and a pope, but who was now stuck in a dull backwater. However, the young Bishop was not looking for pity; he was determined to succeed no matter what. He wrote letters to anyone who might be of help. He offered a sharp mind sheathed in flattery. Of course, the art of flattery is gauging the maximum degree to which it can be applied without arousing suspicion, and this comes only with practice. His brother, Henri, had to pull on the reins occasionally.

Richelieu performed his duties well and composed popular essays on devotion — in French, not the usual Latin. His methods were gentle and persuasive. He demonstrated a tolerance towards the many Huguenots living in his parish. Often he occupied his mind with thoughts of affairs of state and daydreams of serving France as a member of the King's Council. This was not impossible, for he had friends near the Regent and he belonged to an organization that could promote talent in this direction when it saw fit. Church and State were not completely separate entities, in fact they were rather closely knit. High church appointments went to members of noble families like the Richelieus, who ended up with one son in Court and another in the Assembly of Bishops. Cardinals were appointed at the pleasure of the pope, true, but the king provided the short list from which the pontiff had to choose. French cardinals were expected to act as ambassadors extraordinary in royal service. For their part, cardinals demanded a seat on the King's Council and formal precedence therein.

In 1614 the Bishop of Luçon got his opportunity. The Queen Mother Regent was persuaded to call to Paris a rare meeting of the Estates-General. This meant that representatives for the three estates (Nobility, Clergy and Commons) would meet in a prolonged convention for the purpose of coming up with suggestions for the King as to how the affairs of state might be better run. Richelieu was chosen as a representative for Poitou. Mentally he was well prepared to meet the challenge of presenting palatable, fresh ideas, but he was terribly inexperienced. If he impressed those in power, he could advance rapidly. One false move, however, and he might never again have the opportunity of becoming the great rascal the pope had predicted. The climate of Luçon was proving detrimental to his health.

It is at this point in time that our stories began.

CHRONOLOGY — CARDINAL RICHELIEU

Sept, 1585 Armand-Jean du Plessis de Richelieu is born in Paris. Father: The Grand Provost of France, François de Richelieu. Mother: Suzanne de la Porte, daughter of a lawyer from Poitiers.

July, 1590 François de Richelieu dies of typhoid, deep in debt. His widow works hard to pay off her creditors and promote her three sons' careers, especially that of the eldest, Henri.

Sept, 1601 Infanta Ana is born in Madrid, a first child. Father: Philip III of Spain, then the greatest European nation. Her mother: Margaret of Austria.

Sept, 1601 The future King Louis XIII is born in Paris. Father: Henri IV, the greatest king of France, now 48 years old. Mother: Marie de Medici, a 27-year-old bride from Florence.

Easter, 1607 Richelieu is consecrated Bishop of Luçon.

May 14, 1610 Henri IV is assassinated and Marie de Medici becomes Regent.

1610–1614 As Bishop of Luçon, Richelieu writes popular essays on religion. His approach is orthodox, but tending to leniency and flexibility.

Feb 23, 1615 Delegate Richelieu of the Estates-General is chosen to make the closing address before the young King and the Regent.

Nov 25, 1615 Louis XIII marries Anne of Austria in Bordeaux. They journey slowly to Paris, never sharing a bed.

May 16, 1616 The royal party enters a jubilant Paris, where Richelieu now resides. He belatedly takes up his duties as Anne's Grand Almoner.

Nov 14, 1616 Suzanne de la Porte dies at Breye. Armand is too busy to attend his mother's funeral even though it is delayed a month.

Nov 25, 1616 Richelieu becomes Secretary of State for foreign affairs.

Apr 24, 1617 Concini, the Regent's favorite, is assassinated at the King's command. The Regent and Richelieu are banned from the Court.

Mar 7, 1619 Richelieu is recalled from exile in Avignon to act as an adviser to Marie de Medici. She comes to rely on his counsel.

July 8, 1619 His beloved brother, Henri, is killed in a pointless duel.

Sept 25, 1622 Richelieu is made a cardinal by Pope Gregory XV. This is a reward for services rendered to the Queen Mother. It is thought Richelieu will be a staunch supporter of the interests of the Papacy and Spain within France — a mistaken impression.

Apr 29, 1624 Louis reluctantly appoints Cardinal Richelieu to his Council.

Aug 13, 1624   Louis XIII makes Richelieu his chief Councillor. Richelieu remains so for the remainder of his life. Gradually his hidden agenda, the glorification of France, emerges.

May 11, 1625   King Charles I marries the King's sister by proxy at Notre Dame.

May 24, 1625   Buckingham arrives in Paris to escort his new queen to London. Richelieu entertains Buckingham lavishly, but rejects suggestions of an alliance between England and France against Spain.

This is the end of the time period covered by our stories. The Cardinal ruled France in the King's name until his own death on December 4, 1642. He had followed a rational plan which promoted the welfare of France against its great rival, Spain, a plan completed by his protégé, Cardinal Mazarin, who controlled Anne of Austria in a way his predecessor never could. Richelieu had held the infant Dauphin in his arms, but Louis XIV from an early age was taught by his mother to revile the name of the Frenchman to whom he owed the most for his inheritance as the greatest monarch in Europe.

Dec, 1600	Marie-Aimée is born near Tours as a second child. Mother: Madeleine de Leononcourt. Father: Hercule de Rohan, Duc de Montbazon.
1602–1616	Her young mother dies in 1602. She and her older brother are given a 'liberal' education by a series of governesses of questionable credentials, one of whom was a courtesan from Tours, a mistress of the Duc. The guiding principles of their tutelage are pleasure and caprice. Discipline is not a factor. Marie learns to ride, shoot, swim, and play with boys.
1616	She joins the Court as a maid-of-honor.
Sept 13, 1617	She marries Charles d'Albert de Luynes, the King's favorite. He is 39 years old and wields great political power. As a wedding gift he gives her the jewels of the departed Concinis.
1617–1618	She flirts with the King and arouses the jealousy of Queen Anne. Becomes Superintendent of the Queen's Household and Purse and Head of her Council. She performs these tasks very well. Court life is a series of gay parties and extravagant entertainments. Marie-Aimée and Anne become the closest of friends.
Jan 25, 1619	At Luynes' insistence Louis begins normal marriage relations with Queen Anne. Love blossoms. Louis writes poems and songs to her.
Dec 25, 1620	Marie-Aimée bears a son, Louis, whose godparents are the King and the Queen Mother. This son enjoys long life as Duc de Luynes.
1621	Marie-Aimée engages in a series of passing love affairs under the guidance of the conscienceless Princesse de Conti, a lady of wit, intelligence, and considerable experience – a novelist to boot. The less gifted brother of the Princesse, the Duc de Chevreuse, becomes Marie-Aimée's most prominent lover, but Luynes is in the South fighting the Huguenots and he is unaware of it.
Dec 21, 1621	Luynes dies of scarlet fever while on campaign. His daughter is born soon after, destined for the nunnery.
Mar 14, 1622	Queen Anne has a miscarriage after silly horseplay at the Louvre. Louis XIII blames Marie-Aimée for the loss.
Apr 15, 1622	The Duchesse de Luynes is expelled from Court over the Queen's protests. Louis is deeply offended by his wife's 'disloyalty.'
Apr 20, 1622	Marie-Aimé marries the Duc de Chevreuse, a member of the powerful Guise family and a supporter of Louis who was beside the King throughout the fateful day of the Concini assassination.

May 22, 1622	The Duc is rewarded with the title of Grand Falconer of France. He fights fearlessly in the battle of Negrepelisse and persuades the reluctant King to allow his wife back into Court.
July 3, 1622	The Duchesse de Chevreuse returns to Court without a position, but is the Queen's constant companion and friend. The Court is again a place for gaiety, gallantry, frivolity and fun.
Mar 5, 1623	Carnival season in Paris. The Prince of Wales and the Duke of Buckingham secretly observe the Queen's ballet. The Duke is much impressed by the queen's beauty and grace.
Feb, 1624	The English Court sends Viscount Kensington, later Lord Holland, to Paris to negotiate the marriage of the Prince of Wales to Louis's youngest sister, Henrietta-Maria. As a cousin of Charles, the Duc de Chevreuse plays a prominent role. Kensington and the Duchesse become lovers. They promote a flirtation between Queen Anne and Buckingham.
May 11, 1625	The Duc de Chevreuse acts as proxy to King Charles I at his wedding to Henrietta-Maria outside the doors of Notre Dame.
May 24, 1625	The Duke of Buckingham arrives in Paris. There ensues a week of fabulous parties that are to become legend. Queen Anne discovers she does not find Buckingham's attentions to be unwelcome, but is at a loss as to how to react.
June 7, 1625	The Duke escorts the new Queen of England to her new country. At Amiens he manoeuvres to place himself alone with Anne. His sexual advances are answered with screams. The King recognizes this as the handiwork of the Duchesse.
July, 1625	Marie-Aimée bedazzles the English Court with her beauty, gaiety and wit. Despite being nine months pregnant, she flirts with Charles and spends days in seclusion with Buckingham. Years later she confides that Buckingham was the lover she esteemed most. A daughter, Anne-Marie, is born at Hampton Court. Two weeks later, the Duchesse swims the Thames for exercise.
July 25, 1625	The French Court recalls the Duc and Duchesse to Paris. The Bishop of Mende has reported on the queen's entourage: 'it seems as if these ladies have come over to establish brothels rather than serve religion.' Marie-Aimée is said to act shamelessly. The Duc receives the Order of the Garter from a grateful Charles I.
1625 -1626	Marie-Aimée engineers the infamous Conspiracy of the Dames with the Queen Mother, Queen Anne and the Princesse de Condé. The plan is to remove Richelieu and give more power to Gaston. Richelieu survives an assassination attempt. Marie-Aimé flees to Lorraine.

1626 onwards	The Duchesse is frequently in exile, but continues to engage in dangerous court intrigues in support of Spanish and other foreign interests. She fights a losing battle against Richelieu and Mazarin.
Sept 5, 1638	Anne is delivered of a son, the future Louis XIV. Her attitude changes with her new position and she seeks the support of Richelieu, the man she once opposed so vehemently.
Apr, 1643	On his deathbed, Louis XIII points with fleshless finger to the name of the Duchesse de Chevreuse and says in a quavering voice: 'This is the Devil. There. This is the very Devil.'
Nov 7, 1652	Charlotte de Chevreuse, the debauched daughter born in Lorraine, dies in Paris in her mother's arms, probably a suicide by poison – an emotional victim of the political machinations of her mother.
Feb 1, 1667	Marie-Aimée's grandson, Charles-Honoré d'Albert, marries Colbert's daughter.
Aug 12, 1679	The Duchesse dies peacefully at the Benedictine Priory at Gagny, after five long years of prayer, silence, and solitude. Thanks to her iron constitution, she had outlived Richelieu by thirty-seven years.

August 16, 1679 would have marked the fifty-third anniversary of the death of Marie-Aimée's first victim, the Comte de Chalais, whom she had induced in 1626 to join a plot to murder Richelieu. He died screaming on the scaffold at the hands of an incompetent executioner who needed forty blows to effect a decapitation. Perhaps she was happy to miss this anniversary, or, more likely, she had long since disassociated herself from the grim consequences of her self-centered activities. After all, she had not signed the death warrant.

She requested burial in the simplest fashion at the nearby Chapel of the Blessed Virgin. She directed her own epitaph to read as follows:

'Here lies Marie de Rohan, Duchesse de Chevreuse, daughter of Hercule de Rohan, Duc de Montbazon. Humility having long since killed in her heart all the glory of the century, she forbade the slightest mark of greatness and desired to be buried for ever beneath the simplicity of this tomb...'

Her wish has not been fulfilled as her grave site has been lost with, time although the gravestone is still in the possession of her descendants from her marriage to Luynes.

Let her cousin, the Duc de La Rochefoucauld, have the last word:

When our vices finally abandon us, we flatter ourselves with the belief that it is we who have left them behind.

Also by Robert MacKinnon

Samurai Bridge
A tale of old Japan

Romance, adventure, swordplay — and plenty of bridge! This novel is '*Seven Samurai*' as Charles Goren might have written it!

MASTER POINT PRESS
Toronto

The Bridge Publisher

More Bridge Titles from Master Point Press

Bridge the Silver Way by David Silver and Tim Bourke
192pp., PB   Can $19.95   US $14.95

Bridge: 25 Ways to Compete in the Bidding.
by Barbara Seagram and Marc Smith
220pp., PB   Can.$19.95   US $15.95

Bridge, Zia... and me by Michael Rosenberg
(foreword by Zia Mahmood)
192pp., PB   Can $19.95   US $15.95

Challenge Your Declarer Play by Danny Roth
128pp., PB   Can. $12.95   US $ 9.95

Classic Kantar *a collection of bridge humor* by Eddie Kantar
192pp., PB   Can $19.95   US $14.95

Competitive Bidding in the 21st Century by Marshall Miles
254pp.,PB   Can. $22.95   US. $16.95

Countdown to Winning Bridge by Tim Bourke and Marc Smith
92pp., PB   Can $19.95   US $14.95

Easier Done Than Said *Brilliancy at the Bridge Table*
by Prakash K. Paranjape
128pp., PB   Can $15.95   US $12.95

For Love or Money *The Life of a Bridge Journalist*
by Mark Horton and Brian Senior
189pp., PB   Can $22.95   US $16.95

Focus On Declarer Play by Danny Roth
128pp., PB   Can $12.95   US $9.95

Focus On Defence by Danny Roth
128pp., PB   Can $12.95   US $9.95

Focus On Bidding by Danny Roth
160pp., PB   Can $14.95   US $11.95

I Shot my Bridge Partner by Matthew Granovetter
384pp., PB   Can $19.95   US $14.95

Murder at the Bridge Table by Matthew Granovetter
320pp., PB   Can $19.95   US $14.95

Partnership Bidding *a workbook* by Mary Paul
96pp., PB   Can $9.95   US $7.95

Playing with the Bridge Legends by Barnet Shenkin
(forewords by Zia and Michael Rosenberg)
240pp., PB   Can $24.95   US $17.95

Saints and Sinners *The St. Titus Bridge Challenge*
by David Bird & Tim Bourke
192pp., PB   Can $19.95   US $14.95

Samurai Bridge *A tale of old Japan* by Robert F. MacKinnon
256pp., PB   Can $22.95   US $16.95

Tales out of School *'Bridge 101' and other stories* by David Silver
(foreword by Dorothy Hayden Truscott)
128pp., PB   Can $12.95   US $9.95

The Bridge Magicians by Mark Horton and Radoslaw Kielbasinski
248pp., PB   Can $24.95   US $17.95

The Bridge Player's Bedside Book edited by Tony Forrester
256pp., HC   Can $27.95   US $19.95

The Bridge World's 'Test Your Play' by Jeff Rubens
164pp., PB   Can $14.95   US $11.95

The Complete Book of BOLS Bridge Tips edited by Sally Brock
176pp., PB (photographs)   Can $24.95   US $17.95

The Pocket Guide to Bridge by Barbara Seagram and Ray Lee
64pp., PB   Can $9.95   US$7.95

There Must Be A Way... *52 challenging bridge hands*
by Andrew Diosy (foreword by Eddie Kantar)
96pp., PB   Can $9.95   US $9.95

Thinking on Defense by Jim Priebe (foreword by Eric Kokish)
216pp., PB   Can $19.95   US$15.95

You Have to See This... *52 more challenging bridge problems*
by Andrew Diosy and Linda Lee
96pp., PB   Can $12.95   US $9.95

Win the Bermuda Bowl with Me by Jeff Meckstroth and Marc Smith
288pp., PB (photographs)   Can $24.95   US $17.95

World Class — *conversations with the bridge masters* by Marc Smith
288pp., PB (photographs)   Can $24.95   US $17.95